Foolish Fantasies

An April May Snow

Southern Paranormal Women's Fiction

By

M. Scott Swanson

April May Snow Titles

Foolish Aspirations

Foolish Beliefs

Foolish Cravings

Foolish Desires

Foolish Expectations

Foolish Fantasies

Seven Title Prequel Series

Throw the Bouquet

Throw the Cap

Throw the Dice

Throw the Elbow

Throw the Fastball

Throw the Gauntlet

Throw the Hissy

Never miss an April May Snow release.

Join the reader's club!

www.mscottswanson.com

Author's note- This is a work of fiction. Character names, businesses, locations, crime incidents and hauntings are purely imagination. Where the public names of locations are used, please know it is from a place of love and respect from this author. Any resemblance to actual people living or dead or to private events or establishments is entirely coincidental.

Now I believe there comes a time
When everything just falls in line
We live an' learn from our mistakes
The deepest cuts are healed by faith

Pat Benatar-
"All Fired Up"

Chapter 1

"You can't possibly expect me to believe that." I narrow my eyes at Ms. Applewhite.

"It's the truth, dear. I was simply cleaning up. No one ever clears the debris. You can't count on the groundskeepers to do it. They're way too lazy."

"Do you expect me to believe that you're some sort of benevolent grave caretaker?"

She purses her lips. "Oh, I really like the sound of that."

I rub my right temple. A massive migraine threatens to pile onto my already trying day.

It is less than a week until Christmas, and the collective town of Guntersville has lost its ever-loving mind. I have had more misdemeanors and theft charge clients to defend than I can shake a stick at. Still, DA Lane Jameson seems to intend to prosecute every one of them before our Christmas Eve recess.

"Oakville Cemetery claims they put fresh poinsettias out this week for decoration of the mausoleum. I doubt seriously, as a trained florist, you believed the flowers needed disposal."

"Fresh is relative, dear."

I favor Ms. Applewhite my well-learned "I refuse to take any more of your bull malarkey" stare. By how she squirms, creating an awkward squeak sound on the cushion of the pleather chair she sits on, my stare is as effective as ever.

"Well, perhaps I made a mistake." Rhonda Applewhite rolls her eyes. "It's tough to tell how long these arrangements have been out when so many of the fly-by-night florists provide blooms considerably past their prime. Some of them are complete garbage by the time they arrive on site."

I am attempting to be patient, but she is getting on my last nerve. "They were poinsettias. Hello Christmas?"

"How was I to know they were for Christmas? Honestly, dear, I thought they were trying to save money. Poinsettias are less expensive before Christmas. I really believed they were a few weeks old."

I have no clue if poinsettias are less expensive before Christmas or if she is lying to me. However, I do know she is lying to me about cleaning up the gravesites.

Rhonda Applewhite bought one of the local florist shops, Petals and More, three years earlier when widow Warden passed. Widow Warden had no immediate family, and her only surviving relatives, two elderly cousins, lived out of state.

Rhonda Applewhite bought the florist for what I understand to be a fire sale price. Unfortunately, purchasing the business did not extend any of the essential business acumen necessary for the continued success of the florist. It is common knowledge in town Rhonda skimps on all her flower arrangements. Consequently, her clientele was ever-shrinking as fewer people traded with her by the month.

Sitting across the table from Rhonda, I am amazed how her cheerful round figure and bright gray hair belie her true character. At least if the newly installed security cameras at Oakville cemetery are to be believed.

The police had received numerous reports from the surrounding cemeteries over the last year. Oakville, by far the largest cemetery in Guntersville, filed most of the complaints. Flower wreaths were disappearing overnight from newly deceased citizens. Worse, holiday decorations recently put out at the expense of the cemetery were stripped bare of blooms meant to prepare the grounds for the Christmas visitors.

The thefts were not limited to flowers. Oakville lost thirty large jack-o'-lanterns during October and a nativity scene just after Thanksgiving.

What sort of person steals a nativity scene?

As I look across the table at the grandmotherly looking woman, I push out cautiously with my senses. I give a shiver as the nature of her energy melds with mine. Her signature is dark, cold, and hungry.

Ask a stupid question about who would steal a nativity scene—well, I have my answer.

"Rhonda, I'm sure you can justify stealing the flowers you sold to your grieving clients a day earlier. Perhaps you have a cash flow issue. Maybe your suppliers ran out of stock. The point is, I don't care.

"Do you understand? I don't care why you did it. I'm just here to help you mitigate the punishment and get on with your life. To do that, I need you to be honest with me so we can build a defense."

"I am being honest. This is just a malicious lie being spread by one of the other florists in town. They know my work is superior to theirs."

I've had my fill. I'd take care of ten DUIs to one Rhonda Applewhite.

It really gets my goat when people lie to me. It is difficult enough to defend a client's stupid actions. But Rhonda is making it monumentally difficult with her continued lying.

"Fine." I stand too fast. My migraine spikes. I grab the side of my head as I shuffle to the projector and turn it on. "Maybe this will change your mind." I hit the feed from my laptop, and a grainy security picture projects onto the wall.

We watch the film as a minivan pulls up close to the mausoleum. A very round person, who by their walk appears to be female, collects twenty large potted poinsettias and loads them into the back of the minivan. The thief's hair is concealed by a hoodie, their face hidden by a mask.

"Does this look familiar?" I ask Rhonda.

"It looks like it might be Oakview, but I can't be for sure."

I point at the round image collecting poinsettias. "I mean this person."

Rhonda takes her time inspecting the person in the security footage. She moves closer to the image and squints. In a halting voice, she says, "No. I can't say that I do."

This is driving me nuts. "Rhonda, it's you. Stop with the games, please."

"I don't know how many times I have to tell you I'm not playing a game. I have no idea who that is."

Oakview had waited two weeks before reporting any of the incidents as they were waiting to capture the car tag. During that time, their security cameras recorded this thief stealing flowers every night.

Last night they caught a break. Rhonda parked her van right in front of one of the cameras, and the staff was able to record her tag number.

"Rhonda, it's you."

"No, it's not," Rhonda insists.

I point at the decal on the side of the van. "Petals and More. It's your van."

"It doesn't mean anything."

The ice picks of my migraine poke at the back of my neck. I clutch at the base of my skull with my right hand. This round of headaches will be painful and last a while. I can just tell.

"If you can't tell me the truth, Rhonda, I'll have to get with DA Jameson and see if he will transfer your case."

Rhonda crosses her arms as she leans back in her chair. "That will be fine by me. You don't exactly impress me as somebody who can really defend me."

I jerk my eyebrows upward, acknowledging her comment, pack my backpack, and walk out the door. My friend, Jade the security officer, stands outside the door.

"Good meeting?" she asks.

"You might as well fix that one a cell. I don't know how I'm going to keep her from being one of your permanent residents."

"Darn. I was sort of hoping you would take her with you. She's not near as sweet as she looks."

"Tell me about it."

Chapter 2

I decide I'm too busy to work on a case where I have no empathy for the defendant. Rather than head north the two blocks to Snow and Associates, I walk one block in the opposite direction to the DA's Annex building.

I don't have an appointment. Still, that has never prevented me from getting an audience before.

Bailey Nix is working at the DA's front desk. I went to school with her older brother, Brad. "Is he in?" I ask.

Bailey opens her mouth to say something, then clamps it shut as she takes in my aggravated body language. She clicks a button on her phone. "DA Jameson? April Snow is here to see you."

"Give me a minute." Lane's voice crackles across the line.

"How's your brother?" I ask.

My question brings a smile to Bailey's face. "He's great. He and his wife Libby just found out they're pregnant again."

My gosh. I think Brad and Libby are trying to single-handedly repopulate the earth with tall, skinny white people. "Is that, like, their third?"

"No, this is their fifth they're expecting," Bailey says.

Good Lord. And I'm having a tough time committing to having one. I suppose I might need to determine who my baby daddy or husband will be before worrying too much about committing to a child.

"You can send her in, Bailey."

I give Bailey a finger wave as I walk toward Lane's door. "Tell them both hi for me."

Lane is typing on his laptop. His large mahogany desk is placed strategically in the center of the room, his back to the wall and two uncomfortable chairs for guests. The chairs are eight inches shorter than the desk.

I plop down in one of the chairs. My chin is barely level with the top of his desktop.

Lane is stressed and his workload untenable. But anyone who didn't know where to look would only see a calm, taller version of George Clooney. If the networks ever wanted to cast a Southern lawyer, they could do far worse than give Lane Jameson a call for the part.

The desk is the key to knowing Lane's current mindset. Most days, there would only be one, or at the most two folders open on his desk and none on the second desk behind him. Lane likes to keep everything buttoned up and in its place.

Today there are five separate piles of folders stacked on his side desk. In the center of his desk next to his keyboard is one the size of an unabridged dictionary.

"What can I do for you today, Counselor Snow?" Lane says without looking away from his computer screen.

"Ms. Applewhite and I have come to a mutual agreement that she needs to be appointed a different counselor."

"No."

I'm sure I simply overreacted due to my heightened frustration from dealing with Rhonda, but it felt like Lane slapped me in the face. "Maybe I didn't explain it correctly. We can't work together."

"You explained it effectively. I understood your point. And the answer is no," he says again without the courtesy of looking in my direction.

I accidentally let out a frustrated bark of laughter. "I don't think you get it. We can't work together."

He tears his eyes away from the screen. I lean back due to the intensity of his glare. "I would suggest the two of you work out your differences."

"I don't see why you can't just assign her to somebody else," I whine.

"Because I assigned her to you." He returns his attention to his case. "Besides, you're it."

"What do you mean I'm it?"

"I mean, you're it. Monique is on maternity leave, your uncle is in Mobile until Christmas Eve, and Lamar just transferred to the Jefferson County District Attorney's office." He looks at me pointedly. "You're the only defense attorney I have until after Christmas break."

What is it in the water making everybody get pregnant? And why did Lane let Lamar take a promotion when we need him here? "So, you're really gonna stick me with Ms. Applewhite?"

Lane rubs his hands through his perfect hair. It falls back into place perfectly like some physics anomaly. "What are you not understanding, April? You're the last counselor standing in town until Christmas break. I've got two more DUIs and three theft charges I'm giving you today. They all need to be cleared before Christmas Eve."

That's too much work. I can't handle all that. Actually, I'm capable of it. I just don't want to handle all that. "I can work ten hours a day and not be able to clear those up before Christmas Eve."

"Then I guess you better plan on working eleven hours a day. Plus Saturday, if needed." He pushes the stack of folders on his desk to me. Reluctantly I lift them off his desk.

If I thought it would do any good, I would stay and argue longer. Judging by the number of cases on Lane's desk and the situation with all the other defense attorneys, I know there isn't any choice. I don't like it, but I figure I might as well take my sulking elsewhere since it won't earn me any brownie points with Lane.

This bites. Somehow my part-time, mostly a glorified receptionist job has turned into a legal partner position without the title, car, or cut of the profits. Howard will have to come off some serious dough if this is going to continue.

My aggravation dissipates as I walk by the town square back to the office in the blustery forty-degree weather.

There is no point in having a conversation with Howard about a pay increase. I will be transferring to Baltimore or the D.C. area in the next couple of months when Lee returns to Baltimore to start the professional baseball season.

That is the plan. I'm not exactly following Lee. I'm following my dream of working in a major metropolitan area, and it doesn't get much more prominent than the capital. Plus, it will be a fun benefit to have an attractive boyfriend to come home to when the team is having a homestand. Still, there will be plenty of opportunities to work the insane hours required to make partner while he is on the road.

It is all fitting in nicely. I love it when my plans come together.

Even if I cannot find a suitable law firm for my services, I have the offer from agent King in my back pocket. I can always apply for the FBI.

I still feel like I need to pinch myself to make sure I'm not dreaming that Lee Darby and I are a hot number now. It just dills my pickle that we found each other, and the second time around is so right.

It's like Granny always says about things happening for a reason. I wouldn't have been here when Lee moved back home if my career had not gone to heck in a handbasket, forcing me to regroup in Guntersville. We wouldn't have been together to make our connection.

Yes, my life is genuinely coming together now. I'm beginning to feel like the old April again.

His team is located in Baltimore, which is perfect for me. There is plenty of opportunity for me in D.C., and I have a network there as some of my law school friends work in the area.

The fact Lee owns a beautiful gargantuan home on the lake

ten minutes from my parents' lake house means we will be able to spend quality time with my family during the off-season.

If you had asked me last year, I would have said that is not important to me. Still, after the previous six months, it has become vital to me.

See, I can even change my mind and own the error of my ways.

I do feel awful for Howard. I believe he's become too dependent on me.

Recently, he bought another business. He also has a girlfriend, yet I've never met or spoken to her. Still, it's pretty apparent, even though he refuses to discuss the matter with me, his heart is in Mobile.

He did not have time to pursue either the second business or the personal relationship before I began working with him. He must find a replacement for me before I leave in the spring.

Spring is what I have penciled in as my "leaving Guntersville" date. That's when Lee will be returning to Baltimore. It might be a little sooner, but that's the plan for now.

Walking into the law office, I drop the folders on my desk. I decide to pop some popcorn before I begin the arduous task of going through the files and calling the clients.

I'm not particularly hungry. Popping popcorn is just one of the best procrastination ploys.

I watch the popcorn bag spin in the microwave for the first minute. I pull out my phone and hit speed dial.

"Hi, what's up, baby?"

Lee's voice makes me feel warm. "I'm just missing you."

"I know what you mean. I sure wish I was home with you right now."

I scan the small break room in the law office, aware that even if he were in Guntersville, I would still be at work right now. "I wish you were, too. When are you going to be home?"

"Ahh—I hope by Friday. It's not going quite as fast as I was hoping. My velocity is up, but I still don't have the movement I want."

"I thought *I* had the movement you wanted."

Lee chuckles. "That's true, too. Maybe if Coach can help me get a little movement on my pitch, you can show me your movement when I get home."

"That's a possibility."

"You know you're killing me." His tone is joking. We have spent many hours together over the last month, but we still have not taken the final "physical" step in our relationship yet.

"Good things come to those who wait."

"But not to those who wait too late," he grumbles.

"What's that supposed to mean?"

"Nothing. That's the saying. Not to those who wait too late."

My face tightens. "It sounds as if you are trying to make a point."

"You're giving me too much credit. I'm a ballplayer. I don't think that deep."

Lee is a mess. But he's my mess, and he is uber cute.

I know he's sexually frustrated. Mainly because I am, too.

Believe me, I am no prude, and nobody could use a quick sexual fix more than me. It's been a long time, as in—well, when you have to stop to figure out when it was, you know it's been too long.

Still, I feel this is the long-term relationship I have dreamed of my entire life. A relationship that allows me to have my career and the man of my dreams.

And I don't want to mess it up by moving too quickly.

That, and although I'm all in on the relationship, there's a teeny tiny lone voice in my head screaming, "It's not real! You're going to get hurt!" I know it's a random rogue thought as I have zero indication that Lee is anything other than perfect.

Still, it can be a mood killer.

"Well, Mr. Big Mouth, I guess you're fortunate that your girlfriend lets things go so easy."

"Yes, I am very grateful that my girlfriend is easy."

I laugh. "That's not what I said!"

"It's not? It's what I heard."

"No. It's what you hope," I say.

The bell on the front door jingles. A familiar elderly woman shuffles into the office.

"Lee, I need to let you go. Someone just came into the office."

"Oh. All right, I'll call you tonight. Love you."

"Yeah. You, too," I say as I disconnect the line.

"Good morning, Ms. Castle. How can I help you today?"

"Is Howard in?" Her raspberry-painted lips disappear into a fine line as she waits for my answer.

"No, ma'am. I'm the only one holding down the fort today." I know she will take exception to my answer. "Is there something I can assist you with?"

"I need to change my will."

Ms. Castle comes in every six to eight weeks to change her will. It's wise for people to plan their estates so they don't end up in probate and ravaged by taxes. It's even understandable that people will change their minds occasionally about how their assets will be distributed upon their death.

Changing your mind every two months based on what someone did or didn't do for you or say to you is a bit trying. It borders on insanity when your net worth is close to zero.

Ms. Castle's cash flow is down to her Social Security check. She does own a farm on the north side of town that is excellent for growing rocks. Other than that, her wealth resides solely in her head.

Howard insists we continue to change her will for her at no charge. I don't like it, and I feel it is stupid, but it's his firm.

I open my laptop. "So, what changes are we making today?"

She looks around the room as if expecting to find someone else in the office and steps closer to me. She leans over my desk. "I want to sell the old farmhouse, so I need to change my will."

"Okay. Why do you need to change your will?"

She frowns and looks at me as if I'm an idiot. "Because it's presently supposed to be transferred to my cousin Joan upon my death. It would be awfully embarrassing if the will is read and she finds out that I had left the house and property to her but sold it out from under her before I died."

Fair. "Okay, we can change that. I'll delete all references about the property."

"Good. One other thing."

"Yes, ma'am."

"The man I'm selling the property to, he asked when the last time it was platted. Do you know what that means?"

"Yes, ma'am."

"Good. How do I go about getting that done?"

"I'm not positive, but my mama is a real estate agent, and I can ask her and let you know."

Ms. Castle nods her head. "Good. Thank you." She clutches her purse and turns as if to leave. She pauses, turning back to me. "I really don't want to sell."

I begin to tell her she doesn't have to, then realize it must be for financial reasons. I know her home is paid for, but maintenance and the annual taxes alone on the house as large as hers can drain a fixed budget.

"Please don't tell anyone about this. Other than your mama."

"No ma'am, lawyer-client privilege."

She forces a smile that threatens to crack her near-white make-up base. "Yes, lawyer-client privilege."

As Dottie Castle leaves our office, I notice something smells like it is burning. I follow the scent to the break room and move into overdrive as I see the thick smoke rolling out of the microwave.

Jerking my bag of popcorn out of the microwave, I toss it into the sink. I hose it down with cold water until the smoldering subsides.

So much for my popcorn snack. Good thing I wasn't actually hungry.

Chapter 3

I work through lunch on the cases Lane dumped on me. After scheduling my client meetings for early in the morning, I returned to the jail that afternoon to give Rhonda Applewhite the splendid news that we would be working together after all.

It doesn't alter any of the stories she is peddling. This forces me to warn her that if she does not accept some accountability for her actions, she will be looking at some serious jail time as well as being obligated to pay back the cemeteries for the flowers she stole.

She is nonplussed, but I feel better for having leveled with her.

I look at my phone as I exit the jail and am surprised to see it is already four thirty. I'm hungry, aggravated, and need some alone time.

As a rule, I'm not a big drinker—anymore. But today, with it being a rough day and my boyfriend being hundreds of miles away, I could really use a drink.

I get in my IROC and drive out to Jester's. There are better places for a girl to get a drink. Still, I can check in with my friend Winky and see how one of my former clients and Winky's new employee, Sylvester, is acclimating to the workforce.

The smell of stale beer and cigarettes greets me as I enter

Jester's. Sylvester Langham is working as the barkeep. He gestures a greeting to me as he tucks a towel in his back pocket.

Always vigilant now, I notice the three bikers at the pool table and two truck drivers at the bar talking in front of Sylvester.

That makes the bar two people too crowded for me. I head for one of the small tables at the back of the room.

I have only been to Jester's twice since Winky hired Sylvester. It is the first time I've seen Sylvester working behind the bar. He seems comfortable enough. Maybe Winky has made a good decision, giving Sylvester a chance. I hope so for both men.

"How are you, Ms. April?" Sylvester greets me when he makes it to my table.

"Honestly, it's been a rough day, Sylvester. What would you suggest for me to put it all behind me?"

His smile reveals two gold teeth. Either they are new, or he has never smiled in front of me before. "Well, I'd recommend a month at the beach. But we'll probably need to improvise. I know a drink called Naked on the Beach that will make you think you're on the beach in no time."

"You're pulling my leg, Sylvester."

"No, ma'am. True story."

"Right. Then tell me what's in it."

"Pineapple juice, mango nectar, coconut rum, blue liquor, and a shot of moonshine."

"You're crazy. I'm not drinking that."

Sylvester favors me a good-natured shrug. "You don't know what you're missing out on."

"Right. Just bring me some sangria and some fries if you don't mind."

"Cheeseburger and fries?"

"No. I'm trying to watch my calories before Christmas dinner. I'm still working off the Halloween candy and the Thanksgiving feast."

Sylvester gives me an appraising look that leaves me feeling a little uncomfortable. He rolls his lower lip out. "I—don't see—the issue."

"That's sweet. But I do see it."

Sylvester is smart enough to let it drop and retreats to the bar.

While I wait for him to return, four more bikers come in and start a game at the second pool table, and three more truck drivers enter, taking up a table. It looks like it is going to be a busy night.

One of the truckers feeds a bill into the jukebox. A Travis Tritt song begins to play. It fits the general ambiance of Jester's.

Sylvester reappears with a loaded-down tray. "Sangria, cheeseburger and fries, and a Naked on the Beach."

"Sylvester, I'm not paying for all this. I just wanted sangria and fries."

"You're not paying for any of it." He shows me the tab where he has written April across it in red letters. "Winky told me to take care of you next time you came in."

"Thank you. That's sweet of you." I scan the bar. "Where is Winky?"

"He took the old man up to the VFW. One of his friends is having a birthday celebration. They usually can't go because they would have to close the bar."

My stomach tightens, and I hate that I have the reaction. "You're here by yourself?"

Sylvester makes a dismissive gesture. "I can handle it. It's no big deal. Besides, I think the old man is so cranky because he doesn't get out any."

By my calculations, Jester Warner is cranky because he is a mean old jerk who is verbally abusive. Winky, his only son, takes care of him. The way Jester treats him makes Winky a saint in my book.

I hope Winky hasn't put too much trust in Sylvester just yet. It is good that he gave Sylvester a job. Everyone needs a second chance. But Sylvester is only a few weeks removed from being a hard-core thief. Old habits die hard.

If something goes wrong, in my mind, it would be just as much Winky's fault as Sylvester's. It is way too early to be laying this much temptation in front of Sylvester.

I cover my fries with ketchup and begin to eat them with a fork. They are still hot with a crispy shell. Just the way I like them.

The sangria is good too, complete with a slice of orange and pineapple garnish on the glass. Sylvester has brought some flair for presentation to the joint, if nothing else.

Tomorrow is going to be a full day with a total of five interviews. That in and of itself is a lot of work.

But that is just the start. I'll then have to prepare for the hearings, make sure we are on the docket, and sometimes the most difficult of all, make sure my clients show up on time. With Friday being the last court day before Christmas break, I have zero margin for error.

I cut a portion of the hamburger and take a bite. Oh my. That is certainly much better than usual.

One of the things bothering me is if I should move in with Lee when we move to Baltimore. It makes sense, financially and logistically, but I never really thought I would live with someone without being married. I'm not a slave to social mores. I figured I wouldn't ever live with someone.

If we were going to live together in Baltimore, should we try a trial run in Guntersville? That sounds like a fun idea, and a part of me is begging, "Yes!" Still, for some reason, that doesn't seem like a great idea.

I feel like Lee wouldn't mind and might even like the idea. Then again, I like having my own place to retreat to and regroup if I have a rough day or just need to think.

The Naked on the Beach drink is absolutely incredible. I feel warm all over, and yes, it does make me feel like I want to go streaking. No, I'm just kidding.

I mean, it's like thirty degrees outside.

The door flies open, and an attractive young man stands in the doorway as snow blows into the bar over his shoulders.

He shuts the door as he stomps snow off his odd black lace-up boots.

I watch him with interest as he makes his way over to the now-silent jukebox, reaches into his pocket, and drops coins into the machine.

"Blue Moon Kentucky" begins to play.

It causes me to smile. I remember as a young child dancing to that song. My mama always said that it was Nana's favorite song. Something about knowing one of your family members likes something, even if you don't take to it right away, you try to enjoy the same things they do. With time I have come to love the song.

The attractive young man walks toward the back of Jester's past the bikers playing pool. My back stiffens as I realize he is coming toward my table. I begin to panic.

"Are you doing alright tonight, April?" he asks.

How does he know my name? I hate it when I have forgotten someone's name, yet they remember mine. "Sure. How are you?"

The young man pulls out a chair and sits down at my table.

"Be my guest." I don't try to hide the sarcasm. I don't want to be rude, but I also don't feel the need to entertain anybody. Especially somebody I can't remember.

"Mighty friendly of you." He stares at me, and I am transfixed by his hazel green eyes. It feels like we are touching even though the table separates us.

Ah, to heck with it. A little bit of conversation with somebody that I don't remember isn't gonna kill me. "You come here often?"

He looks over both shoulders as if taking in Jester's for the first time. "Actually, my first time."

"The best pointers I can give you is the beer is cold, the wine gives you a headache, and you don't play pool with any of those biker dudes."

The man's lips twitch into a smile. I suddenly realize he is at least five years younger than me. His youth was initially masked by the severe expression on his face.

"Why are you nervous?" he asks.

"I'm not nervous. Why would you say that?"

He shrugs nonchalantly. "You always make light of the situation when you're nervous."

Who is this dude? And who is he to say that about me? I wave my hand in front of me. "Excuse me, do I know you?"

"Not in the sense that you mean. But I do know you."

Okay, so maybe talking to weird strangers isn't the best decision. "Okay, how about you do both of us a favor and move your riddle game to a different table. I was here trying to just chill out, and you're causing me to stress."

"No need to stress." He took the glass with the Naked on the Beach and slings back the last of it. "In the end, you'll figure out that almost everything you stressed about is pointless, and a lot of the time, the things you took for granted are the few things you *should* have stressed about."

Between the long day and the alcohol, I'm not in the mood for attractive weird dude's riddles. "Okay, I'm sure you got a great future writing fortune cookie sayings, but I say this in the kindest way possible. Please move your butt to another table before I have to call somebody over to do it for me."

He locks eyes with me a second time. Again, it feels like he is physically touching me. "You want me to prove to you that I know you?"

"Heck no." I'm way past creeped out and fumbling for my purse.

"Wait. Give me a minute of your time."

It's probably lousy decision number two, but I pause with my purse in my lap.

"You can do something that you're extremely proud of that only a couple of people in the world know you can do."

"Yeah, attract the attention of wackadoodles. Only you're wrong; I'm not proud of it."

"Nervous again. Making light of the situation."

Now he's ruffled my feathers, and I shoot to my feet. "Listen

—" I realize I still haven't remembered his name. "I've asked you nicely. This is your last warning. You need to move on."

"Shhh—sit down. You don't have anything to prove to me."

I want to argue. I want to tell him he needs to head right back out that door before he gets his butt whupped. But we lock eyes again, and I feel my breathing and heart rate regulate. Calmness washes over me as I sit.

Grinning, he leans forward while cupping his hands together in the center of the table. "You'll like this," he says.

I'm in a daze. I am overly tired, have a nice buzz from the moonshine, and feel almost tranquilized in the presence of— whatever his name is.

There is a yellow light glowing from inside his cupped hands. Slowly he opens his hands just enough for me to look inside. The rotating ball of flame, orange-yellow and blue, between his two cupped palms looks like a miniature sun. "This is what your Nana is trying to teach you. Control. Total control of the uncontrollable things in life. The person who can do that rules their destiny."

The miniature sun contained in between his hands is too fascinating to ignore even though I have to endure another fortune cookie bit of wisdom while I watch.

I'm racking my brain to think of how this man can know I dabble in fire creation. The only people who know are Nana, of course, and the paranormal team. Sure, I had a little mishap with fire creation in Birmingham last month. Well, I burned a house down. Still, nobody outside the team was the wiser that it wasn't another case of an abandoned home burning down from a random lightning strike.

"So, you know my Nana?"

Again, the hauntingly familiar smile that made him appear to be only a few years out of high school, "Yes. I know your Nana very well."

"What's your name?"

He hesitates. "Robert."

"Does Robert have a last name?"

"If you plan on asking your Nana if she knows me, you won't need the last name."

This game has gone on long enough. It's time to get the information I need.

I reach out with my energy in an attempt to get a power reading off the man. It is as if my field stops its progress six inches in front of Robert, then circles around him. It never touches him.

That's a first. I've never felt that before.

Still, I'm not receiving any negative readings from him. No positive feelings flow to me, either. He is an enigma.

"Why are you so concerned about these cases if you're headed to Baltimore in three months?"

Excellent question. "Because my reputation matters to me. I'm going to continue doing my job to the best of my abilities until the day I leave."

"That's admirable. At your core, if nothing else, you are honorable."

"Thanks," I say with a surprised tone to match my feelings.

"You can also be feckless, materialistic, and driven by other people's measurements of success."

Dang, that's harsh. "I disagree with you."

"I know, the truth hurts. But we can't stay in denial forever."

I am one more fortune cookie saying away from messing up his pretty face. "You're sort of over the line now."

"You need someone to be over the line. Let's face it, you don't do subtle."

I'm struggling to understand what I am dealing with in Robert. I am past thinking he is some random chance meeting. I also have dispelled any belief that I am in the company of a human.

If Robert is a ghost, he is the most complete apparition I've ever encountered. There is the possibility that I am asleep in my car. I was tired enough to fall asleep before entering Jester's. I might even be passed out on top of the table from the Naked on the Beach drink.

The fact remains that this man, Robert, understands things about me that a normal human being could not even begin to know. This leads to another possibility.

Robert might be a demon or an angel.

I don't like either prospect. Regardless of which team he is on, the chance of dealing with something besides witches and ghosts does not sit well with me.

"You don't need to worry," he says with a perturbed tone.

"I beg your pardon?"

"About who I am. You're concerned about it. The only thing you really need to know is that I have your best interest in mind."

This is rich. "Do you, now?"

"Yes."

"You just met me. How can you possibly know what's in my best interest?"

He leans back in his chair. "People hire consultants for businesses all the time. The consultants come in and study the operation and give their best assessment. Just think of me as your personal consultant. A consultant who has already studied every aspect of your life."

A chill runs down my spine as if someone just walked across my grave. If I had more juice, I might set up a defensive barrier. Still, I'm afraid my mind is already too scattered to do that effectively. "What do you mean you studied me?"

He frowns. "Don't make it all weird, April. You really shouldn't worry about it. It's all semantics after all, anyway."

I can continue to argue the point that it does matter. But to what end?

It won't get me anywhere. He is only going to tell me exactly what I need to know. I will have to turn the table somehow.

"You're not from around here, Robert. Where are you from?"

"I'm from here, and my people are from here. Just because we run in different crowds doesn't mean I'm not a Guntersville native."

My understanding of the situation comes in a rush to me. I

know exactly whom I am speaking to now. I try to contain my emotions and can sufficiently tamp down my fear. Still, I am unable to corral my curiosity.

"Nana still bakes a cake for you every year on your birthday."

"No. We're not going to make this about me. It's about you, April."

"I don't see how you separate the two. Your history is a big part of me."

Robert narrows his eyes as he crosses his arms. "Okay. Fair enough, I suppose. But I don't understand how it might help."

Grandpa Hirsch left for Vietnam in late 1969. He wasn't aware that his new bride, Pauline Hirsch, was five weeks pregnant when he shipped out.

I knew I had seen the striking young man's face before. I had seen him in at Nana's. Two photos in her foyer and one of her and this young man cutting up and laughing sits in solidarity on her nightstand.

I asked Nana on numerous occasions why Grandpa had gone to war. She always replied that he didn't have a choice. But every time she said that, I got the distinct impression she was lying.

"I never understood how you could've left Nana."

"I left her with a heavy heart." There is no mirth in his answer.

"She still loves you."

"I love her to the end time."

I suppose that should make me sad given the situation, but instead, it makes me happy. I guess it affects me because I like the idea that Nana's love is reciprocated.

Reciprocated love is a powerful thing. Reciprocated love can transcend the grave.

"Where are you? I know it still bothers her. She doesn't mention it, but I can tell."

"Of course, you can."

I raise my eyebrows in anticipation. I want him to know that I expect an answer.

"Caisson Delta, but it's not important, April. Too many years have passed. I won't be coming home. Pauline knows that. She's good with it now."

His answer tweaks something in my brain. "Do you two communicate?"

He smiles, and the stern expression melts from his face again. "I visit Pauline in her dreams when I can. I would more often, but I know it puts her in a bad place. I never want to hurt her, but sometimes I need to see her. I still have needs too."

"Why have you been spying on me?"

Robert, *Bob* Hirsch, purses his lips and wags a finger side to side. "It's customary that you ask a question, and then I ask a question."

My anxiety level rises considerably. I have been able to identify who the entity is, but I still am not sure of Bob's intent.

I know he can say he is here for my benefit, but the forces of evil are deceptive in nature. If he is evil, that is precisely what I would expect him to say.

"The flower cannot bloom while riding on the air."

Here we go with another one of his Chinese proverbs. "I beg your pardon?"

"You have begun to sprout the start of roots in the fertile grounds of your hometown. Yet you're about to rip up those new roots and follow a young man you barely know to a land that is a mystery to you."

When Grandpa says it like that, it sounds almost unseemly, if not stupid on my part. "I think I'm in love."

"Your very answer shows that your actions are premature if not ill-conceived."

I frown and jerk my head back. "Wait just a darn a minute now. Lee is a good man."

"This has nothing to do with Lee. This is all about April and April's heart."

"So, what? You've come from beyond the grave to question my life decisions? If you don't mind, no thanks. I've got this."

"I beg to differ. I don't think you've given this decision its due level of thought." He shrugs his shoulders. "You may come to the conclusion that you do love Lee, not that you *think* you do and follow him to Baltimore after all. Or you may take any number of other trajectories with your life. That's not my concern. What is my concern is if you have taken a deliberate decision on what April's life trajectory should look like."

"Of course, I have. I'm not gonna take these decisions willy-nilly."

"You've already set things in motion, April. I am here because there is still time for you to change course, but your decisions in the next few days will significantly impact the rest of your life. I'm here to ensure you are evaluating those decisions into the full context of your life."

You know, you go to the local bar to have a drink, and somebody just has to mess with your buzz.

How about this for standard operating procedures. I just got my head straight about what's going on in my life and feel great about it. Leave it to a family member to come and mess up my quiet time and the peace in my heart. In this case, the family member happens to be a man who had been dead and disappeared for forty years. A man I have never met before tonight.

"Listen, I appreciate the concern. I really do. It's just I'm working through my life fine, and I'm not looking for input from family. No offense but especially a family member who is dead and never met me before today."

Robert lays a hand on his chest. "I'm sorry. I must not have explained correctly. This isn't advice. This is an event. I've come to tell you that before Christmas morning, you will be visited by three mentors."

What the heck. "Mentors? Do you mean ghosts? Is this like some sort of *Christmas Carol* joke?"

Robert's expression hardens. "This is no joke. And for the record, ghosts can be mentors, too. Again, semantics, young lady."

That's it. I've had it. I'm out of here. I gather up my purse and stand to leave.

"Are you going?" Robert asks.

"Yes, way, way far away from you."

I stop as I pass the bar and wave to Sylvester. "Sylvester, thank you for taking care of me tonight."

He appears alarmed. "Are you sure you're okay to drive?"

"Sure I am. Again, thank you."

"I can call you a cab." Sylvester shouts at my back.

I wave a hand in the air as I continue toward the door. "Thanks. I've got this."

Stepping outside, the brutal northern wind cuts through my clothing. A few bits of snow land on my face for additional effect.

"Semantics, young lady. I'll semantics his butt. That 1960s version of a pretty boy. Thinking he can come here and tell me how to run my life."

I unlock my IROC. The leather seats are unbelievably cold.

Starting the engine, I take stock of my present level of inebriation. I don't feel drunk, but I'm probably pretty close to the limit. As long as I pay attention and take it slow, I should be okay, though.

Checking the time on my phone, I calculate the amount of wine I had and the amount of time that has passed. Oh, I'm way good. Wait, the moonshine—but I only had a sip or two. Robert—*Bob*—finished that drink.

I pull out onto State Highway 72, driving back toward Guntersville. It is already dark. It gets so dark so quick this time of year. The snow isn't sticking to the road, which is still too warm, but it has reduced visibility.

I give my total concentration to getting home safely, slipping into my PJs, and going to sleep. This evening has not gone to plan.

Who the heck is Grandpa to be questioning whether or not I really love Lee? Of course, I love Lee.

I loved him when we dated in high school. I'm highly attracted to him.

It just goes to show that family should never get involved

with matters of the heart. You love who you love.

I am miffed at Nana, too. All these Thursday classes for the last few months, and she's never mentioned that her dead husband occasionally talks to her through her dreams? I mean, given that I have had dreams where I transferred in time and place, I don't know—maybe it might come up in our conversation at some time. Like perhaps somebody would've thought that could be helpful information for me?

And how about the fact that Nana isn't the only one with skills on Mama's side of the family. Bob alluded to several things that make me think he has the same skill set as Nana.

That wouldn't exactly surprise me. I can see where I might be attracted to somebody that had the same skill set as I do just because it's easier to be weird if your partner is a freak, too.

She really didn't think that would be something of interest to me? I'm seriously disappointed in her.

It is all so aggravating beyond imagination. The last twenty years have been bad enough hearing random voices whenever I pass by a cemetery or a location where someone died in a car accident or was murdered. Now I'm actually having apparitions walk up to me and strike up a conversation?

No. This has to end, and Nana's going to have to help me with it. If she says she can't, I'll tell her I'm going to get Granny to help me. That'll put a fire under her butt.

"You really shouldn't be driving in your condition."

My heart stops and my head jerks to the right, as does my hand on the steering wheel. Grandpa is riding shotgun in my car. I pull the wheel back to the left as I tap the shoulder and am able to stabilize my vehicle.

"What are you trying to do? Kill us?" I scream at him.

"I'm already dead."

"I'm not! Besides, don't be obtuse. You know what I meant." I alternate glares between him and the increasing snowstorm.

"I don't understand why you're angry at me. I'm just trying to get you home safely."

"What? You nearly scared me into the ditch. Great job!"

"You left out before you confirmed you understood about your mentors showing up."

"About three ghosts showing up? How about no thanks."

"You need this."

"Like a hole in my head. I'm telling you, you start sending ghosts my way, and I will put up a barrier that's gonna take until next Christmas to get through. So, tell them just save their energy and leave me alone. That goes for you, too, even if you are family."

"Pull over," Bob says.

"I'm not pulling over for you to get out. You popped into that car seat. You can pop right back out."

"No, pull over. You are in no shape to be driving."

"I'm fine. If somebody would quit distracting me, it wouldn't be any problem at all."

"You're falling asleep," he insists.

"Am not."

The light is reflecting oddly back through the snow. It takes me a second, but I finally realize it isn't my headlights. It is the headlights of the car coming directly at me.

My brain and body freeze with fear of the impending impact when the steering wheel suddenly wrenches hard to the right, throwing me against the driver's door. The steering wheel then twists back to the left, sliding me into the console, and I feel a cold chill as my arm passes through Bob's arm—his hand on the steering wheel.

Chapter 4

I feel someone staring at me. I'm lying on my left side and open my right eye halfway. Puppy is sitting on his haunches, looking at me with great expectations.

Unless Puppy is the one of the Christmas ghosts, I must have dreamed that whole Grandpa Hirsch episode.

"What do you want? You can use your door if you have to go potty. If you're hungry, go to Mama's. I'm sure someone is cooking breakfast."

Puppy barks at me. That catches me off guard. He will growl sometimes and whine often, but barking is like his emergency mode.

I scan my surroundings. I'm in my apartment, no strange visions in the full-length mirror, no one in the bed with me besides Puppy, and no random voices in my head. Those are all good things.

"Hush, boy." I push against his furry mane. He quiets, but it is obvious he doesn't want to abide by my command.

With him silenced, I consider rolling over and going back to sleep. I feel like I have the flu or something and need some extra rest.

As a matter of habit, I pick up my phone on my nightstand and check the time. "Eight thirty?" Every muscle body contracts as my eyes go to the clock on the microwave oven to confirm the time.

Yes, it is eight thirty. My first interview is at nine o'clock.

I jump out of bed, my head dizzy from hopping up so quickly, or maybe it is this flu bug. I slide into the bathroom and begin to brush my teeth as I rifle through my cabinet for hair gel. I'm going to need something to help force down this cowlick on the right side of my head, and a ponytail alone isn't going to accomplish the job.

I spit out the toothpaste and rinse as I run my gel-ladened hands through my hair.

"Why did you let me sleep so late?" I ask Puppy. He hops off the bed and disappears through his doggy door. He must not have appreciated the tone of voice I used.

I pull on a somewhat unwrinkled black skirt and a blouse that I'm not wholly sure if it is clean waiting to be hung, or worn and not yet made it to the laundry hamper. I have ten minutes left for makeup.

That's the genuine concern. Normally I would throw on some quick minimal necessities, but I did something last night I never do. I slept in my makeup.

What in the world was in that drink Sylvester gave me?

I waste a few seconds considering my options, which are all bad. I begin to touch up the makeup left on from last night.

As I apply, I can't help but judge that it makes me look like a burlesque girl, but the only other option is to wash my face and be done with it.

I'll deal with the multitude of blemishes this makeup disaster will create later. I focus on finishing the rehab to the best of my ability as quickly as possible.

I give up on my face, jog into my kitchenette, and scoop up my purse. No laptop. Where's my stupid backpack?

Dropping to my knees, I check under my bed. It's not there, and I make a frantic circle in my apartment, searching the closet then behind the shower curtain. In a last-ditch fit of desperation, I open all my cupboards.

Nothing. There are only so many places you can hide something in a 300-square-foot apartment.

I want to sit on my bed and cry. But that option is not open to me this morning.

If I slept in makeup, I could have left my laptop in my car, as unbelievable as that seems. I jog out to my car as my blouse begins to stick to me from the nervous sweat I have worked up.

I pull up short, in front of my car. It's backed into its parking slot, and I never back in. As I walk toward it, as if it will detonate as I get closer, I see my backpack on the passenger seat.

Lord, I don't need to give myself a heart attack like this. How stupid of me to leave my laptop in my car.

I reach into my purse for my keys. Now they're gone.

A niggle at the back of my mind makes me look up. My car doors are unlocked.

"No, no, no—" I mutter as I pull the driver's door open.

Car backed into its parking space and vehicle left unlocked —such a dude thing. I reach in and slap the driver's sun visor down. My keys jingle as they fall onto the floorboard.

"Fudge!" I scream.

Every male in my family does the exact same annoying thing when parking a vehicle at the house. I want to ignore last night and push it from my mind. It was much more comfortable when I had willingly accepted my self-deceptions that I had only dreamed up my meeting with Bob Hirsch. That he was just some indigestion from the hamburger, *which I didn't ask for.*

Snippets from my evening with Grandpa come rolling back, and I can't deny that I spent the evening with a dead ancestor. I especially will never forget how he admonished me for not taking a cab home—he might have been right on that. I also remember his warning that three more of his preachy buddies would be coming around to show me the error of my ways. Oh goody.

I get in my car and drive downtown. I search with renewed purpose through my purse for any sort of ibuprofen, Tylenol— morphine—for my booming headache.

There must have been something more than moonshine in that drink Sylvester gave me. My grandpa wouldn't just show up after not having been in my life. That's just inconceivable. No, there was just something in my drink.

The Tylenol bottle's cap finally comes off in between my teeth, and I palm four capsules. Darn it. I didn't get a water before I left.

Throwing them into my mouth, I swallow. The capsules stick in the back of my throat. I try to swallow again, but with a dry mouth, that doesn't work. One of the capsules dissolves and triggers my gag reflex.

On the positive, that helps with the dry mouth, and I succeed in clearing them from my throat. Although pills now seem to be stuck just above my sternum.

The struggle is real, and my eyes are watering profusely. Taking a quick look in the mirror, I am horrified to see the small runs the tears have made in my just-applied mascara.

"For the love of..." I shake my head as I study my juvenile makeup. "Why do I even bother."

Subconsciously deep down, I know I had too much to drink last night and an encounter with Grandpa's ghost. But I feel it better to remain in a firm state of denial.

I came home last night and fell sound asleep because I was exhausted. Then I had some odd dreams. That is my story, and I'm sticking to it.

But so help me, if some preachy old ghost shows up tonight, I'm going to be seriously ticked off. The last thing I need is one more person trying to tell me what I should or shouldn't be doing.

I find a parking space on the backside of the Municipal Annex Building. I check my phone as I trot into the building with my backpack slung over my shoulder. Eight fifty-eight. I can't hide my pleasure.

True, I might look like I slept in my clothes and a mortician did my makeup, but by gosh, I'm on time. I am a professional.

Chapter 5

As I finish interviewing my last shoplifter at one o'clock, I'm so hungry my stomach thinks someone cut my throat since I missed breakfast and lunch. Lucky for me, since I'm on this side of the square, I can walk across the street to Petit Fours & Pimento.

Normally, I don't eat there. Mainly because all the men I know call it a "chick food" establishment and would never frequent it with me. Given I don't have a girlfriend in town, I would have to eat by myself. Which is sort of pathetic.

Still, they have some to-die-for chicken salad, and the last I looked, there are still park benches on the square.

As I step out of the Annex, I'm delighted to see Jacob get out of his squad car and come toward the Annex. Jacob is my best friend from school and a great officer of the law.

I wave him down. "Hey, Jacob."

He is concentrating on the notepad in his hand. "Jacob!" I yell.

Jacob finally looks at me, and his brow creases. "Hi, April."

"Hi yourself. Where have you been? I haven't seen you in weeks."

"Ah, you know, just busy with the job."

"Well shoot. I started to think my best friend was avoiding me." I laugh.

Jacob's ears flush red. "No. It's nothing like that at all."

Okay, so it is something like that. What? "Is something bothering you?"

"No. I told you just the job. I'm sorry if it upset you." He points toward the door. "I'm sorry. I've got an appointment I got to get to."

"Oh, okay. Well, good to see you," I offer.

"Yeah, you too. See you around."

I watch him disappear through the double glass door. I'm not sure what's eating at Jacob, but he's almost as bad of a liar as I am. Something is definitely wrong.

My brief encounter with Jacob has put me in a weird mood. I know that the issue is his, whatever it is. Still, it creates a need for me to eat some comfort food.

I order the Southern sampler plate, which has two types of chicken salad, pimento cheese, and Jell-O salad. It's okay. I think it's under 5,000 calories. Who's counting anyway?

Jacob is not only my best friend. He is the longest-running relationship I have with anyone not from my family. He and I have been thick as thieves since elementary school. In all that time, he's had to be brutally honest with me on numerous occasions, just like any good friend should be. But he has never been short and dismissive.

Before today.

I finish my Southern sampler platter and am glad nobody timed me. If they had, word would've gotten around that April Snow is a complete pig. I leave a tip on the table and waddle out of the restaurant. I need to retrieve my car from the Annex parking lot. As I walk over, I try to be thankful for the exercise.

I drive over to the law office, hoping that possibly today is quiet so I can do the necessary prep work for all six of my cases. There was a time when I was begging for at least one case of my own to work. Now I have six hearings tomorrow. Of course, it is extenuating circumstances since it was driven by the fact that Lane wanted everybody to have had their chance before the judges before the court's Christmas break. But it is still an almost insurmountable task.

The jolly old St. Nick that hangs on the Snow and Associates door is badly faded and in desperate need of repainting. I'm not about to throw shade at the old door decoration, given the current state of my makeup.

Seeing Howard's office door closed as I enter the lobby causes some less-than-charitable thoughts about my boss's vacation planning. I attempt to force my opinions back, but I could really use his help now.

He has always been there to answer the tough questions as I got my lawyer's feet under me and even counseled me when I let things become too personal. But this is different. This is not the difficulty of the cases but the sheer volume of them. A phone call to Howard isn't going to help with that.

I stow my purse in my bottom drawer and fire up my laptop. I start to sit, but I swear I can feel the pores in my face beginning to create blackheads and decide to wash my face immediately.

It feels good to wash the grime from my face. I dry my face with a threadbare hand towel and move closer to the mirror for a better look. To my pleasant surprise, I don't see any blemishes erupting under the skin—yet.

What I do see are thick, puffy black pillows under both eyes and crow's feet wrinkles with ruts deep enough to have been caused by a monster tractor pull competition. "Good Lord. You look like you haven't slept in a week," I whisper.

Under any other circumstances, I would just go home and take a four-hour nap. Maybe I'd get up this evening and study the cases once I was fresh. But as it is, even without resting, I'm not sure I will be able to get all my prep work done before the hearings.

I admit it. I'm probably also a little blue. Plus, feeling sorry for myself.

I'm in love, but my boyfriend is out of town, and I'm not a hundred percent sure when he will be back. My boss, who I actually enjoy working for, has left me to take care of everything in his absence, and I could really use his help right now. Then there is the case of my best friend who has done everything but say don't ever talk to me again.

Okay, maybe I'm being overly dramatic about Jacob. But I'm not going to kid you and say that it doesn't hurt my feelings that he doesn't have time to talk to me after not seeing each other for the last few weeks.

Maybe that's just how guy friendships go. Maybe guys don't really check up on each other. I think I always assumed that people, regardless of their sex, are all sort of alike. Now I am seriously reconsidering that.

I need to talk to somebody my own age about what I'm feeling with Lee. Not the lust part, but the one percent part that is holding me back from a total commitment to moving forward. Is that normal?

I could ask my brothers, but that would be *so* awkward. Especially seeing as they're sort of protective, and I believe both know I'm not a virgin anymore but are still in a state of denial regarding that bit of truth.

I'm sure both Nana and Granny would welcome a conversation about relationships. Still, whether I'm right or not, I feel their information might be a little dated. For example, the "whole live together before being married" thing would probably shock Granny. Nana would be like, why bother getting married unless you have kids.

Mama or Daddy? I'd sooner die. I would have to give them daily updates on the situation until it was resolved if I had a conversation with either of them. Besides, it's not Mama or Daddy. Those two are like a team of covert agents, and they share all ill-gotten information with one another.

Oh, this is so frustrating. I want to talk to Jacob about it. He would be able to tell me right away what the problem is, as well as he knows me.

One thing is definitely apparent when I get set up in Baltimore, I'm going to have to work on finding some girlfriends. This whole not having anybody to bounce things off of is making me feel isolated, and I don't like it.

Chapter 6

Diving into my work has helped to chase the blues away. Bonus, I'm making such good progress that I realize the prep work will not take nearly as long as I first thought. I may even be finished sometime this evening.

The front door opens.

"Hello?"

I'm not believing this. I will never forget that voice. It will be the sound of April's shame and embarrassment for all time. "He's not here, Patrick. Can I help you with something?"

"Hey, April." His eyes squint as he tilts his head. "Are you feeling okay?"

Nothing like having a former boyfriend catch you at your worst. At least if he still has any hang-up over it not working out between us, he can now feel like he dodged a bullet. "It's just been a real grind to get everything done before Christmas."

"I know what you mean. I finally got caught up on all the furnace emergencies, and now I'm working around to my maintenance accounts so that I won't have any call-ins on Christmas." He walks over to my desk.

"Howard has you on a maintenance contract?" I ask.

"Yeah." He gestures over his shoulder. "That unit is at least twenty years old. After what happened this summer, he decided he would rather me baby it along for a few more years rather than pay to replace it now."

"Sounds like Uncle Howard. Why pay for something today that you can pay for later or leave for the next tenant."

"Something like that." Patrick laughs.

Funny, his laugh still makes me feel light and airy, but it doesn't have the same sexual underpinnings it held during the summer. He is as attractive as ever, but there is no longer a sexual pull between us.

"How's your son?"

Patrick's face lights up. "Awesome. A-B honor roll again. He didn't get that from me. He also played quarterback on his Junior League team this year. They mostly just run option, but they did really well."

"Oh, that's so cool. I bet that was a blast to watch."

It was like he had turned into a bobblehead doll. "The best thing in the world. Seeing your child be successful beats any success you ever had personally. It's hard to explain."

His smile dims as he continues to stare at me. I'm at a loss as to where the conversation should go from here. I'm relieved when he again gestures over his shoulder. "Well, I'm going to go change the filter, test the heat pump, and inspect the heating elements. Then I'll be out of your hair."

"Take your time. I'm going to be here awhile."

I sneak a look at his butt as he walks to the unit in Howard's office. What? He's got a nice-looking butt.

Chapter 7

It is six in the evening before I realize it. I have standing dinner dates with my grandmothers most weeks. Granny is Tuesday nights, and Nana is Thursday nights.

It serves two purposes. One is to enjoy my time with them while I am still local and have the opportunity to get to know them better. Two is to get advice on the paranormal "gifts" I received from each side of our family. "Gifts" is their word for the wackadoodle skills, not mine.

I feel it best to check in with Granny before I show up on her doorstep. It's best to be respectful that even though we have a standing date—life happens—something may have changed with her schedule.

Her phone rings several times, and I prepare a message to leave on voicemail in my mind when she picks up. "Yes?"

"Hey, Granny. I'm checking to make sure we are still on for tonight?"

"It's almost six, April. Are you not almost here?"

I knew I should've called earlier. "No, ma'am. I'm still at the office."

"Well, bummer. I just took the cornbread out of the oven. You know it's always best right as it comes out. I thought you'd be here at six."

Cornbread is like a magic word. Granny uses buttermilk in

hers, and there's a hint of sweetness to it, but she swears she never puts sugar in her recipe. I'm not gonna call her a liar as long as she keeps making them for me.

"I'll be over before it cools," I tell her as I gather my laptop and shove it in my backpack.

"Don't you be speeding in that demon car your brothers put together for you. I'm still mad at those boys."

"I won't. I'm a responsible driver." A shiver crosses my chest.

I hang up my phone, lock the office, and drive out of town in my "demon car." I keep my word and drive the speed limit. I turn down County Road 7 toward Granny's farm. I'd only gone half a mile when the glare from rotating red and blue lights cuts through the darkness.

My curiosity piques immediately. I pull in behind a truck and a sedan in front of me, waiting for the county deputy to wave me through. As I pass by the fire truck, I see several more sheriff vehicles and a couple of Guntersville police cruisers down the dirt driveway.

I pick up my phone and hit speed dial number five. He picks up on the second ring.

"What's up?" Jacob's voice is short and clipped.

"I was just wondering if you went commando today," I tease.

"No. Black boxer briefs. Anything else? I'm busy here."

"So, there's like this thing, down the county road my Granny lives on—"

"Can't tell you much yet, but a surveyor was out here working on the Castle farm, and they think they found a body."

I get momentary vertigo and have to pay closer attention to my driving. "Dottie Castle? The widow of the car dealer?"

"Yeah, do you know her?"

"Sure, she's one of my repeat customers."

Jacob sighs. "Hopefully, she won't be needing your services for more serious things tonight."

"Do they know who the body is?"

There is commotion and some close-by voices to Jacob. "Hey, listen. I have to catch you later."

"Just tell me if you think it's her husband." Jacob hangs up.

It is the one thing I remember from the Castle case in the late 90s on TV. Gil Castle, the owner of several large car dealerships in the Guntersville area, was brought up on tax evasion charges and rumored to be part of an organized crime ring.

Considering Gil was a pillar of the society, it was a big enough scandal that he was being charged with crimes. When Gil disappeared, it became the story of the decade in Guntersville. Initially, the police thought that he had met with foul play. But as the leads dried up over the next two years, they became of the mindset that he had faked his own murder and then skipped town.

It would've been nice if my friend could've at least given me that bit of information. At least my mind wouldn't be running rampant with conspiracy theories.

I get out of my car to open Granny's gate. Maleficent, Granny's goat that seems to have claimed me, waits for me at the gate.

"Don't you run out while I pull through." I shake a finger at her.

It is apparent I will need to keep my eye on her. Her bright gold eyes shift from me to the opening and back. I know what she is thinking.

My warning her must've been enough to give her pause. She doesn't flinch a muscle as I pull my car through and then relock the gate.

I want to scratch her ears as praise for minding me. As I approach her, she turns her back to me, raises her tail, and wags it three times violently before leaping into the woods.

That's one peculiar goat.

The scent of vegetable soup and cornbread is heavy in the air when I step into Granny's foyer. "Granny, I'm here."

"About time." She appears in the hallway wiping her hands on a dish towel. "I thought I was going to have to send the Marines out to find you."

"I'm pretty sure the Marines don't do that, Granny."

She raises her eyebrows. "They would if I told them to."

I can't contain the laugh that bubbles up from inside me. Granny is five foot two with a bright white helmet-shaped hairdo that makes her five foot six. Granny is a big woman trapped in a small woman's body.

"Hurry up now. I think the cornbread might still be warm. I'll go ahead and ladle a bowl of soup for you."

"Is it vegetable?"

"Yes, it is."

How impressive is that? Not only am I a clairvoyant and a manifestationist, but I can identify soups by their smell.

We sit and enjoy a relaxed, tasty meal together. Granny really does have a knack for cooking.

She catches me up on what is going on at the farm, not much —the sewing circle, a lot of gossip—and church, a possible mission trip to Guatemala next year. I hope I'm as engaged in the world as Granny is when I'm in my seventies.

"Granny, did you know Dottie Castle?"

Granny's face twists as if she has bitten into something rotten. True to form, she catches herself before she says anything ugly.

"Yes. Dottie and I used to be in the same lunch club at one time."

"Was that before or after they lost their dealership?"

"Before. I don't think any of us kept up with the Castles after the indictments." Granny pushes her chair back and begins to gather up the dishes.

"Let me get that," I say.

"I'll let you get them next time." She carries our dirty dishes toward the sink. "You want some coffee? I've got some pecan pie if you have a sweet tooth."

Man. Granny doesn't make it easy for a girl to be good. "Want, yes. Need, no."

"Eating something that makes you happy is never a bad thing. It always sends up positive vibes."

I lean against the counter as she is rinsing the dishes and

then placing them in the dishwasher.

"What was Dottie like? I mean back then."

Granny hesitates before answering. "I don't care to malign her character. Still, it is common knowledge, she wasn't ever in danger of winning any Ms. Congeniality awards, if you understand my meaning."

"Well, I don't think time has really changed her. That's my general opinion of her as well."

"What made you bring that woman up anyhow?"

Granny's use of "that woman" does not escape me. "She's a client of Howard's, but also she's got a bunch of police on her property tonight."

Granny's hands stop moving under the water. "Really?"

"Yeah. I tried to get Jacob to tell me what was going on, but he was too busy. He said that they might've found a body out there on her farm."

Granny shrugs her shoulder and continues to rinse dishes. "Some people have skeletons in their closet. Dottie has them on her farm, I guess."

I bark a laugh. "That's pretty harsh judgment coming from you, Granny."

"Not really. Gil was too connected to this community to just up and leave. Not only did he have his three car lots, but he also had several properties to manage and a different married woman each day of the week to take care of. If you know what I mean."

I believe my jaw bounced off the kitchen counter at her words. "Granny!"

"If I'm lying, I'm dying. He was a big, good-looking guy, way too slick for my taste, but half the women in this town wouldn't have turned him down if he had asked for a date. And when I say date, I'm not talking about going down to the buffet."

"Did Dottie know?" This is getting juicy.

"Of course, she knew. She's not stupid or blind, although I think his money helped blind her to some degree. They were a real odd match at best."

"So do you think that Dottie like—" I make my fingers mimic a gun and slam my trigger-thumb down.

Granny takes the cover off the pie. "Oh, I don't know. It's all rumor and conjecture. Do I think Dottie could have killed Gil? Depends on how mad she got. But if I was a betting woman, she would be more apt to pay somebody to do it."

I raise a finger. "But then you have a loose end, and you have to worry about keeping that person quiet."

Granny looks me up and down as she hands me a piece of pie. "I think you've been thinking about this too much."

"Maybe. It just intrigues me that they never found him. That seems so weird that somebody could just drop off the face of the earth."

"He didn't drop off the face of the earth. He's either buried in it or skirt chasing down in Mexico. It's only odd to you because your generation has grown up in a time where you can't pull your pantyhose out of your butt crack without being on five security cameras. Things weren't like that back then."

"But they didn't get along?"

"They put on a good front at the Rotary clubs and church functions. But I can't think of a single time they held hands or gave each other a hug that wasn't on cue. I also never saw them argue in public."

"No chemistry." For some reason, it is essential for me to identify the issue.

"I guess you could say that." Granny takes a bite of her pie.

"You and Grandpa had chemistry, right?"

Granny's neck flushes red. "I'd call it more biology, but we clicked."

That might've been more information than what I was bargaining for—still, I did ask the question.

I take a bite of my pecan pie, and my body relaxes into satiated bliss. It is the best thing to happen in my life ... this week. "This is awesome."

"Thank you, dear."

"I wish I could cook like this."

"It's not that hard. I could show you," Granny offers.

"I can't boil water. But it sure would be cool if I could make this."

"Can't never did anything." Granny lifts her coffee mug and blows on it. She peeks over the rim. "You really like this Lee boy?"

Granny's got the heat cranked way up in her house. I feel a bead of sweat trickle down my spine. "Sure. He's attractive, nice, has a good career, we have history together—what's not to like?"

She smiles into her coffee. "I was just checking. You've always been a flavor of the month sort of girl. It surprises me that you're sticking with one person all of a sudden."

"You make it sound like I'm fickle."

"No, you said that. All I'm saying is that you typically fall in and out of love like in a three-to-four-week time span." She holds up a hand as I start to argue the point. "There's nothing wrong with that. It just means you're searching for what you think you want your mate to be. It's a lot better than just hooking up with the first person you like."

That's where the one percent is bothering me. If I have broken my normal dating tendencies, why wasn't I one hundred percent gung-ho about this relationship? Why was I excited and looking forward to it, but also hesitant and procrastinating on making any commitment?

"Did you ever have any doubts that Grandpa was the one for you?"

"Not after the first thirty years of marriage."

My facial expression must've been full of shock because she laughs as she places her hand on mine. "I'm just kidding, baby. No, if it wasn't love at first sight for me, it was definitely within the first week that I knew I wanted to be his wife."

"I wish I could have that level of certainty with Lee."

"Maybe you will, maybe you won't. But I hope you don't make a lifelong commitment if you don't get to that level of certainty. I feel that would be a mistake."

"Yeah, but the shot clock is getting a little short on time. If I don't pick somebody soon, I might live the rest of my life by myself. Not to mention missing out on kids if I decide I want any."

"You always did worry too much." Granny shakes her head. "It must be exhausting to be you, April."

I snort a laugh. "It is."

"Did anything come up this week you had questions for me about?" Granny asks.

Immediately the miniature sun Bob held in between the palms of his hands comes to mind. I would give anything to be able to do that.

"I don't know if this is something in your realm of skill or if I need to ask Nana about it. I would like to be able to control fire in between my hands and make it appear like a miniature sun."

Granny's color drains from her face, her skin now as white as her hair. "What made you think of this?"

Her anxiety makes me nervous. "I just had seen it some-where."

"Where?" She leans forward.

"In a dream."

"A dream?"

I can't tell if she is buying it or not. I double down. "Yes, ma'am."

She pauses and gathers herself. She has placed a calm façade over her expression, yet I can still tell she is shaken. "I wouldn't be able to show you that. That level of control, hypothetically speaking, is reserved for angels and demons."

I knew it. I knew Grandpa Hirsch wasn't a ghost. Of course, that still leaves a rather important question unanswered.

"Are you sure it was just a dream?" she asks again.

I briefly consider telling her the truth. Very briefly. I can tell by her focus that if I were to admit to her where I saw the spherical fire, I would get a sermon that I don't care to hear. Be-sides, I'm not positive any of the sequences after I had my glass of wine at Jester's the other night happened. For all I know, I passed out cold from the moonshine and was left drooling on the tabletop dreaming about a grandfather I had never met.

"Are you going to your Nana's Thursday?"

Granny and Nana don't care for one another. So, the question catches me off guard. "Yes."

"You mentioned before about traveling in dreams. An animist would know much more about that than I would. Still, I will need you to tell her what you dreamed of so she can advise if it could possibly be a demon or if she feels it was only a ghost. If she feels it could be a demon you dreamed of—" She frowns as she shakes her head. "It may be one of those rare incidents where her heathen religion intersects with the one true God."

I feel my lip drop open. "Granny, it's not like that."

"You do as I ask." She shakes her finger, inches from my face. "I warned you that your energy will draw them. Good and bad alike. All things are drawn to energy, and yours is abnormally high. How many times must I warn you?"

Geez. Why is everybody so tense today. First Jacob and now Granny. I blow out an exasperated breath. Granny has knocked my pie-buzz down a few notches. "Okay," I mumble.

"I can't hear you."

"Alright already. I'll talk to Nana about it. Satisfied?"

She returns to rinse the dishes. "I will be once you tell me what she says."

"She's probably going to tell me I'm nuckin' futs."

"Oh. We already know that, honey," Granny says without missing a beat.

Chapter 8

It is midnight, and I haven't slept a wink. I'm not worried about the cases anymore. I believe I have those under control, and I can finish up everything tomorrow for the Thursday hearings.

I'm not even perturbed at Howard anymore for abandoning me. It is actually empowering to be able to work through the situation on my own.

Puppy is snoring loudly at the base of the bed. All four of his paws are reaching for the ceiling.

Old man in the lake, Him, tapped on the boathouse pylons earlier, but he hasn't whispered "Get out" in my ear in over two months. I guess even ghosts get acclimated.

My laptop has gotten unbearably hot on my thighs, and I set it on a pillow in front of me. I'm doing something I rarely do since I entered law school. I'm scanning the social media posts of all my friends.

They are friends because their pictures appear under the heading of friends. At least a couple hundred of them I couldn't have placed if you offered me a hundred-dollar bill to tell you their name and where I know them from.

Given my age, many females are either pregnant or have one and even two babies on their hips. They are all taking sweet photos of their families.

One thing is sure, my girlfriends seem to be weathering their pregnancies better than their husbands. Almost all the new dads come complete with their new dad bods, making them look like a rectangle with stick arms and stick legs. Who are these guys? I don't remember any guys in college being built like that.

I consider checking the job market in the Baltimore, D.C. area again. But I'm just not that interested in "work life." At the moment. I know there will be plenty of time to take care of that after Christmas. Who interviews during December anyway?

Is that really the reason? Or is it the one percent "off" feeling? I don't know, but the whole thing is making me highly frustrated.

Then there is what Vander said. Just like Vander, check out for a few months and still feel like you have the right to throw shade. What was it he said after I confirmed that the rumors he had heard were true, that I was dating Lee?

"Watch your six."

What the heck does he mean by that. I mean, he's obviously alluding to something. Why not just come out and say it instead of talking in code?

Watch my six, indeed. If I don't get to sleep soon, I'll be wishing in the morning I *slept* six. I close my laptop and punch my pillow as I try to clear everyone else from my mind.

Chapter 9

I wake up thirty minutes before my alarm is set to go off. Rather than fight my awake state, I decide to grab a shower and go on to work.

As I pull my slacks on, Puppy raises his head as if he has heard something that alarms him. He leaps off the bed and hits the puppy door at full speed.

So help me if I go out there and he's killed a chipmunk or a squirrel. I'm going to tear his furry butt up. He's a Keeshond, not a rat terrier. The dog is about as confused as I am.

I finished blow-drying my hair and put minimal makeup on. Stepping outside, I am greeted with a frozen tundra. There is a thick layer of frost on everything, including my windshield. So that's why I got up early.

I start my car, turning everything to defrost. I have a quarter of a tank. I'll need to get gas later, but I should be okay for now.

I can see Dusty in the kitchen. I can hang out with him for a few minutes while I let the defrost do its work. Besides, I realize that what my dog probably heard was the silverware drawer being opened. The silverware making that distinctive clanking noise when it shifts would have been music to his ears.

"Good morning," I greet Dusty as I enter the kitchen.

"Hey. I just made your dog some scrambled eggs. Do you want me to make you some?"

I gesture over my shoulder. "I gotta be heading out. I was just waiting for the defrost to work on my car."

"I can wrap it up in a tortilla for you."

I'm not a huge fan of the breakfast burrito thing. Still, it seems rude to turn it down. "Sure. Thanks."

"Mexican cheese?"

"Lots, please."

I watched my brother scramble fluffy eggs with more ease than me warming up a frozen pizza. Sometimes I think it's the rest of my family that works the real magic. At the very least, they have the tastier magic.

I am getting anxious. I really should learn how to cook a few dishes. Especially if things lean toward domestication with Lee.

It is embarrassing that I was the only person not to bring a dish to the Thanksgiving feast last month. How embarrassed will I be when Lee realizes that I cannot even cook spaghetti if we don't want to eat out one night.

Why am I even worrying about that? He's a major league ballplayer, and I'm going to be a high-dollar D.C. attorney. We'll just order delivery from a fine restaurant when we want to stay in for movie night.

Dusty slides the scrambled eggs onto the tortilla and sprinkles the cheese liberally over the top. He looks out the glass door in the direction of my car.

"That was a heavy freeze last night. I doubt if your defroster has had time to work yet. You might as well eat it the way it was meant to be enjoyed."

I take a glance out the door. It does still look like my car is trapped in a winter wonderland. I pull my eggs towards me. "I might as well make good use of the downtime."

My whole plan of action about eating out collapses as I take the first bite of the eggs Dusty whipped up for me. Oh my gosh, what my brother can do with a plain egg. Wealthy, a genuinely nice guy, and an incredible cook, Dusty will get snatched right off the market if he ever puts himself back out there.

"This is seriously delicious," I praise him as soon as I clear enough of a bite not to be talking with my mouth full.

"Good, glad you like it." He cracks three more eggs into the skillet.

Puppy pushes his plate across the floor before deciding the eggs are all gone. He proceeds to belch and trot off to the den. I assume he is going to go back to sleep on the sofa.

"You got anything planned Saturday night?" Dusty asks out of the blue.

Darn it, I knew these eggs couldn't be free. "You mean like the eve of Christmas Eve?"

Dusty wrinkles his forehead in thought. "Is that even a thing?"

"It is if I'm exhausted. Howard hasn't been at work all week."

"Is he back down in Mobile?"

"Either that or dead in a ditch. I swear it's like trying to get a thirteen-year-old to check in."

Dusty chuckles as he adjusts the heat of the eye. "I'd say that's karma biting you on the butt."

"I'll have you know I checked in all the time with our parents. Except maybe once or twice."

"Uh-huh. So, what's it going to be?"

"I don't know, Dusty. I've got six cases this week, and I thought I might go Christmas shopping Saturday."

Dusty slaps his hand, still holding the spatula, to his chest. "Christmas shopping? You've never given gifts."

That is a sad truth. It sounds really horrible when Dusty says it. "I'm trying to turn over a new leaf."

"A little cash might come in handy when you're playing Santa."

Isn't that the case? My student loans kicked into full force last month, and they make Uncle Sam's income tax look minuscule. Every payday, I seem to have just enough money to make my student loan notes and buy a soda. "There are more important things in the world than money."

"Forty dollars an hour, including travel time. I buy all the eats, and guess what?"

I don't want to take the bait. I'm not going to take the bait. "What?" Dang it.

"I'll throw in a free double feature," Dusty promises.

"What, are we going to a drive-in?"

"No, the old Imperial movie theater in Shelbyville, Tennessee."

"Shelbyville?"

Dusty waives his spatula. "You know, sort of between Fayetteville and Murfreesboro, Tennessee."

That doesn't help at all. "Oh yeah."

"It's light-duty. It is just sounds and an occasional cold spot." He makes eye contact with me. "What do you say? You know you want to go."

Lord help me, I do want to go. I exhale loudly and act as if I'm being forced against my will. "I suppose if you need me to go with you. Still, you're going to buy me some popcorn."

"Okay," Dusty agrees merrily.

"And some of those chocolate-covered malt balls."

"Sure thing," he agrees.

I wonder what else I can throw into the deal while he has such an agreeable nature. I decide to call it quits, though. I don't want to appear greedy. Plus, he has been nice enough to cook me breakfast.

Dusty's face is in total concentration as he slides his eggs onto his plate. He sprinkles a pinch of cheese across them.

My mind slides back to my situation with Lee, and I wonder if talking to Dusty might offer me some clarity. I'm curious what made Dusty decide to ask Bethany, his ex-wife, to marry him when they were younger. He doesn't like to talk about her. But I figured I could glean some direction from Dusty if he would open up.

"Dusty, can I ask you a question?"

"Sure."

"How did you know you wanted to marry Bethany?"

He shoots me a glance as his features tense. It seems like he isn't going to answer me, and I rephrase the question. "What made you sure it was time to marry her? That she was the right one."

"Honestly, I haven't even thought about it."

"You don't know when it was that you decided she was the right one?" That seems so out of character for my uber-analytical brother.

He looks toward the ceiling as if the answer is written there. "No. I don't think I ever thought about it like that."

Wow. "So, you never thought about whether or not she was the person you wanted to spend the rest of your life with, is that what I'm hearing?"

"Yeah, pretty much. Kind of funny now when I think about it." He takes a bite of eggs as if that ends our conversation.

"Seriously?"

"What? It was her idea. She kept saying she wanted to get married."

"And that was a good enough reason for you to marry her? I mean, what was it about her that made you think you loved her? Did you think she was smart? Did she make you laugh? I'm just wondering."

"I thought she was hot. Plus, I didn't want to disappoint her," he says.

I'm in complete shock. I expected so much more from Dusty. Dusty is my smart brother. I thought everything he did was laden with cerebral reasoning beyond reproach. Yet he's telling me that he married his first wife because she was hot and he didn't want to disappoint her. I might expect that from Chase but not from Dusty.

"You know that's pretty stupid?" I say.

"Hindsight being twenty-twenty, it was probably not my most stellar decision."

Dusty just qualified for the understatement of the year. "I hope this answer makes more sense to me. When did you know that it was over?"

His body language changes, and I know I won't be getting

the truth. "When I signed the divorce papers."

"Aw, come on, Dusty. It's not going to hurt you to tell me what blew it up. There's always that last straw that breaks the camel's back."

He sets his fork down and seems to contemplate the question. His eyes focus on something miles away before he comes back to me. "I was up in New York three years ago. I had an appointment that week with both my agent and my publisher.

"We were hammering out the details for a contract for books two through five. I got a call from my bank. They wanted to confirm that I was moving four hundred thousand dollars from the joint account that Bethany and I shared to a private account in her name only.

"I asked them how that could even happen over the phone. That's when the bank manager told me that I had been in there thirty minutes earlier making the transaction. Yeah, I suppose that's when I knew."

"The guy?"

Dusty rubs his temples. "Just one of the guys she was sleeping with. He had gotten some false IDs made up. The bank was just on their toes enough to realize it wouldn't make sense for me to take my name off the account when she had access to it on the joint account.

"If they hadn't called, she would've been able to lift almost every dime I earned on the first book."

"I bet she wasn't too happy when she saw that the bank had reversed the transfer."

"Nope. She's been trying to take every dime of my royalties ever since."

"Why does she think that she's due that money. What did she ever do to help further your career?"

Dusty gives me a look as if he thinks I have lost my mind. "She doesn't think she's earned it. Bethany just wants it. She'll tell you straight to your face that she thinks my books are crap. She's always thought they were stupid. But she has a decent angle on some cash, and she's taking it. It's just Bethany."

"See what hot got you."

He laughs. "Yeah, well, maybe you should remember that and learn from your older brother's mistakes."

"What's that supposed to mean?"

"Just saying there's a big difference between lust and love. And take it from an expert. Lust is a lot more expensive."

Chapter 10

I'll be a few minutes late arriving at Snow and Associates. But the skies are a perfectly clear powder blue, and the sun sparkles off the lake's surface, making it look like the water is coated in tinsel.

It is Wednesday, I have a handle on my cases, and I'm only three days away from a four-day weekend. Life is good, and it would be hard for anyone to mess it up.

As I drive past the town square, I notice Gadsden's Channel 3 News truck is parked in front of the courthouse. That's never a good sign, but I'm sure it's somebody else's issue to worry about. Let them deal with Chuck Grassley.

As I pull into my parking spot in front of our office, I see Lane's car two spots down. My happiness falls into my stomach. I try to imagine something positive, as Granny always instructs me. Something like Lane is coming to give me a gift certificate for having taken so many cases on last-minute notice.

Despite all the forced happy thoughts, I must think Lane being at Snow and Associates first thing in the morning cannot be a good thing.

I unlock the front door and wave at him to acknowledge his presence. He is talking on his phone, and he holds up a finger toward me. I resist the urge to show him a different finger but am professional enough to slip inside the office. I bump up the thermostat since Patrick has made sure I'll have heat in the office.

Lane strides into the office. "Good morning, April."

"No doughnuts, District Attorney Jameson?"

His happy face crumbles as he rocks back on his heels. "I could go get you some," he says with a halting voice.

I can't conceal my giggle. "I was just jerking your chain, sir."

"Oh, yeah." He shoves his hands in his trouser pockets and grins. "I knew that."

Right, sure you did. "What can I do for you?"

"Funny you should ask. I'm sure you know what happened up at the Castle farm last night."

Finally, I will get the scoop. I lean forward attentively. "I know the police were out there, but that is about it."

Lance licks his lips and shifts his weight. He doesn't usually act this nervous. "There's a good possibility that we found the body of Gil Castle last night."

"That case has been open for over two decades. Finding the body is a good thing. Well, it sucks for Mr. Castle, but it's good to be able to have finally found his body."

"Yes, it does make it where we have a better shot at finally solving the cold case."

I give a slight shoulder shrug. "Thank you for filling me in?"

"We've brought her in for questioning, Dottie that is. We need to compare her story to her story from the nineties."

That isn't exactly a surprise. It sounds like standard police operating procedures to me, and I can't figure out why Lane is going through them in such painstaking detail. "Spouses are usually good suspects to start an investigation with."

"Yes." He repositions his hands behind his back. "I need to interview Ms. Castle right away, and she is demanding her attorney. She tells me that you are her lawyer."

A bark of laughter escapes me. I stop as I realize Lane is serious. "For real?"

"Yes. She insists that you're her lawyer."

I shake my head. "Oh no. I simply help her change her will

on the laptop whenever she has a dispute with her family. I can't possibly be her lawyer because she's never paid me a single dime."

"Well, she's probably never paid anything because she's flat broke," Lane informs me.

I think I always suspected that. Still, having Lane confirm it really gets under my skin. "Then what's with the will thing?"

"Oh, don't get me wrong. She has a few pieces of property around town that she draws rent on. It's enough to pay, or mostly pay, her monthly expenses. But if Dottie has any cash lying around, it's going to be spent in a matter of minutes. She was that way even when Gil was alive."

Here I had been beating myself up because I would cringe when the elderly woman came into the office. I had always found her condescending and a general pain in my derrière. Something you deal with when it is a paying customer. Still, if my hopes were to cultivate our relationship into her becoming a client, I was delusional. "You seem to forget you laid six different cases on me for Thursday."

"I haven't forgotten. But this is a client request. I don't know if she will talk if I am forced to bring in a different attorney. Besides, it shouldn't take long."

"Lane, I'm holding this office down by myself. You need to get her somebody else." It isn't just the time aspect. Changing a will, which is basically cutting and pasting paragraphs, is one thing. Defending someone in a capital murder case, someone you don't particularly care for, is another level of commitment. I know I sound like it's personal. Maybe it is. Perhaps Dottie has said one too many insensitive things to me or talked down to me one too many times for me to be able to mount an effective defense for her.

Lane's lips narrow. "Okay. I'll call in a favor and get someone to handle the DUIs and the shoplifting cases I gave you yesterday. I just need you to sit with Dottie today while she is being questioned and then take care of Rhonda Applewhite's hearing Thursday."

I shoot up out of my chair. "No!" I'm talking with my hands by this point. "I spent the better part of the day prepping those cases, Lane. You can't pull them out from under me now."

"Just bill the hours. Why do you care?"

"Because I started it, and I want to finish it."

"I don't see what the big deal is. If you want to keep the cases, fine. I was just trying to lessen your load."

"If you want to lessen my load, how about you come up with a plea bargain for Rhonda Applewhite that I can get her to accept."

Lane shakes his head side to side vehemently. "No. Rhonda Applewhite will get her day in court. I'm not cutting a plea bargain with her. What she did is beyond despicable, and I will not reward it by cutting a single day off her sentence."

"Don't get too far in front of your skis there, District Attorney. You still have to convict her."

"I've got film footage." He points a finger in my direction. "I'm not going to cut one single day off her sentence."

I point a finger back at him. "I'm not sitting down with Dottie Castle for one moment."

We stare at each other as if we are playing a mental game of chicken, trying to see who is going to break first. I am not going to break first because Lane isn't offering me anything I necessarily want, the best I can tell.

Lane blinks first. "Howard would do this for me."

I wrinkle my nose in disgust. "Then give Howard a call. Have him do it."

"You know that's not an option."

"Then why bring Howard's name into the conversation? All I'm saying is you can free up a significant amount of time for me by coming up with an acceptable plea deal we can all live with on the Applewhite case."

"I can't do that."

I sit back down and wave my hand at him. "Then go find somebody else to bully." I return my attention to the contract in front of me.

There is such a long silence I forget Lane is still there. "I'm a bully?"

I meet his eyes, my neck and ears heating from my aggravation. "Only when you don't get exactly what you want, Lane. Other than that, you're a real peach the rest of the time."

He pulls up a chair and sits. Lane isn't looking at me. He's staring in the general direction of the baseboard in front of him. It seems as if he has a lot on his mind, and I don't want to interrupt him, so I go back to editing my contract.

Bless it. It isn't even my fault, and yet *I* feel guilty for having called Lane a bully. Accurately, I might add. I tell myself I'm not going to apologize—and I apologize.

"I didn't mean to hurt your feelings, but sometimes when you don't get your way, you just try to steamroll the situation. I need to let you know that it makes me feel bad, and I don't want to participate."

His mouth opens slightly as he nods his head quickly. "No, I apologize. You're right."

He runs a hand through his salt-and-pepper hair. "I was desperate to get all our cases taken care of before the Christmas break, and the Castle situation has thrown a major wrench in my plans."

"I need you to know that I think what Rhonda Applewhite did is one of the most reprehensible things I've ever heard of, driven by greed. It truly makes me ill just thinking about it." I hold up a finger. "Still, in the grand scheme of things, she didn't endanger anybody like those DUIs, and she didn't steal anything with a price tag on it, and she didn't kill and bury anybody on their farm."

"It's still disgraceful," Lane mumbles.

"Yes, it is. It's shameful, but it didn't put a single person in harm's way. All I'm saying is that with the given circumstances and all of us wanting to get out for a Christmas break, is it such a bad thing to offer her a plea bargain? Not because what she did is excusable, but because it didn't endanger anyone."

I chuckle. "Heck, Lane. Do it because it's Christmas."

"Is that how you plan on defending your clients in the future, April? Figure out what the closest holiday is and propose that your client get to walk free in the spirit of that holiday?

"If it becomes effective, I would have no problem using it to help my clients."

"Manipulation over litigation?" he snipes.

"They're dead, Lane. I really don't think anybody at the cemetery cares anymore if someone took a bouquet off their gravestones."

"I believe the grief-stricken families would strongly disagree with you."

He might be right about the families. But I know first-hand the dead don't care.

I can't walk through a cemetery without gleaning hundreds of mumbling thoughts from the dead. In all the times I experienced this horror, I have never heard a ghost complaining someone lifted flowers off their grave.

As a rule, most ghosts are simply stuck on this side of the veil in confusion. They are not watching their grave.

"I'm not sure what you're complaining about anymore, Lane. You can get what you want by authorizing a simple plea bargain for Rhonda. Or you can spend hours interviewing Ms. Castle because she won't talk to you. The choice is yours, not mine."

"I don't like this. I don't like this one bit," Lane complains. "I swear it feels like blackmail."

How dare he. "It's called negotiating, Lane. You know, I give you something you want in exchange for something I need. No one is forcing you to make a plea bargain for Rhonda Applewhite, but if you want me to handle the Castle case, that is what I require." I add one of my patented eye rolls to drive home the point. "Blackmail. Honestly?"

The coloration of his neck and cheeks darken to a painful-looking purple. "Fine. I'll get you a plea bargain for Ms. Applewhite. But mark my word, it's going to include parole time, and if she breaks the parole agreement, she's going to serve the fullest sentence I can charge her with under the law."

I turn back to the contract again. "See. That wasn't so difficult."

The office falls silent again. Lane isn't standing to leave, which is annoying. I meet his glare. "What, Lane?"

Lane gestures toward the door. "Are you going with me to interview Ms. Castle?"

"Now?" I point at my laptop. "I was working on this, and I was going to wait for the plea bargain."

"I need you to come now. Besides, I'll work on the plea bargain tonight." He must've understood my icy stare as he adds. "Honest. I'll get it done tonight."

"Fine," I say as I shut my laptop and load it into my backpack. "Let's get this over with, then."

Chapter 11

Lane wants me to ride with him the two blocks to the county jail. I refuse, explaining that I don't want to have to bum a ride back to the office.

Even securing the promise of a plea bargain for Rhonda Applewhite is not sufficient for having to sit down with Dottie Castle. It's a fool's bargain at best.

I follow Lane to the Annex and accompany him into the jail. There is a sad three-foot Christmas tree in the far corner of the lobby.

The guard buzzes Lane and me into the registration office. We log in and follow our escort toward the interrogation rooms.

"Reynolds and Bill have been assigned the case. We must get Ms. Castle talking as soon as possible."

By my reckoning, Gil has been dead for about twenty-five years. I'm not exactly seeing what the urgency is in getting Ms. Castle to talk immediately. "I understand."

We turn down the hallway to the left and enter a room labeled "A." Jane Bill is staring through the one-way glass when we enter.

Jane is in her early forties. I know she plans to retire from the force in the next couple of years.

She cuts her eyes to us then back to the glass. "Ronnie is in there just making small talk with her."

Unbelievable. "I thought she had requested a lawyer?"

Jane extends her five-foot-three height as she moves toward me. "She's scared. We're only keeping her company."

"I bet," I say as I walk by, bumping shoulders with her. I try the doorknob, which is locked, so I do the ladylike thing and hammer on the door with my fist.

"April, calm down," Lane says.

"You know better than this." I direct my words at Jane. Before she can answer, the door clicks and opens.

Ronnie Reynolds is staring at me as if I have gone crazy. "What's up?" he asks.

"Your game," I say as I push past him.

"Are you okay?" I ask Dottie as I approach the table in the center of the room.

Dottie's usually impeccable appearance is in shambles. Her well-coifed hair is now lopsided on her head as if she were pulled from her bed. She has no makeup on, and for the first time, I see that her skin has an eerie yellow discoloration.

Dottie is not a well woman.

"I think so, dear."

I pull my laptop out and turn it on. "What were they asking you just now?"

She shakes her head. "Honestly, I don't know. Did you hear that they think they may have found Gil's body? On the farm?"

"I did." I hear a noise behind me and am surprised to see Ronnie still in the room. "You can leave, Detective Reynolds."

His carefully cultivated three-day stubble beard fills in with additional color at the cheeks. "I would prefer to stay in the room. Just in case."

I scoff. "In case what, Ronnie? She pulls out a needle and tries to embroider something for me."

He stammers, "I just thought—"

"Don't. Don't think, just leave me to talk to my client and make sure to turn off your speakers."

I wait and watch the door close behind Ronnie before turning back to Dottie. "Now, that's better."

She does not respond to me. Dottie stares at her hands clasped in her lap.

"Have they fed you anything?"

"They offered to get me a biscuit earlier, but I couldn't possibly eat anything knowing that Gil is gone."

"Well, we will have to get you something to eat before too long. This is all a very stressful situation, and we don't want you to get sick."

"They say he was there all along."

Her eyes are glazed. I believe she might have said that out loud even if I were not in the room. "Most likely. But Doc Crowder will be able to get us more details.

"All that time we spent looking for him. He never left home."

"I'll admit it is odd."

"It's sort of like finding your glasses on top of your head when you been looking for them all morning," Dottie says.

"No, Dottie, it's not the same. Finding your husband in your backyard is way different. Was there not a search of the farm at the time Gil went missing?"

Dottie rubs at her temples. "I remember there was. I think there was a search party. But it's so long ago now I really can't remember."

"The area that they found him in, do you remember if they searched that area?"

Dottie shakes her head. Her eyes begin to glisten with the makings of tears. "I don't know. I just don't know anymore. I think they did."

I'm not even sure it matters at this point. But for some reason, I need to know if that area had been searched.

True, Doc Crowder will probably be able to tell us whether or not the body has ever been moved. Still, I am curious how a freshly dug grave could be missed with cadaver dogs and a search team.

"Am I going to jail? I can't go to jail. I'm too old, and I don't belong with *those* people."

I feel the hairs on the back of my neck stand up when she says "those people." I can't help it. I've never suffered elitists well. They're right up there with liars, thieves, and hypocrites for me. Dottie is a strong candidate for all four.

I can't do it. There is no way I can defend Dottie. I won't. Professionalism is just going to have to take a backseat on this one because this woman gets under my skin and makes me break out in hives.

"I'm so scared. You're the only person in the world left who can help me." Dottie's lower lip trembles as she speaks.

Fudge nuts. I'm going to end up defending her.

I will hate every minute, and if I end up losing, I'm going to despise myself for not turning down the case. I watch the mean-spirited, diminutive woman crumble before my eyes.

She does indeed look frightened. I suppose I would be, too, if I were being accused of capital murder.

"Dottie, you're gonna have to level with me. Did you kill Gil?"

"My word! How could you possibly ask me that?"

Wrong answer. "Dottie, you're going to be asked a lot more than that if we don't establish an alibi in the timetable that makes it impossible for you to have killed Gil."

As I explain the situation to her, it dawns on me just what a colossal undertaking it will be to develop an alibi from twenty-five years ago. It isn't even known what date the man was killed. Thankfully the burden of proof is on the prosecution. Still, I can't hang our hopes just on that. I will need multiple items to cast doubt on any accusation that Dottie killed Gil.

"So, I'll ask you again, did you kill your husband?"

An eerie calm cast over her face as she locks eyes with me. "No. I did not kill Gil."

"Did you hire someone to kill Gil?"

"No. As a matter of fact, I never knew what happened to Gil. One day he was there, and the next, he was gone. Overnight he was replaced with hundreds of people looking for him and the police asking a bunch of questions."

"Do you have any idea who might have killed Gil?"

Dottie grabs a Kleenex from the box on the table and dabs at her nose and eyes. "Not exactly. Gil had a lot of business partners and a lot of people that competed against him. Who's to say that one of them didn't kill him to get rid of him?"

"Right, but is there anybody in particular that stands out more than the rest to you?"

She takes a moment and appears to be accessing her memory. "I don't know for sure. But if I had to say, I bet it was Johnny Lee Raley."

The name doesn't mean anything to me. "Johnny Lee Raley?"

"Yes." She leans across the table. "He was always asking Gil to sell his dealerships to him. A real creep of a man. He even had the audacity to hit on me once."

It doesn't sound like a perfect suspect, but there is definitely some motive *if* what Dottie says is true.

But I have my doubt. Even though I live in a small town, I don't know everybody in our county. Still, a businessman successful enough to buy a car dealership with a name as unique as Johnny Lee Raley almost seems like she is making him up.

"Did the police interview Johnny Lee when Gil first disappeared?"

Dottie screws her face up. "I don't think I mentioned him to them. But again, it was so long ago I can't be certain of what I did say or do."

It comes to me in a rush that makes my ears burn. Dottie thought she could play me like she plays everyone in her life. Every time she tells one of her lies, there is a funny electrical charge that crackles in the air.

I believe, subconsciously, she knows it and is fighting hard to try and conceal her deception. If she were dealing with any normal person, she could manipulate them at will. This is one of the few times that my "gifts" actually are an asset.

"Dottie, you need to remember as much as you can about what took place twenty-five years ago. I don't think you fully understand the severity of what's going on here. The police have just dug up a body, the body of your husband, that they had been searching for the past twenty-five years. Don't think for a moment that they're going to just rebury Gil and get him a nice tombstone and consider it a done deal. They will be searching for his murderer or murderers."

"As they should, dear."

"But he was found on your property, Dottie. We have to come up with a credible reason why you couldn't have been present when Gil was killed. We need a plausible alibi for when Doc Crowder comes back and tells us when Gil died."

"The doctor can tell when Gil died?"

There it is again. That little something tweaking my mind saying that Dottie isn't being truthful. For one, why is she showing so much interest in whether or not Doc Crowder can determine the time of death?

"Oh yes, with today's scientific capabilities, he should be able to tell us what day he died, possibly down to the hour. Every once in a while, he gets lucky and can tell us to the minute."

"I think I have seen that on TV," Dottie says.

"Dottie, tell me about the case against Gil. What impact did it have on y'all's relationship?"

"Well, I never. I just thought that you would be more respectful than that."

"No, Dottie. I ask the same hard questions you are going to be asked by the prosecutor. That's why you mustn't lie to me. I need to know the real story."

"I am telling you the real story. I don't lie."

Oh, Lord, please give me strength. "Did Gil's verdict cause the family financial trouble?"

"What would it do to you if you lost your job today?" Dottie asks.

"It's not about me, Dottie. It's about defending you. Please answer the question. Truthfully."

"It caused some sore feelings in the relationship, alright? I had held up my end of the deal. I held the parties for his business fleet leasing clients. I turned a blind eye to all the floozies he stuck his pecker in. Basically, I played the socialite wife, and he provided me with the props to complete the visual."

"Props? How do you mean, Dottie?"

She screws up her face as if I asked the dumbest question ever. "Honey child, Gil and I had little in common, except for the fact that both of us grew up too poor to paint and too proud to whitewash. The farms our people worked had fields that had a hard time growing hay. We both knew what it was to be poor, and the first chance we got to get out of poverty, we took it and never looked back."

I still don't understand. "What does that have to do with props?"

"Spoken like a true young lady of privilege." Dottie crosses her thin arms across her bony chest. "That old saying about 'it takes money to make money'? There's a lot of truth in that. Gil and I both understood that at an early age. Here's another saying for you. 'Investors only loan money to people who don't need it.' *Now*, do you understand?"

Nope. Totally lost. "No, ma'am. I can't say that I do."

"Honestly, child. To be so smart, you sure aren't very experienced. Do you realize how much money it takes to open up an American-made car dealership?"

She cuts me off as I start to answer. "Huge amounts of money. So how do two country bumpkins too poor to pay attention end up with a car dealership? Investors. Investors who are under the impression that the Castles are loaded and have the Midas touch. That means—" She ticks off fingers one by one. "Luxury cars, a sprawling lake home in a gated community, furs, jewelry, and designer clothes. It was all necessary to make the mark. Once investors saw us living the high life, they quit looking at the investment. They just wanted in.

"Greed is a powerful thing. It can cause people to temporarily lose their minds and do things they never thought they would do."

I don't really believe Dottie's assessment of investors.

Ninety-nine percent of the financial majors I knew at Alabama would have seen through the Castles' ruse in a matter of seconds. Still, on second thought, it only takes one percent to invest in a project to make it a reality.

"So, what went wrong?"

Dottie rolls her eyes. "Darn government as usual. They were eating up fifty percent of every dollar in profit. I suppose Gil finally decided that Uncle Sam was taking too large of a portion. He started ratcheting down the quarterlies. By the time the IRS came calling and finished with their investigation, we owed ten million dollars in back taxes and had virtually no assets available to us."

"I don't understand how that ended up with charges against Gil. There are people who don't pay their fair share every year, and then when they're audited, they have to pay up."

"That's true. But those individuals don't have a second set of accurately detailed books that back up the fake books they show the IRS. The only thing the IRS dislikes more than people who don't pay their taxes are people that have multiple books."

Yes, something tells me that most accountants wouldn't find that very amusing. If anything, it would send them into search and destroy mode.

"And when the indictment came down?"

Dottie sighs. "Everything we owned went away overnight. We were fortunate that we had a couple of older homes on Henry Street we had put into his mama's name, and we were able to move into one of those. But the eight-thousand-square-foot lake house was seized, as was Gil's Jaguar and my Denali." She laughs. "I'm sure they were pretty ticked off about that when they realized that both cars were upside down."

There is no humor in this to me. If anything, it is just sad. These two people were on the cusp of pulling themselves out of poverty forever but never set enough money back for longevity. I mean, I'm broke, and my net worth is negative when you factor in my student loans, but I sure as heck wouldn't make the kind of money they were making and not be able to retire in my fifties.

"You had this farm at the time?"

"Yes, it was his mama's. It's forty acres that's best crop is solid rock."

Except for the area someone buried Gil. "How long before you moved here?"

"Not quite six months. We had only been in it for a couple of weeks when Gil came up missing."

"Did Johnny Lee Raley know where your farm property was?"

"Yes. Johnny Lee and Gil were pretty close during that time. He knew we had moved back to the old homestead."

So, Johnny Lee would have had the opportunity as well. "Dottie, do you happen to know where I could find Johnny Lee?"

"Old town cemetery. He died in 2007 of prostate cancer."

"I'm sorry, Dottie."

She waves her hand. "Johnny Lee was no friend of mine."

"I need you to be crystal clear on these background items when we let the detectives in to talk to you."

She exhales loudly. "I thought that's why I was telling you. Why do I have to talk to them?"

"Because they're the police, Dottie. They're trying to get to the bottom of what happened to your husband."

She shakes her head side to side. "He's been dead twenty-five years. Finding out what happened to him is not going to bring him back from the dead."

"No, but in some cases, just letting the parents and family know how they perished helps them get over the tremendous loss."

She scoffs. "Again, it was twenty-five years ago. I'm the only family left that even knew him. Everybody else is dead except for our two nieces, and they were children when he went missing."

"Second cousins."

"Excuse me?"

"They're not his nieces. They are his second cousins, and he has a cousin surviving him." I have deleted and reinserted their names in the will enough times I will never be able to forget their relationship.

Dottie's eyes narrow. "I know what they are. My point is that nobody cares anymore."

I shrug. "Actually, the state still cares, Ms. Castle."

Chapter 12

Detectives Reynolds and Bill interview Ms. Castle for four hours. When they roll around to repeat their line of questioning for the third time, I let them know that we are done for the day.

Jane is more than willing to call it a day. She has been acting distracted looking at her watch the last hour of the interview.

Ronnie Reynolds is a bulldog. He is tenacious and is reluctant to bring the interview to a close. I remind him that Dottie is an elderly woman who has not eaten today. I remind him Channel 3 News has a van parked outside the police station. It would be unfortunate if he were forced to explain why Dottie passed out from exhaustion during their interrogation.

Elder abuse is still frowned upon in these parts.

As the detectives leave us, Dottie says, "I am hungry now."

"I'll make sure they bring you your dinner as soon as they get you back to your cell."

"Cell?" Dottie's eyelids blink in such quick succession it looks as if she is having a seizure.

"Are you okay?"

"What do you mean cell?"

"Uh—you didn't think they were going to release you, did you?" I ask.

"Yes. I talked to them, didn't I? Why do I have to stay the

night in this dreadful place?"

"We'll get an opportunity to request bail tomorrow, but there was no opportunity today."

"I can't sleep here. There are criminals in here!"

It is all I can do to choke back a laugh. "You'll be fine. Besides, it will be great motivation why you need to work with your attorney so she can successfully get you out of jail."

"You're really going to abandon me in here?" Dottie asks in an accusatory manner, making me feel like I'm leaving her to be executed.

"I don't have a choice in the matter, Dottie. There were no openings with the judges today, and we'll have to post bail tomorrow. It's really not that bad. You just don't mess with anybody, and they won't mess with you."

"Why don't you get in here and spend the night with me?"

Not enough money in the world, and it has nothing to do with the rest of the inmates. "I still have a few hours of work to do to be prepared for your hearing tomorrow. You do want me to be prepared when I go in front of the judge, don't you?"

She doesn't answer me. She favors me a spectacular "death stare" as I pack up my equipment. "I promise you I'll be back tomorrow."

"Don't you worry about me. I'm sure I'll be just fine all on my own."

Chapter 13

I check the time on my phone as I leave the police station. There is still half an hour left in the workday, but I'm toast and choose to head home.

It is tough for me to feel empathy for Dottie. It would be horrible for your husband to come up missing without knowing what happened to him for twenty-five years. I suppose I should cut her slack for that, but the fact of the matter is I always feel like the woman is lying to me. Almost like she is playing me like she and Gil played the investors, according to her, to get their dealership.

It's my experience that manipulative people aren't manipulative just once. If they get away with it, they continue until somebody calls them on it. I really don't feel like being the one to call Dottie on her poor human interactions.

The sun is just beginning to drop below the horizon when I turn onto the peninsula my parents' neighborhood is built on. The sun flashes between the pines, playing havoc with my eyesight.

I turn onto my parents' driveway and am surprised to see a monstrous amount of chicken wire on my daddy's twenty-foot, low-bed trailer. All three of the men in my family, plus Miles and Patrick, are wrestling with the chicken wire.

I want to sneak off to my room and sulk about what a crappy

day I had, then review my case files one more time for the extensive courtroom time I will be spending tomorrow. I don't have time to ask them what sort of happy horse manure they are into today.

Really, I don't care to know.

All of them have their backs turned to me as I walk to my apartment. Ah, crud muffin. My blasted curiosity won't let me leave lying dogs lie.

"Hey, what are y'all doing?" I say as I saunter over to the trailer.

All five men turn and stare at me as if I appeared magically out of thin air. Chase and Dusty crack a grin while everybody else goes back to work.

"Were making the largest baby Jesus manger we can fit on the trailer," Chase says proudly. "It's for the children's hospital wing Christmas parade this weekend."

"With chicken wire?" I ask.

"Chicken wire to form the frame. Then we'll push colored tissue in between to fill it out," Dusty explains.

"And you're gonna make baby Jesus out of chicken wire too? That seems sort of sacrilegious. Did you run that one by Granny?"

"No, that's just it. The manger will be so big we won't even have to put a baby inside of it. Nobody can see into the box to see if baby Jesus is missing."

I'm not sure how that works, but if there isn't a likeness of Jesus in the manger, I don't see how it can be blasphemous.

Patrick walks around the edge of the trailer. We lock eyes momentarily. My face warms up, and I become angry with myself. What's that about? I'm all but a married woman now. "Patrick."

"April." He nods his head. Then he breaks eye contact and returns to his task.

That's twice in short order he's paid no attention to me. Good for him. He is entirely past our *almost* fling. Maybe one day he can forgive me for how it ended.

"Is Mama home?"

Daddy looks up and fields my question. "No. She had to go to Nana's for something."

"And you just let her go?"

Daddy's eyes shift back to me. "Have you lived with your mother? I'm curious, because I don't think it would be a good idea for any of us to try and stop her from doing something once she has her mind made up."

Daddy makes a fair point. Unfortunately, that means I don't have anyone to talk to unless I want to construct a twenty-foot-high manger.

Nah. I'm good.

I walk to my apartment and unlock the door. I shut the door behind me then notice something amiss.

There is a faint, yet distinct, smell of leather and old Rebel cologne. That is disconcerting for two reasons. First, there has not been a man in my apartment in the last week. Second, that is the cologne my Grandpa Hirsch wore the other night when he visited me at Jester's.

That forces me into a round of searching every closet cabinet and under my bed for an out-of-place ghost. It's one thing to be looking for ghosts and see one when you are investigating. But to have a spirit suddenly appear when you're all relaxed is asking for a heart attack.

I check the cupboard drawers and notice a notebook sheet lying on top of my counter. I pick it up and do not recognize the handwriting. It is small print with very exacting letters.

The note reads, *"Everything is arranged. Expect your first visit here Friday at midnight."* Instinctively I wad up the piece of paper and throw it in the garbage. As if that will solve the issue.

I don't know what is so scary about this encounter. I've seen ghosts my entire life, and enough in the last six months for another lifetime. Why would my grandpa, who allegedly means me no ill will, be frightening the bejesus out of me?

Why? Because it is evident this is not some sort of across-the-veil social call. It is too much of an elaborate design not to be meant to change the trajectory of my life.

The odd thing about it is that if this happened a month ago, I might even welcome it. Because I felt lost, aimless, and without a plan. I could've used some sage advice then.

But now? Now that I have a destination in mind? A boyfriend that I feel pretty serious about, and a new drive to be as successful as possible? Now does not seem like the opportune moment for an ancestral intervention.

Yet here we are. I walk over to the trash can and pull the note back out. As I flatten it to its original form, the script begins to fade and then disappears altogether.

Great. So now I can't even ask Nana or Granny about it. It's like it never happened.

I think it might be some sort of invisible ink. I turn a stove eye on and hold the crumpled sheet over it. Even with the heat, the script does not reappear. The center of the sheet bursts into flames. I pivot to the sink to douse it, but all that remains is a charred corner.

Nothing spooky about that. I just held it too close to the heat. I think.

A loud clang comes from my front door. I turn as my body tenses with fear, afraid that an apparition is coming through my door.

Puppy tilts his furry head and examines me. He must not like what he sees since he comes into the apartment, does a U-turn, and leaves.

"Coward! Some best friend you are." He's the worst kind of male dog. The type that galivants all over town and doesn't pull his weight at the house.

At least he is enough of a distraction to get the note off my mind. If Grandpa wants to communicate with me, I suppose I would rather it be via disappearing letters rather than interrupting my drinking time in the future.

Chapter 14

Since mama isn't home and the boys are all intent on building their float for the Christmas parade, I know I'm on my own for dinner. I consider ordering a small pizza, but the delivery fee and tip would double the cost. That seems like a waste of money.

Luckily I've had a domestic streak ever since I met Lee. I remember I recently went to the grocery store. I open my cupboard and ponder my options.

Do I want the can of chicken noodle soup or the can of Chicken and Stars? You would think I'm deciding on my college major. It is no easy decision for me, and I change my mind at least twice before grabbing the can opener and starting on my meal preparation.

If Puppy returns and thinks I'm going to share after he abandoned me, he will be highly disappointed.

Baltimore is an hour ahead of us, so I give Lee a call. I dial his number as I watch my soup bowl spin in the microwave.

"Hello?" There is a tremendous amount of background noise on his end.

"Did I catch you at a bad time?" I ask him.

"No. It's never a bad time to hear from you." I hear a door open and close. The noise is muffled. "Me and Charlie Rankin had just gone to catch us a bite after mechanics training and treatment."

I have studied his team enough to know that Charlie Rankin is one of the catchers on their team. Geez, I really must have it bad if I'm learning his team's roster. "What are y'all eating?"

"Charlie's having a huge sirloin steak. I'm trying to be good. I opted for the grilled chicken and rice."

"It's easier to stay in shape than have to get in shape during spring ball." Where did that come from?

"That's the truth. What are your dinner plans?"

"Oh, me? I'm just finishing up on some soup I've been working on."

"Oh, wow. That sounds awesome. My mom used to make a couple of different soups. The idea of some good homemade soup just makes me miss you and home that much more."

He misses me. And I'm going to have to learn how to make soup. "I bet you haven't thought about me once since you've been up there," I tease.

"Not true at all. I wish there was some way you could've come with me. You should be up here interviewing for jobs while I'm working."

"It's Christmas, and if we stick to our plans, it'll be the last Christmas I spend in Guntersville."

"I know. I'm sorry if I'm being selfish. I just wish you were here. Plus, you would be better company than Rankin, that's for sure."

"It doesn't sound like you set the bar very high for me."

"You don't know the half of it. You haven't sat across Rankin while he's eating one of his medium-rare steaks. Yuck."

I don't want to ask for fear of sounding desperate, but I need to know, and he still hasn't committed. "Do you know yet when you're going to be home?"

There is a pause on the line. "Unfortunately, no. My agent has another ad we are supposed to be shooting tomorrow. Plus, I probably could still use a couple more days of training with our new pitching coach."

It isn't what I want to hear. "I understand. I just—I don't

know. I could use a hug and some company."

"Me too. Weirdly, I've never really missed anyone. Even my mom and dad when I went off to college. I thought I was going to be homesick, but it never seemed to phase me. I feel like I'm missing a part of me right now when you're not with me."

"Come home to me, then." I didn't mean to say that. It just sort of popped out there.

"Don't. I want to, but you know I have a job to do."

"I know. I'm sorry."

"Don't be sorry," he insists. "It's just when you say it, it becomes too much of a temptation. It's important what I'm doing right now, and even though I would rather be with you, to do my job well, I need to take care of my business."

"I understand. I'll let you get back to your dinner."

"I wish I was coming home this week. I'd ask you to save me some of that soup."

"Come home soon, and I'll just make you a fresh pot."

Lee laughs, and it makes my stomach tickle with desire.

"I think that may have been the sexiest phone talk I've ever heard," he says.

"You're silly. Have a good night," I say.

"You too, baby."

I hang up the phone. All I can think is, having a boyfriend to call is a good thing.

Chapter 15

The sun is so bright I must hold my eyes in a permanent squint to combat the glare. I can feel the part in my hair beginning to itch from the first stage of a painful scalp sunburn. Sweat trickles down my spine as thorns scratch my exposed legs and arms. I hold out the front hem of my purple-stained T-shirt to form a bowl while I pick plump blackberries from unruly canes with my other hand.

I feel buoyant and joyous.

The raucous laughter of my brothers comes up on me. Chase is running and laughing, blackberries splatted to his T-shirt. Dusty is in pursuit, his puffy cheeks red from exertion.

Dusty stops and throws three blackberries at a high rate of speed in quick succession. One bounces off the back of Chase's head.

I watch them in a stupefied bliss before I realize they appeared as thirteen-year-olds. I look down at my own knobby-kneed legs and flat chest, realizing I must be eight years old again. Oddly, I'm okay with it.

Collecting a small handful of the plump blackberries, I toss them back into my mouth. I bite down, and the tangy tart flavor explodes in my mouth. Now I am beyond joyous.

Scratches be darned; this is heaven.

"You two rascals are going to waste all the berries. Granny

won't be able to cook you a cobbler."

Despite the scolding tone, the voice makes me feel warm inside. I turn to search for him. I see my Grandpa Snow's tall, sturdy frame in his coveralls through the high, tangled canes.

"Oh, Homer. Leave the children be. We have enough berries in here to feed an army." Granny's voice is so much younger with none of the trembles she sometimes has in it now.

"Loretta, you let those boys run too wild, and they'll turn into hoodlums."

Granny comes into view and puts her arm around Grandpa. "What kind of trouble are they going to get into out here, Homer? They're just burning off energy."

"I could burn off some of that energy by putting them on moving the hay bales," he grumbles.

"Oh, hush up, you old grump."

"Where's that little one anyway. Those two boys always running wild, waking the dead, and that baby quiet as a church mouse."

I raise my blackberry-stained hand. "I'm in here," I call.

They both peer through the canes for the longest time before they see me. I wave my hand, and they nod simultaneously.

"Baby, there's snakes back that way," Granny cautions.

"Do you have your work boots on like I taught you?" Grandpa asks.

I want to lie and tell him yes. I always hate to disappoint either one of them. "No, sir."

"What do you have on, baby?"

"I'm barefoot, ma'am."

I close my eyes tight and wait for the scolding. I can't remember when either one of them laid a hand on me in anger, but I know I have lost a few inches of skin off my face from them hollering at me.

The scolding never comes.

Something cold and wet lands on my forehead. In quick succession, something else cold hits my cheek. I open my eyes, just to slits, so the sun won't blind me. It's nearly pitch dark.

Snow is spitting in the air. A consistent frigid breeze races down the damp street I'm on. The buildings are brick masonry, three to five stories tall, and old. They look like the type of buildings that got revitalized when downtown cities were gentrified. There has been no gentrification on this street.

I shiver against the cold and realize I'm barefoot on the damp asphalt. There is nobody around. Not just nobody I know, but no human being in sight. It is entirely silent, too.

For lack of a better plan, I walk down the street. My tender feet are rebelling with every stone I accidentally step on.

My desperation builds inside me. Bubbling right below that is gut-wrenching loneliness. In some ways, this seems to be worse than being lost in the void.

In the void, I saw and felt nothing. Here I see everything that reminds me of what was mankind, but now there is no trace of the people who should be around me on the street.

Through the silence of the night, I hear a loud crack followed by joyous cheering. I begin to run down the paved street, the soles of my feet slapping the brutal rough surface of the blacktop.

I come around the corner and stop in my tracks. The entire city block is lit up. As I stare at Camden Yards, I become the biggest baseball fan in the world.

My feet slap the wet road in double time as I run the three blocks to the first gate I come to. Chain-link is pulled and locked across the front of the entrance. A huge handwritten sign on cardboard is taped to the gate. *Sold out, no admittance.*

As the loneliness settles in again, I inspect the cuts on my feet. For the first time, I realize I am now a grown woman. I am now a very sad grown woman.

I wake with a start, and one of my binders falls off my bed. I must've fallen asleep while I was looking at my cases.

There isn't much more I can study. I pack the folders in my backpack and slip into my PJs. I feel myself floating off to sleep in a matter of minutes.

Chapter 16

My shoplifting and DUI cases are in the city court at nine o'clock sharp. Unfortunately, for my clients, I drew Judge Isaac Phillips.

Judge Phillips is a consistent and fair judge. However, his sentences tend toward the excessive. Not a good thing for my clients.

"Counselor Snow, I see you have filled most of my docket today. Are you planning on bringing me much holiday joy?"

Judge Phillips doesn't typically joke, so this has me a little off center and uncomfortable. "I hope so, your honor."

"Then let's see what you have, Counselor."

The planets must have been in a millennial alignment or something. The judge sees fit to assign each of my shoplifting cases two hundred hours of community service and require they pay restitution. Two of my three DUIs had their license suspended for thirty days and a two-thousand-dollar fine. One had their license suspended for six months and was required to spend a week in jail.

By Judge Philips' standards—a slap on the wrist.

"Counselor Snow, does this mean that I'm done with your docket for today?"

Judge Phillips never chit chats. This is just one more addition to the twilight zone day in his court. "Yes, sir. I'm all done for the day."

"I'm sure I won't see you before Christmas, so I'll tell you now. I hope you and your family have a wonderful Christmas. Don't do anything I wouldn't do."

Elizabeth Johnson, the prosecuting attorney brushes against me and whispers. "I think he's already been doing something he shouldn't be doing." She holds her right index finger to her thumb and mimes taking a puff.

"I know, right?" I say.

She motions toward the door with her head. "Let's go to lunch. I'll fill you in."

"I don't know if I have time." I slide my laptop into my backpack.

"Girl, there's always time for Petit Fours & Pimento."

My mouth waters as I remember my lunch from earlier in the week. Great, Pavlov didn't need a dog; he could have just used me.

"Okay, but I really do have to be at the county courthouse by one."

"It's not even eleven. I said, let's get lunch. I wasn't looking for a date."

Elizabeth Johnson is the city prosecutor. She is in her late thirties and dresses like she is in her early twenties. She is my height with an even fuller figure, long, relaxed curled hair, and enough attitude for three women. We have talked in passing before. Still, this is the first time either of us has extended an offer to go to lunch together.

"What do you think that was about today?" I hold the door open to Petit Fours & Pimento.

"The man be tripping. Rumor is he came home a few weeks ago, and Ruth met him at the front door with a shotgun."

I realize other than his name, I really don't know anything about Judge Phillips. I assume Ruth is his wife.

"She told the old coot she was tired of being talked down to, and if he couldn't do better than that, she was going to end his miserable existence."

"His wife?" I thought I better make sure it wasn't his house-keeper.

Elizabeth's full lips tighten on her face as she nods. "Um-hmm. Woman been married to that man for nearly thirty-five years. Heck, I guess even a good-natured dog will turn around and bite your hand if you slap it long enough."

"He's been beating his wife?"

Elizabeth nearly drops the lemonade off her tray as she laughs. "No. He's just mean and nasty to her." She shakes her head. "Thinking a judge is hitting his wife."

"I didn't know."

We sit at a table near the plate-glass window. Elizabeth continues, "The story is, the only thing that got that shotgun away from Ruth was Judge Phillips convincing her he would go to counseling."

"Did he?"

"Oh yeah. He's been going every other day for the last two weeks, from what I hear. I don't think it's fixing anything, though. I think it's just making him weirder."

I can't help it. An involuntary shudder comes over me. "I know what you mean. It's sorta creepy."

Elizabeth raises her eyebrows. "Amen."

"I think I prefer predictable over his new nice. I kept thinking it was some sort of a joke."

"It is sort of a joke. He's been mean for so long that when he's being nice, it seems unnatural."

"I guess we should give him credit for at least trying," I say.

"More like give him credit for evading buckshot to the gut," Elizabeth says as she takes a bite of her sandwich.

We eat in companionable silence for a few minutes. As we finish, Elizabeth says, "I got to hurry up and finish today, so I can get over to B-Mart. My daughter's wanting that new video game called *Star Masters*. Unfortunately, that means that she needs a new gaming system too, because they didn't make it for the system she has."

"That is such a racket."

Elizabeth smiles. "Your baby girl wants it. What are you gonna do? I know it's a racket, but it makes her happy, and she's a good kid. She gets good grades, and she's not any trouble."

"What's her name?"

"Amber. She's ten. It's sort of an awkward phase for her. She's taller than all the boys in her class right now." Elizabeth wrinkles her nose.

"That's normal for that age," I offer.

"Sure, it is. It doesn't make it any easier for the girls, though. Her daddy is all about sports, so he's always telling her it's a good thing." Elizabeth sighs. "And that's fine. She's a good athlete. But she likes to read more than she likes to play ball. She just plays to please her daddy."

"Well, it's good he's involved with her."

"When he's in town. Jimmy's a concrete engineer. He goes to sites where they're pouring for high-rises. He's usually gone for ten days and home for four. So, we have ten days of calm, just us girls, followed by four days of this manic pace while Jimmy gets his time in with everybody."

I'm not sure what I'm supposed to do with that. I'm surprised Elizabeth is talking about her family when we have not been on a friendly basis before today. "That would be tough."

"Yeah. I guess I should just be happy that he loves us and always comes home. But I have to admit I would do anything for him to have a job locally."

Without changing professions, that isn't going to be an option. There are currently—zero high-rises being built in the county. "Has he always traveled like that?"

"Oh yes. I went into this with my eyes wide open. This wasn't like something that snuck up on me. I just thought I would be able to handle it better. I did handle it better when I was younger. But now? Now I really would like my man to be home every night. Or at least most nights."

What Elizabeth is saying forces me to reflect on Lee's career. Is this what I have to look forward to in ten or fifteen years down the road?" How would I handle it? Could I manage to raise a child mostly on my own while still working full time?

"I think I've got similar concerns. The guy I'm dating right now is a major-league pitcher."

Elizabeth rolls her eyes. "You definitely don't want to be talking to me, then."

"Why do you say that?"

Elizabeth suddenly becomes interested in her pocketbook. "Never mind. Not my place. I shouldn't have said anything."

"No. I'm serious, Elizabeth. What were you going to say?"

"I'm sure your boyfriend is totally different. But my older sister was married to a professional basketball player for a couple of years. She got used to him being gone for the road trips but never could quite get used to his girlfriends calling his cell phone when he was home."

"Oh. Well, Lee is not like that."

"We all thought that about Colin, too."

She flashes a sardonic smile as she slides her purse strap onto her shoulder. "But I'm sure you're right about your boyfriend. Like I said, there's a gaming station waiting for me to spend half a week's salary on it."

"To make your little girl happy."

Her face lights up. "Anything for that. I enjoyed having lunch with you. We'll have to do it again sometime."

"Yes," I say. "I enjoyed it, too."

"Well, have a Merry Christmas."

"You too, Elizabeth."

As I watch Elizabeth leave the café, my stomach knots up. The reality of Lee's lifestyle might be the one percent that is holding me back in our relationship. Up until a few seconds ago, I had only been considering the travel aspect. The inconvenience of missed anniversaries, missed birthdays, and if we have kids, the inability for him to coach little league soccer and football.

I had forgotten about the lifestyle that many of the young athletes led when on the road. For some, it meant excessive partying at times. For others, it meant giving in to the temptation of curious female fans.

That isn't Lee. Lee isn't like that. And if he was, he wouldn't be acting like he wants a long-term relationship with me.

Sure, I'm not gonna be blind to the fact that he could be out with his buddies and get tempted and do something stupid. But I know Lee, and he isn't wired like that.

I pick up my backpack and head for the door. Amid the poinsettias and stuffed elf dolls that decorate the entry is a sign I had not noticed on the way into the café. "Do you believe?" At the moment, I'd like to say I do, but the jury is still out.

Chapter 17

Judge Rossi appears tired as she takes the bench. A diminutive woman, she usually is highly animated and forceful in her nature. Today she is sluggish.

I make eye contact with Lane at the prosecutor's table and draw my eyebrows together in question. He purses his lips and shakes his head. I take that to mean she is not in good health, but I will want the details later.

The judge calls for Rhonda Applewhite's case and reads the four counts of grand theft charged against her. Rhonda stands next to me as I reply, "Not guilty," to Judge Rossi.

Judge Rossi narrows her eyes then turns to Lane. "Isn't Ms. Applewhite the defendant that you have those hours of security tape on?"

"Yes, ma'am," Lane responds.

Judge Rossi turns back to me. "Not guilty? Are we sure about that, Counselor?"

No. But that's what my bonehead client wants to claim. "Yes, ma'am. We believe that the quality of the tapes is in question. Therefore, the identity cannot be confirmed as Ms. Applewhite."

The corners of Judge Rossi's lips tick up in amusement. "I see. Or at least we will see pretty soon. Counselor Snow, I'll remind you the court does not take kindly to defendants claiming their innocence if there is overwhelming evidence of their guilt. Our sentencing is much more favorable toward clients who have remorse for the wrongdoing and are accountable for it."

"Yes, ma'am."

"Would you and your client like to take a moment to reconsider the plea?"

I look to Rhonda, and she immediately gives me an "as if" look. "No, Your Honor. We stand on our not-guilty plea. We would like to request that Ms. Applewhite be released on her own recognizance."

Judge Rossi looks to Lane. "District Attorney?"

"She's a first-time offender, and I wouldn't consider her a flight risk. I suppose I don't have an issue with it."

Judge Rossi takes off her reading glasses and rubs the bridge of her nose. She then cleans her glasses with a tissue. "It's Christmas time, folks. I'm genuinely trying to be charitable. But maybe it's because I'm old, and before too long, I'll be in the ground. Still, the idea of someone coming into a cemetery and stealing the flowers that a loved one may have put on my grave horrifies me. No. It repulses me.

"I'll agree, Ms. Applewhite did not do anything that endangered anybody else, and she is a first-time offender. I also believe that because of her long-standing in the community, she is not a flight risk.

"However, she is coming here today aware of the preponderance of evidence against her and still she refuses to be accountable for her barbaric ghoulish act."

Judge Rossi replaces her glasses. "I'm setting bail at five thousand dollars. Not because I think it's an absolute necessity, Ms. Applewhite. I just want to inconvenience you like you're going to be inconveniencing this court and the families whose flowers you stole."

Before I can say anything, Judge Rossi hammers her gavel against the sounding block. "I believe you have another bit of business to take up with me, Counselor Snow. We'll take a thirty-minute recess and then reconvene."

I look to Lane, and he shrugs. Turning, I watch Judge Rossi disappear into her chamber.

"That's a ridiculously high bail," Rhonda complains.

I hold up my hand toward Rhonda. "Don't even."

"What? It is," she whines.

"Did you not even listen to the judge? Once she sees the security tapes, she's going to charge you with the maximum sentence, and you will have four felonies. You had a chance to negotiate them down to misdemeanors."

"Those grainy tapes aren't going to be able to show anything."

I'm relieved when Hal Joiner, Judge Rossi's bailiff, takes Rhonda by the arm. "Come with me, Ms. Applewhite."

Hal moves Dottie toward the exit. I step over to Lane's table. "Hey, what's up with Judge Rossi?"

Lane moves closer. Putting his mouth next to my ear, he whispers, "The cancer is back."

There is a sense of vertigo that flashes through me, and I must put my hand on Lane's table to steady myself. I assumed he would tell me she had a cold or bronchitis. I had no clue she had ever had cancer. Heck, for all intents and purposes, Judge Rossi is a 5-foot-tall version of "ten foot tall and bulletproof." I would think cancer would back off such a formidable opponent.

I suppose even our heroes have frailties.

"I didn't know," I whisper back to Lane

He nods his head. "We'll talk later."

I sit down at the defender's table and stare ahead at the Marshall County seal on the wall behind the too-large chair that is Judge Rossi's throne. I'm numb, in shock, and sad. If there is anyone in Guntersville outside of my family that I would most like to emulate, it is Judge Rossi.

She is a strong, confident woman who knows who she is and bent the world to her liking. All the while collecting friends and admirers along the way. It takes a special person to be able to accomplish those two things simultaneously.

Hal Joiner returns to the courtroom with Dottie Castle at his side. Orange is definitely not Dottie's color.

"Hello, Ms. Castle."

"April, you have to get me out of here."

"Yes, ma'am, that's what we're going to try to do."

"No, I don't think you understand. I can't spend another night here. Try is not sufficient."

"I understood perfectly. We'll do our best to get you released today, and then we'll have to build a case to prove your innocence."

"I thought I was innocent until proven guilty."

I motion for her to have a seat. "Yes, ma'am. You are. I should've worded it differently."

The way Lane is railroading this case through, I think my original wording is correct. Ever since they found Gil's body on the Castle farm and he assigned Ms. Castle's defense to me, I have the feeling the burden of proof is on the defendant.

The discovery period will be particularly fascinating. For the life of me, I can't see how, after the case is cold for twenty-five years, a body pops up and they have Ms. Castle charged a few hours later.

There is no rush. Why not take your time and make sure all your I's are dotted and T's are crossed?

Judge Rossi returns from her chamber. She climbs the stairs laboriously to take her seat. I can tell her color is much lighter than usual. My heart breaks, thinking that she is in pain and might be leaving us in the future.

When Judge Rossi reads the charges of lying to police and obstruction of justice, I lock eyes with Lane. This is a curveball, as I understood his intent to be to charge Dottie with manslaughter.

Even though it sounds like a win for Dottie, given she is involved with a capital case, it is still a felony. A felony much easier for Lane to prove, giving him time for the charge he really wants to level against Dottie.

"Counselor Snow, how does your client plead?" Judge Rossi asks.

"Your Honor, there has been a slight adjustment to the charges. May I have a moment to confer with my client."

Judge Rossi removes her glasses and rubs the bridge of her nose. "DA Jameson, are we playing fast and loose with the charges again?"

"No, Your Honor."

"Take a moment to talk to your client, Counselor Snow. But please be aware that the court does not have an unlimited amount of time today."

"Yes, Your Honor."

"What does that mean?" Dottie asks as I turn my attention to her.

"I was under the impression that you're going to be charged with manslaughter. But the district attorney has changed it to lying to obstruct an investigation." I have limited time, so I'm blunt. "Dottie, did you lie to the investigators?"

"No!" she says indignantly, while gesturing with her hands. "But I also didn't kill Gil, and they think I did that, too."

It is a fair point. "You're sure you did not lie to them?"

"I didn't kill my husband, and therefore I have no reason to lie to anybody about anything. I don't understand any of this."

There is still murky, blurred energy that I don't care for emanating from Dottie. She could, like Judge Rossi, be in poor health, or she could be lying like a true sociopath. But for now, her statement will have to be enough.

"Judge Rossi, my client pleads not guilty."

"Very well. District Attorney Jameson, is there any reason why we should not extend bail at this time?"

"Your Honor, the state would prefer that the defendant stays in custody until the conclusion of her trial," Lane says.

"I understand your preference, District Attorney. Still, the holiday season is a lousy time for anyone to be in jail unless they're going to harm somebody. Is it your opinion that Dottie Castle might commit a violent crime while she's out on bail?"

"It's always a possibility."

Rossi smiles and looks like she might laugh. "Yes. It is always a possibility. The court will take your opinion under advisement."

She turns her icy stare back to me. "I'm releasing Ms. Castle into her own recognizance. She is not to leave the city, and she is not to make any excessive withdrawals from any of her accounts. Can you abide by these rules of release?"

Dottie is nodding her head profusely.

"Yes, Your Honor. We thank you for your understanding," I say.

"Don't thank me, Counselor Snow. Just make sure that your client shows back up the first week of January."

"Yes, Your Honor."

Rossi strikes the sounding block. "We are adjourned. I wish all of you a merry Christmas." She turns and disappears into her chamber before any of us can respond.

"I can go home?" Dottie's eyes are bloodshot. Her usually crystal blue irises appear cloudy today.

"Yes. The bailiff will take you back to get your belongings, then they will release you. You need to make sure to abide by what Judge Rossi told you. It is a real gift that she's releasing you. If she finds out that you broke your promise, I assure you she will be ruthless in your punishment."

"I understand," Dottie says. She steps toward Hal as he comes to collect her.

I crowd into Lane's space as Dottie leaves. "What was that about?"

"What?"

Lane doesn't play stupid very well. "The charges. Why did you change the charges? You told me you planned to charge her with manslaughter."

Lane closes his briefcase. "And I will. Just as soon as I have enough evidence to convict her for it."

"So, what was this all about today? Why not just wait to charge her?"

"Because she's being uncooperative, and she doesn't take it seriously. I figure a night in jail might give her some needed perspective on the situation."

"You don't have anything." It surprises me when I hear the epiphany tumble from my mouth. I thought I was just thinking it.

"Not concrete. Not yet, but I will."

I'm not sure why that rubs my fur the wrong way. I suppose it has more to do with Lane's arrogant mannerisms that crept into his conversation. I decide to let it go. Dottie is going home for the holidays, and Lane just admitted that she wasn't truly a suspect yet in Gil's death.

All good news.

What isn't good news is Judge Rossi's condition. "Can you talk about—" I gesture toward the bench.

Lane nods his head and points toward the exit. "Not in here."

I pick up my backpack and follow him out of the courtroom.

Chapter 18

"Care to share a cup of coffee?" Lane asks as we clear the courtroom double doors. "I'm buying."

"Sure." I follow him out of the municipal courthouse and into the bitter cold.

"It's hard to remember I live in the South with this north wind cutting through my coat," Lane remarks.

"Well, it is December."

"True that."

I stamp my boots in an attempt to warm my feet as we wait for the holiday traffic to break across Gunter Street. The little shops up and down the main drag are busy with locals as well as out-of-towners who have come to try and find a unique gift for the one they love.

My body tenses in horror. I hadn't even thought about getting Lee a gift.

Oh, how stupid.

I've left myself only three days to figure out what I'm going to get the professed love of my life. I'm such an idiot.

What's wrong with me? If I'm so in love with Lee, wouldn't I already have thought of some perfect Christmas gift for him? Isn't that what girls do?

As we walk across the street, I'm racking my brain about all of our conversations. Hoping, searching for any dropped hint about something Lee might want or need.

Who am I kidding? He is a professional ballplayer who just bought a lake house as a secondary residence. What am I going to get him that he needs? Man. I'm so screwed.

"Before we talk about Judge Rossi, I want to ask you about your status."

Lane is staring at me with that familiar look of expectation as we walk the sidewalk. "Status?"

"You have had a lot of opportunities posed to you lately, and I'm wondering if you have made a decision on any of them."

"Opportunities?" Lord, I sound like a stupid parrot.

Lane favors me a smile as he opens the door to Hot Mugs and gestures for me to go in first. "The FBI, a possible prosecutor's position here in the county—"

"Oh, that."

"Yes, that," he says as he motions for me to get in front of him in the line.

"I really haven't taken time to think about all that right now. You know the holidays and the workload—"

"April, you can't neglect the important because of the critical. Otherwise, you're going to wake up in twenty years and wonder how this became your life."

Heck, I already wonder daily how this is my life. "Yeah, my daddy tells me that all the time."

"Your father is a smart man."

"Yeah, that's what he will tell you anytime you ask him." Did I say that out loud?

Lane chuckles. "He'd probably also tell you he has a brilliant daughter. I just hope she takes the time soon to reflect on her career options."

"Touché," I agree.

There is another part of the Lee equation that is slightly problematic. Everybody is aware that Lee and I are dating. However, we haven't yet mentioned to anyone that I'm considering moving to Baltimore to live with him.

Considering? I have all but promised Lee I would.

The idea of broaching the subject with my parents sends shivers through my body. I like to hold onto the possibility that they will be happy for me. Still, I have a gut feeling it will be a long, arduous process to bring them around to the idea. Especially since there isn't going to be a ring—or a wedding—involved.

Lane selects a quiet booth in a dimly lit corner of Hot Mugs. He scans the area making sure nobody is seated within earshot of our conversation.

"Margaret's touchy about who knows about her illness," Lane says as I slide into the booth.

"I'll say. I didn't even know that she had cancer before."

"You wouldn't. She had breast cancer fifteen years ago and fought it into remission. Unfortunately, it's back, and from what she tells me, it's terminal."

I get vertigo again. My world spins on the word "terminal." I'm thankful for the back of the booth that I lean against. "That's awful."

"Don't rule her out just yet. Margaret was supposed to be terminal last time, too. The woman's doctors were absolutely amazed when her test came back clear. They went from amazed to condescending when she began to tell them her recovery had nothing to do with their medicine and everything to do with prayer."

Lane seems highly amused by Margaret's belief that she cured herself with prayer. Given my recent revelations regarding manifestation, I'm not laughing.

But I am sick at heart over the news.

I know it's the natural order that people die. I'm not some eight-year-old.

But I'm also not old enough to have gotten used to death. I don't want to get used to it, and I sure don't want to lose one of my real-life superheroes at this stage of my career.

"Hey, chin up. If Margaret were to see you acting like that around her, she would know I told you."

I exhale as my shoulders slump. I feel defeated. "Did she say how her son and sister took the bad news?"

Lane raises his eyebrows. "Oh, no. She didn't tell either of them last time, and she's not telling them this time."

"She's got to tell them."

"Not according to her. She says that she already lives her life like it's her last day and has been doing that for fifteen years. If Margaret loses this round, they'll definitely be able to tell before she heads out. At this point, all she's focused on is making sure that she gets every moment she can get out of this life." He chuckles again. "She told me she paid full-price admission to this amusement park. She isn't resting until they turn out the lights on her."

My face tightens with anxiety. "But not telling anybody just seems wrong. Doesn't she want to give her family a chance to prepare?"

"If she told anybody fifteen years ago, she never would've made judge. It was already an uphill struggle because she is female. Include the fact she is a minority—if they knew she had a serious illness, there would be no way she would've made judge."

All the wise rulings I had experienced in her court go through my mind. "That would've been a travesty."

"On way too many fronts. I'm sure you can understand why she is playing it close to the vest again this time." He makes a slight shrug of his shoulder. "She's well into her seventies. If they thought she was ill, they would pressure her to give up the bench. If she beats this, she will want to stay on the bench until she can't work anymore. It's who she is, what she does."

"Why are you telling me all this. It sounds as if it's all supposed to be a secret."

Lane tucks his hands under his chin, his elbows propped on the table. "It's not obvious?"

"No. It's not."

"District attorney is political by nature. It's a good position for someone looking for a stepping stone to a higher political office. At one time, I thought I might want that in my life.

Things have changed, and my goals have changed."

I nod my head because it seems required, and I certainly can empathize with plans changing in your life. Still, I have no idea where this conversation is leading. Curiously, I'm beginning to feel uncomfortable with the direction, even though it does not pertain to me.

"I've been thinking about it for a while. In the next year or two, I would like to move into a judgeship if possible. Which would leave a district attorney position open for a young bright attorney." He inclines his forehead toward me. "We can't pick the next DA, but we can influence the decision, and in our mind, you are one of the most talented people for that role."

My head feels like it is going to explode. First the news about Judge Rossi and then that she and Lane are secretly plotting my career? I want to just say, "No, that's not happening!" Luckily for once in my life, I'm too shocked for my mouth to go on autopilot.

"That's high praise, Lane. I appreciate you saying that."

"It's not just praise. It's how Margaret and I feel about you. True, you're still young and inexperienced. Still, you have the natural instincts it takes to be a highly successful district attorney."

All I can think is what a fraud I am. Lane is heaping praise on me, and the flattery is making me both grateful and self-conscious. I am grateful that my work is appreciated, but self-conscious because I still feel like a fraud deep down.

It is as if there are two universes in the world. My universe is cobbling together a couple of part-time jobs to make ends meet. At the same time, I interview for jobs outside of Guntersville. In the Guntersville reality, everyone suddenly believes I'm planning to throw down roots, fully engage in my work, and do my utmost for my clients.

Most days, I know I'm just winging it.

I must've waited too long to respond. Lane adds, "We know that you have other opportunities available to you. I'm just saying that if you wanted to give it consideration, you have some fans who are willing to work to help it materialize for you. I can tell you from personal experience that it's a good gig if you can get it."

I begin to get my bearings back. "I'm sure it is. I just have never really considered myself as a district attorney before."

"I understand. You're going to be successful. Regardless if you choose to work prosecution or defense. From the prosecutorial side, I just like the way that you're able to look at things. Instinctively you know if a client is innocent and caught up in a bad situation or if they're trying to lie their way out of justice."

Lane's observation hits a little too close to home. I immediately become concerned about using my clairvoyance "gifts" too often on my clients. I always promised to never use it, but I have accidentally read my clients a couple of times.

Okay, a few times. "Again, thank you, Lane. I'd really have to think on it."

His brow creases. "Oh, sure. It wasn't like I was expecting a commitment today. I just needed to let you know where Margaret and I were on the topic. Also, I want you to at least consider your local prospects when you're considering your next job opportunity."

"I will, and you will be one of the first people I tell."

Chapter 19

Saying I'm emotionally spent is an understatement. By the time Lane and I finish coffee, it is five o'clock. I have an overwhelming desire to go home and slide into bed. I don't need the extra sleep. It's that everybody is so needy that they are sapping all my energy.

I sit down in my car, and my phone rings. As I read the caller ID, I groan, realizing what night it is. I want to bang my head on my steering wheel but manage not to. "Hey, Nana."

"Hi, honey. Can you do me a favor and pick up some tea bags on your way over?"

Oh boy. If I could only tell Nana I can't come tonight. If she weren't calling asking for something, I would beg off, but if I don't pick up the tea bags for her, that will mean that she will be eating dinner alone and without tea. That just won't do.

"Yes, ma'am."

"Thank you. Oh, and by the way, I hope you have your eating pants on."

Unwittingly I look down at my skirt. I guess it wouldn't be a big deal to undo the top button. "Yes, ma'am."

"Good, because we're having country-fried steak, biscuits and gravy, and mashed potatoes. I've got a splash of green beans you can put on your plate if you need some color."

It is impossible to eat that sort of food and not end up

chunky dunkin' in the lake instead of skinny dippin'. It is also impossible to turn that menu selection down and not regret it for three days.

Sometimes you have to undo your waistband and enjoy life.

"That's definitely one of my favorites," I tell Nana.

"Mine too. I'm just about to put the biscuits in the oven, so I hope you're not gonna be long."

Putting the biscuits, cookies, and fresh bread in the oven is how passive-aggressive cooks get things done. It is a very effective phrase to get favors done lickety-split, albeit over-used.

The sun has set as I come upon the Willoughby covered bridge. I don't see my nemesis, the drowned little girl, and pick up speed so that maybe I can get across the covered bridge before she realizes I'm there.

I'm fifty yards away from the bridge when she floats up the left side shoulder, hovering three inches above the asphalt.

Locking up my car's brakes, I slide into a forty-five-degree angle on the road while I watch the little girl glaring at me. I pull forward until I can straighten my car. A puddle forms below her on the asphalt as the lake water trickles from the hem of her dress. Her chin is nearly touching her chest, forcing her wet hair to hang slack about her face.

I rev my engine in preparation to speed through her and cross the bridge. I shift my IROC into gear, and the eerie little girl points a bony finger in my direction, lifts her doll, and rips its head off.

I don't know sign language. Still, I'm pretty sure I get her meaning.

Slamming the accelerator to the floor, my rear tires squeal, sending up a plume of smoke behind me. My tires grab the asphalt and my car catapults forward, pressing me into my seat as I drive through the ghost. My tires lose grip on the old damp planks, sending me fishtailing across the old bridge.

As I hit the lip of the asphalt on the opposite side, my car lifts into the air. I'm screaming in jubilation over my hard-fought freedom as I wait for my car to come back to earth.

It crashes onto the road, forcing my forehead to bounce off my steering wheel, and I bite my tongue. Still, I'm grinning like a loon.

Take that, creepy little girl!

I'm incredibly thankful for all the dream catchers blowing in the gnarled old oak trees while driving up to Nana's house. I know the drowned girl will never follow me this far, or at least to date she hasn't, but if she did, I sure hope she gets all tangled up in the web of one of Nana's magical creations.

It is an impossibility, but I swear I can smell the biscuits as soon as I get out of my car. Lord, help me. I need this meal like I need a share-size candy bar all to myself.

I open the screen door. "Knock, knock, Nana."

"Back here in the kitchen, sweetie. I'm just taking the biscuits out."

I cross through what passes for her living room in the double-wide. She has three, eight-foot folding tables filling the small room. Each has a hundred small pint-size colored glass bottles.

As I walk to the kitchen, the scent of hot grease, pepper, butter, and fresh biscuits envelops me. My stomach rumbles as if I hadn't eaten in a week.

"I can't think of the last time I had country-fried steak," I say.

Nana lays a clean dish towel over the biscuits, "Really? I'm surprised there's not a restaurant down in Tuscaloosa you could've got it at while you were in school."

"Well, they do. But it's sort of like how once you have a vine-ripened tomato from a garden, those tomatoes at the grocery store aren't worth eating."

"I know that's right. If you try to make a BLT with one of those, it's a waste of good bacon and bread."

"What about the lettuce?"

Nana rolls her upper lip. "Never been much of a fan for lettuce on a sandwich. I could take it or leave it. Do you have the tea?"

"Yes, ma'am." She gestures toward a saucepan of boiling water. I take out eight tea bags and drop them in the pan as I move it off the eye. I take her tea pitcher, fill it half full with water, and put a cup of sugar in it.

"Anything exciting happen this week?" she asks.

I tense and have an odd sensation that somehow she knows about Grandpa's visit. That is silly. There's is no way Nana could know. I've told no one. "Hmmm, not really. My welcoming hostess at the bridge made another appearance."

Nana rolls her eyes. "Child, I still haven't seen that ghost. I wonder what in the world she has against you."

I pick the top off one of the biscuits and alternate it between hands as it cools. "I wish I knew, but one thing I do know is she has anger issues."

"Obviously only with you. Are you at least taking precautions when you encounter her?"

"Yeah. I'm making sure my car is going at top speed so she can't catch me." I take a bite of the biscuit and close my eyes as it melts on my tongue.

"I'm not sure that's the most effective protection."

I want to disagree with her and tell her it has worked just fine so far, but I'm busy finishing off the rest of the biscuit I pinched.

"That's exciting stuff about your mama selling the old Sinclair bed and breakfast," Nana says.

"She did?" I realize I have not seen Mama all week.

"You didn't know?" Nana hands me an oversized plate.

"I knew it had been placed with her earlier in the month, but no, I hadn't heard anything about it."

Guntersville was at one time home to six bed and breakfasts. The Sinclair was by far the most opulent.

It occupies the tallest crest in Guntersville and has a commanding view of the main channel. The home was built by Brody Sinclair in the 1930s. The Sinclair family made their money in dog food.

The plant still survives on the southern shore of the lake. In the 1980s, the family sold the home. It became a maintenance money pit for every homeowner until the Tinkers bought it ten years ago. They refurbished the entire house, including the landscaping, and had what we thought was a thriving bed-and-breakfast business.

It would have been except for a tiny detail. The Tinkers, while excellent business people and great cooks, didn't like people. Unfortunately for them, it's hard to run a prosperous bed and breakfast and not like people.

"So, someone else is going to take on the bed and breakfast?"

Nana lifts her plate. "No. Some hotshot executive out of Birmingham bought it. He's supposed to have a whole tribe of teenage grandchildren that talked him into buying a lake house."

"Oh, that'll be a blast."

Nana grins. "You know the drill. They'll have it for seven years, it will slowly go to seed, and when it becomes a party house for the college grandchildren, they'll up and sell it one day."

Yes, that is often the way of the out-of-town money. Once they realize that a lake house has as much if not more maintenance than a typical house, it starts to bleed the fun out of it. The only out-of-towners who end up staying long-term are the ones who want to retire to the lake.

Why is it that nothing tastes as good as the things that are bad for you? Why can't spring mix lettuce and carrot sticks taste like homemade gravy and creamy mashed potatoes? How easy would it be to stay in shape if it weren't for that one fact?

It isn't long before I reach down with my left hand and undo the button to my skirt. That should have been a sign to me that it was time to quit. Instead, as the pressure eases on my stomach, I continue shoveling delicious bites of country-fried steak into my mouth.

As my pace slows, I remember all the bottles in the living room. "What's up with the bottles in the living room?"

Nana rolls her eyes again, exhaling loudly. "That silly Internet site I'm on. It's covering me up with orders."

"Those are all for the hair removal?"

"Oh, Lord no. Hair removal still sells relatively well. But it's my number three producer now."

I'm afraid to ask, and being part of the justice system, I'm not sure I want to know. My curiosity gets the best of me, though. "What are your top two producers?"

"The herbal weight loss tonic is a pretty good moneymaker. Still, the one that is driving me *crazy*, and I can barely keep up with the orders, is the male enhancement tonic."

I choke on my last bite of biscuit. Please let me have heard Nana wrong. "Male what?"

"Enhancement. You know." Nana puts her hands toward her crotch and opens her hands wide. "Make it bigger, stronger, and longer."

My lower jaw is hanging slack. I can't believe we are having this conversation.

Nana's eyes narrow. "That's a great slogan. I might need to change my banner to that."

"Do they drink this, or like rub it on their thing?" I'm not sure which would be worse.

"They drink it. I don't know if it would do anything if they rubbed it on themselves. I don't know that anyone has tried that."

"I hate to ask this, but how do you know that it works?"

"Oscar Branch tried it out for me."

In his late seventies, Oscar Branch is about one hundred pounds overweight with yellow-stained white hair and tobacco-stained teeth. His usual attire is heavily scarred pull-on leather boots, denim coveralls splotched liberally with oil, and no shirt. I know the dating field thins as you get older, but I can't imagine Nana having to settle for Oscar Branch. "You didn't—" I wrinkle my nose without thinking.

"Didn't what?" Nana's shoulders convulse. "Oh no! Please. That's so gross. I tried it out on his pig."

"For the love of—Nana! What's the matter with you people?"

"It didn't hurt him," she says.

"Stop! I don't want to hear any more of this. It's just too weird and gross."

Nana purses her lips as her ears turn red. "What is so gross about feeding an old boar male enhancement?"

"Wait, are you saying 'boar' like b-o-r-e or 'boar' like a pig?"

"Pig. I told you he tried it out on his pig."

I'm relieved we're still on the pig and haven't moved on to Oscar. "Why?"

"It makes perfect sense. Oscar said his boar had lost interest in the females and was afraid he would have to artificially inseminate his sows this year. Everybody knows that pigs have ninety-nine percent of the DNA that humans do, so we thought it would be a good idea to try the tonic out on his boar."

I suppose, all things being equal, I would rather Nana poison a pig during the pseudo-lab trials. It's better than one of her tonics killing some unsuspecting Internet rube from across the country. "Did it work?"

Nana lifted her right hand and rocked it left to right.

"Maybe, sorta, what does that mean?" I ask.

"It worked. That pig was making love to every sow in sight— three times. Oscar had to put the sheep in a different part of the pasture because the boar kept trying to tear down the fence to get after the sheep."

"I guess, all in all, at least you know that the product works and it's safe."

"Oh, it works all right. The safe part is sort of subjective. That pig stayed after it three days straight, and then he just fell over dead."

We lock eyes. Neither of us makes a peep for the longest time. It's as if I'm waiting for a punchline. A punchline that will never come.

"Dead," I say.

"I'm afraid so." Nana shakes her head slowly. "According to Oscar, he just fell over on his side and never moved again."

"And this doesn't bother you? You're not worried that one of your customers might have the same thing happen to them?"

"Of course not. It was a pig, not a human."

"But you just said ninety-nine percent of same DNA."

"Yeah, but ninety-nine percent leaves room for differences."

At this rate, Nana is going to need a stellar defense attorney. I'm positive I'm not good enough. "You can't pick and choose, Nana. You can't say because they're ninety-nine percent the same that the enhancement part works. Then say because there's a one percent difference, humans won't have the same catastrophic death event as that poor boar that y'all fed this tonic to."

Nana stands and gathers the plates. "That's the thing about you, honey. You just borrow too much trouble. Always worrying about things before they even happen. I've been sending out that male enhancement for three weeks now, and I haven't had the first complaint."

"Have you had any reviews at all posted on the website about the product?" I ask.

"No, not yet."

"That's because they're all dead, Nana." I'm only half-joking.

"That's just silly." She rinses the dishes. "You can get you a bottle for your boyfriend if you want."

"No, I think we're good in that department," I say.

Nana flashes a grin over her shoulder. "Oh. Well, good for you."

I feel the heat creep up my neck, and my cheeks flush. "No. Not like that."

"Oh."

I have no desire to go into explaining Lee's and my love life, or lack of it, to my Nana. For one, I don't understand it. I say the first thing that comes to mind. "Grandpa Hirsch visited me the other night."

Nana stops washing the dish in her hand and turns the water off. She leans all of her weight against the counter.

I watch and wait for her to turn and respond. Of all the reactions I had expected from Nana, silence is not it, and it frightens me. "Nana, did you hear me?"

Chapter 20

What I'm sure is only seconds feels like an eternity while I wait for her response. Her silence only amplifies my own concern regarding the unexpected visit.

"Yes, child. Give me a moment." With her left hand remaining on the counter, she walks down to the pantry on the end, opens it, and retrieves an amber-colored bottle.

She brings the bottle and two shot glasses to the table. Without a word, she fills both glasses and sets the bottle down.

Time stands still as I watch Nana staring at the trembling surface of the golden liquor in the shot glass. "When? When did you see him?"

I pull my shoulders in and stare at the table. "Earlier this week."

Her eyes meet mine briefly, then return to the liquor on the table. "Monday?"

It is hard to remember precisely. It'd been a difficult week, and all the days were running together. "Yes, ma'am."

Nana appears to finally make up her mind and snatches one of the shot glasses up and empties it in one fluid motion. "You never knew your grandpa. How could you be sure it was him?"

I can tell by her whispered tone she is hoping I'm wrong but convinced I'm right. "The pictures in the foyer and the one you keep on your nightstand. It took me a little while to figure out why his face looked so familiar."

Nana takes the second shot glass and downs it. I thought she had poured it for me, but I wasn't in the mood to drink anyway.

"What did he want with you?"

"Mostly, he just seemed to want to talk. But when I went to leave, he appeared in my car."

Nana's light bronze skin takes on an ashen color. "You invited him into your car?"

"No, ma'am. He just sort of appeared."

Nana refills the shot glasses. I notice the bottle's neck is shaking as she pours.

"He said I would have visitors soon. What do you think he meant?"

Nana cradles her head in her hands. "Lord, child. Why does everything have to be so attracted to you?"

"I don't know."

Nana gives a slight shake of her head. "It was a rhetorical question, April. The spirits are attracted to you because of your power. They feel it, and they crave it. They know with your level of power they can cross the veil easily and possibly even affect things on this side."

"But it's my grandpa. He wouldn't hurt me, would he?"

"How do you know for sure it was your grandpa?" Nana raises her eyebrows in that manner that tells me I wasn't thinking things all the way through.

"Because he looked like the picture on your dresser, and he told me his name was Robert?"

"And there's never been an evil entity that would stoop so low as to disguise themselves and lie about their name."

Maybe she is right. Perhaps I hadn't thought it all the way through.

Until this conversation, I had really considered the meeting with Grandpa Hirsch and his pronouncement that I would have three visitors as more of a nuisance than a problem. But if Nana is correct, which she could be, it might be some manner of a trap.

We sit in silence for a while longer, both staring at the full shot glasses. I'm beginning to change my mind and think that I might want a shot of whiskey.

A question comes to me. "How did you know it was Monday?"

Nana answers it as if she has expected it all along. "He visited me that night and told me he had talked to you."

"Why didn't you tell me that?"

"I hoped I was wrong?" She folds her hands on the table. "I thought maybe it was something I just dreamed."

"No. I don't believe that you thought it was a dream."

Nana takes another shot of whiskey and slaps the tumbler to the table. "I didn't say I believed it was a dream. I said I hoped it was a dream. It's not a crime for somebody to hope."

"What does it mean? I asked Granny about it, and she told me that you would be better able to tell me."

"Loretta knows more than what she's letting on," Nana grumbles.

"It's your dead husband, so I figure you would know more than Granny."

Nana closes her eyes. "You know, I just wanted to teach you how to control your animism and how to direct it so that you could have a little fun with it and be able to use your skill to your advantage. If I had ever thought that it would wake my dead husband from the grave, I never would've broached the subject with you."

"Could've, would've, should've, but we are here now, Nana. Tell me what I need to know. Please."

She bites her lower lip for a moment before she speaks. "First off, you have to understand this puts you in grave danger."

"Like being stuck in the void?"

"Different, but the same results of not being in control of your soul anymore."

Great. I wanted to learn how to make fireballs in my hand, and random ghosts are trying to steal my spiritual freedom. Once again, the "gift" seems to have a higher price tag than its value.

"Is there any way I can block them from coming to visit?"

"I doubt it. Ever since you've been back, your energy has been increasing each week exponentially. That would mean that your blocking spells would be more potent, but in a way, attract even more attention from the other side of the veil. In the end, I don't think you'll be able to stop this from moving forward.

"Suppose Bob's ghost followed you from one location to another, as you say. In that case, he is very passionate about your need for these visits. Given his level of energy about the idea, I wouldn't think there's any way to prevent it."

I make a twirling motion with one of my fingers. "Why am I getting the sense that you're not telling me something?"

Nana snaps up the last full shot glass and downs it. "Your grandpa was an incredibly powerful medium. Similar to your power level. It does not surprise me that he's able to come to this side of the veil in a full apparition. It wouldn't surprise me if his apparition might even be able to move physical objects in our plane."

"He can."

Nana's eyes narrow. "How do you know?"

I frown. "He opened the door to Jester's, pulled out a chair to sit in, oh, and he also wrote me a note."

"Do you have it with you?"

"No, ma'am. I held it too close to the stove. It burst into flames."

Nana shakes her head as she draws in a deep breath. "It scares me that he's walking on this side now. Being on the dark side of the veil has a tendency to drive spirits mad. He's been over there too long now. Which in my book makes him not fully trustworthy."

"You're talking about your husband," I whisper.

She shakes her head vehemently. "No. My husband is dead and has been dead for over four decades. What you and I are visited by is a spirit.

"The same spirit that used to inhabit the body of your grandpa, but things change with time. Once the spirit left Bob, it doesn't necessarily hold to all the relationship and family norms it built up while he was alive."

"But it could," I insist.

"It could," Nana agrees begrudgingly. "Still, there is too much at risk. We have to take precautions where we can, even if it is your grandpa, and not forget it could be a different entity up to mischief."

"Precautions are good," I agree.

"When are these visitors due?"

"He didn't say. Just that it would be before Christmas."

Nana rubs her lower lip. "So, soon. Real soon."

Goodness, I keep forgetting. Christmas morning will be here in only three days. I nod my head.

Nana's expression takes on a higher level of seriousness. "You can accept nothing from them."

That seems simple enough. I can't imagine what a spirit would offer me that I would *want*.

"If you accept a gift from them, you are beholden to them. Once that takes place, you will have to gift them something of greater value. First, it's a complication we don't need. Second, if it is an entity up to mischief, they will likely refuse your reciprocal gift. That will doom you to be their instrument to control."

Talk about abusive relationships. "Yes, ma'am."

Nana acknowledges my agreement and continues. "Most importantly, you cannot allow them to embrace you. They might touch you or guide you with their hand on your shoulder or back. This is typically harmless, but if it is a ghost with ill intent, they might be doing this to lower your guard."

All our prior training and Nana has never mentioned this before? Not that I would ever allow an apparition to hug me. Still, I have the distinct impression this bit of information might have been helpful to have before tonight.

"What happens if they embrace me?"

Nana closes her eyes while clenching her fist. "April, for once, just do as I ask without the questions. The important thing is that you don't let them. I'm making many assumptions, but the three visitors have something specific to show you if Bob has scheduled this. This may require them to guide you to a different place and/or time. In that situation, they may probably need to hold your hand or arm while you travel. All I'm saying is don't let them turn it into an embrace."

"What happens if they embrace me. You've never told me this before."

"Sugar, April. You just can't help yourself, can you?"

I shrug. "It helps me. I don't understand why you have never mentioned it before."

"Can't you see? You've never had a ghost approach you directly. A visitor from the other side of the veil seeking you out. Mind you, I know Bob passed to the other side. He's not one of these poor entities you and your brother go and investigate. Those are souls trapped on this side of the veil by their deeds or confusion over their death.

"Bob sought you out. He came to you. It's his agenda. That makes it different, April."

"And if they embrace me..." I continue to chip away with my persistency.

"They absorb your power."

I'm expecting her to tell me their embrace would cause me some sort of unbearable pain or long-term nightmares. I imagined something along the lines of a spiritual posttraumatic syndrome. "All things being considered, it might be a blessing to let them take my powers. Then I wouldn't have to worry about all this."

"You don't understand." Nana's lips remain parted as she glares at me. "There is no separating your 'gifts' power from your life power. When I say they will take your power, I mean they will drain you. And once your energy forces have been drained, there's nothing left. Just the husk that your energy and spirit animated before their embrace."

Well, that is sort of sobering. Basically, Nana tells me that I'm a battery-operated doll, and I have to make sure the spirits don't pull my double A's out.

This drastically alters the complexion of the impending visits. Their arrival will not be just an aggravation. They put me in mortal danger.

I preferred when they were just an aggravation.

"So, how do I stop that?"

"For one, remain vigilant. Be expecting it. If it doesn't happen, consider yourself fortunate. If one of them does try, use whatever force you have to escape them. It would be what Chase always says about fighting."

"There's no such thing as a fair fight," I whisper. I've heard it a thousand times if I've heard it once from him.

Nana turns the water on again and scrubs the remainder of our dishes.

"That's it?" I ask.

"That's not enough?" she asks.

Yes, it is plenty. It is plenty more than what I want to deal with.

For the millionth time, I want to feel sorry for myself. I curse the genetics that has bequeathed this nightmare on me that I must live with every day. Life is hard enough without having to deal with things that most others don't even see.

"Is there anything special you want for Christmas?" Nana asks.

Nana moving seamlessly from my mortal danger to something as trivial as my Christmas gift discombobulates my brain. "Ma'am?"

"Is there anything in particular you want?"

"Besides somebody stopping these visits?"

"Anything from *this* world that I might do for you or get you?"

Maybe she has the right of it. Just thinking about Christmas takes away some of the stress that is building in my chest. "I really haven't thought much about gifts. I have been trying to get through to this weekend. I'm also hoping that Lee can make it home for Christmas."

"Is there a possibility he won't be able to?"

I frown. "He says he will be home in time. Still, he said he would be back on Monday, and here it is Thursday."

"What's holding him up?" she asks.

"His agent has a couple of advertisement deals ready for him, and they want him to get them done before he leaves town."

"That sounds reasonable. Some of those athletes have such short careers I'm sure they want to maximize their earnings while they're playing."

"Yeah. I suppose. But on the other hand, it's Christmas. I don't mean to be jealous or anything, but there's 350-some odd other days of the year to work besides the week leading into Christmas."

"I understand." She turns to face me. "I know it's disappointing."

"Yea." I shake my head. "Maybe I'm just tired and grouchy."

"You do look terribly tired. Maybe you should go on home and get to bed early."

I feel awful and am embarrassed—I am the worst of company. "Are you sure you wouldn't mind? I hate to eat and run."

"Not at all. Besides, we're going to be together all day Monday, too."

"I do think I could use a couple extra hours of sleep."

Nana closes in and gives me a hug and a kiss on the cheek. "Quit worrying so much. You're strong like the oak and as resourceful as a beaver. Your star will light the sky."

I smile because I know she thinks she is being sneaky. "Thank you for the blessing."

"You're welcome. Now go get some sleep."

"Yes, ma'am."

As I walk toward her screen door, my eyes zero in on the eight-foot table full of blue Mason jars labeled "Male Enhancement." "Hey, Nana. If you don't mind, I'm going to take one of these male enhancement tonics after all."

"Take two, honey."

That's not a bad idea. If it works, we'll need a refill. This way, I can take care of Lee's gift and give myself a gift in the process.

Chapter 21

I don't relax until I pass through the Willoughby bridge. For whatever reason, the drowned girl doesn't put up near as much of a fight when I'm leaving as when I'm coming to Nana's. She doesn't even bother to make an appearance tonight.

Nana's new instruction regarding my need to avoid the embrace of a spirit weighs heavily on my mind. I think back through the excursions I've had with Dusty and his team. I realize there were at least three instances where an apparition had ample opportunity to embrace me if they so wished.

That is the nature of my "gifts." Even if I want to learn everything I can about them, the only valuable resources for information are people who have like "gifts."

There are no textbooks to read and no charts to cross-reference your actions by. At least not the type you can read online or checkout at the library.

Everything is either learned from an experienced cohort or learned the hard way by trial and error.

I am not happy about Nana forgetting to tell me about this safety tip earlier. Still, it is understandable that she forgot, given the sheer volume of knowledge she has been attempting to impart upon me. A pragmatic person would say I have not been embraced; therefore, the information would've been superfluous anyway.

I don't care to think about it anymore. Besides, there is no guarantee that any of these visits are actually going to take place.

For all I know, Grandpa might be a practical joker and the whole three spirits visiting was just to get a laugh at my expense. I can see him on the other side of the veil yucking it up right now.

I choose to instead reflect on what is going right in my life. The things I can control.

It would have been impossible for me to choreograph today's events during court any better than they turned out. It was like I was writing one of those cheap crime novels that folks like to read but never tell their friends they're a fan of reading. As if I wrote up the ending where everything falls into place for the lead attorney. Still, that's precisely what happened.

I was charmed with all eight cases. Even when Ms. Applewhite tried to blow up her own defense, I was able to save the day.

I'll never know if it is my skill as a litigator or just blind luck. Truthfully, I really don't care which it is; I just like winning.

What winning affords you is slow days at the office. I'm reviewing my cases in my head. I have nothing pressing tomorrow. It certainly doesn't hurt my feelings that the Friday before a holiday, I can spend half the day on paperwork then check out early if I wish.

I pull into my parents' driveway. The only car home is Dusty's.

Unlocking my apartment, I call for Puppy. I call again after hearing nothing. I run a quick check of my apartment, concluding he must be over at the big house.

Slipping out of my now too-tight skirt, I pull on a holey pair of sweatpants, a hoodie, and my furry slippers. I flip my hoodie up and head out of my apartment in search of my missing child.

The glass door is unlocked. As I slide it open, I'm greeted by the scent of pizza drenched in garlic butter. It smells good, but I'm still full.

I holler for Puppy. I get no response, so I head toward the noise coming from the basement.

I'm two steps from the bottom when I see Dusty in the far left-hand corner of the basement, watching a big screen with Puppy rolled up against his left ankle.

"So, he's with Uncle Dusty."

Dusty turns, and his eyebrows shoot up. "Oh, hey. I didn't know you were looking for him. If I had known you were home, I would have texted you."

"I hadn't exactly sent out an APB on him yet. I figured he was over here."

Dusty runs his hand over the top of Puppy's head. "I hope you don't mind us having a boys' night. He's already eaten. Meat lover's pizza. No onions."

"I smell garlic."

Dusty lifts a plastic container from the pizza box. "Garlic butter dipping sauce just for me."

"Thank you. And thank you for keeping him company. I'm sure he enjoys hanging out with you." I take a closer look at what Dusty is watching on the big screen. "What are you watching anyway?"

Dusty looks at the screen, then back to me. "It's a 1948 movie with Ted Barker in the lead role. It's called *Shadow Over Heaven*."

"Did your cable get canceled?" I quip.

Dusty laughs. "No. It's research. Ted Baker was a native of Shelbyville, Tennessee. When he was sixteen, he left Shelbyville for LA and got a role as a supporting actor in the movie *Pinstriped Blues* a few years later. The movie was a flop, but the female patrons really liked Ted, and he started to be in more movies as the leading man."

"Is he a good actor?"

Dusty rubs his eyes. "He's hideous."

I watch the film for a few minutes and confirm Dusty is

being truthful. "And how is this research?"

"Ted Barker is thought to possibly be one of the entities at the Imperial Theater. It's always helpful to review old footage and see what you are dealing with. Besides, it's a great reason to have pizza and hang with your boy."

I watch a few more minutes of the black-and-white movie. The best description I can give is it was like a poor man's version of *The Maltese Falcon*, without the suspense.

Dusty jerks his head around. "Oh, hey. I forgot to tell you. We want to leave tomorrow at noon. Are you going to be available?"

"Darn, Dusty. Thank you for the advance notice."

"Are you?"

"Well, yes, but that's not the point. You can't just be popping these things on me. I like to work with schedules," I grouse.

"So do I. But it's Christmas, and the guys' schedules are getting loaded up by family activities their parents are shaming them into attending. We want to make it a quick up-and-back."

"That'll never work," I say with a brief snort.

"It should. It's one of those single-screen theaters you see boarded up in a lot of the small towns. There's just not that much territory to cover in one of them."

"I hear you, but it seems like we have been getting more than we have bargained for on all our excursions this year."

Dusty shakes with a laugh he is holding in as the crow's feet at the corners of his eyes deepen. "You have the right of that. I'm grateful, mind you. It's great material for the business. But somedays I'm like, 'Really? Again?'"

"It's like in that movie when the villain turns off the Ecto-Containment System, and all the ghosts they caught are flying around town, causing havoc," I say.

Dusty laughs harder. "I had forgotten about that movie. Maybe I need to check if anyone in the Southeast recently turned their containment system off."

We feed off each other's laughter. Puppy joins in with a few barks.

I catch my breath. The words pop out of my mouth. "Nana says they, the ghosts, are attracted to my powers."

Dusty sobers and nods his head. "I believe she has the right of it. I'm beginning to think we may have been in the presence of ghosts during excursions before you, where the entities simply chose not to expose themselves."

"I guess you guys are just boring without me."

"We are definitely low on juice without you," Dusty agrees.

"Well, I wouldn't want to make it too hard for you to gather your material. First, because I like reading your books, and second, because I wouldn't want you to starve," I tease.

"That's kind of you, Sis."

"And you do an admirable job of babysitting my dog."

"Thank you."

I exhale as if I'm being put upon considerably. "Here's the deal. I will go and even be on time for when the van leaves, but I am not sleeping in that van on the way home. If, when we are done, we can't make it home by eleven, you are spotting us all rooms and a pancake breakfast before we come home."

"There are not that many hotels in Shelbyville." Dusty's forehead creases.

"Not my problem, big boy. Home by eleven or a room." I raise my hand. "Separate room and a pancake breakfast."

"Bless it, woman." Dusty's eyes open wide. "Is there anything else I can get you? Maybe some jewelry or a new car?"

I shrug my shoulders. "No. I'm grateful for the car you've already gotten me, and I'm not much on jewelry."

"Good thing. You sure do drive a hard bargain."

"The way I see it, I am rare skilled labor. I should be able to demand a premium."

Dusty rocks his chair back and crosses his arms. "Point taken. Just for the record, you're worth every penny I pay. It's just I worry that the rest of the team will be wanting the same perks as you negotiate."

I grin. "Again, your problem, big boy, not mine."

"Fair enough. Don't be late tomorrow."

"Come on, Puppy. We got to get in bed now, so we don't run late tomorrow." Puppy sits up and cocks his head as if trying to decide if I'm serious. "It's not a negotiation, young man."

Dusty reaches down and scratches Puppy's neck. "Sorry, boy. The fun is over. I'll catch up with you next weekend."

Puppy looks up at Dusty, yawns, and trots over to me. I guess he is ready for bed after all.

Chapter 22

I get my bags packed for the excursion, put on my PJs, and brush my teeth. I should go straight to bed. There isn't much work at Snow and Associates tomorrow, but to make a showing and get back to the house by noon, I need to leave for work at 6:30 in the morning.

Still, a pang in my heart forces me to pick up my smartphone and hit Lee's speed dial number.

"Hey, babe, I didn't think you would still be up, or I would've called you," Lee says.

"It's not that late. You're an hour ahead of me."

"True. I always forget about that."

"How did the advertisement go?"

Lee clicks his tongue. "It was okay. I only had one line in it, so it was sort of boring. I guess it's a paycheck."

"If it makes you feel any better, nobody's paying *me* for saying one sentence."

"It's not really that anyway." His voice sounds aggravated with a hint of sadness.

"Is everything okay? You're not getting traded or anything, are you?"

Lee laughs as he answers. "Not unless you know something I don't. But no, it's not the job. I had some great sessions earlier in the week, and we're all looking forward to this next season. I think I can contribute a lot to the team."

"I know you can." I haven't actually seen Lee pitch since high school, but I have no doubt that his skill has only improved since then. In school, because of his ability to throw hard and with a quick release, he was behind the plate catching when he wasn't pitching.

"No, the problem is I'm just ready to come home."

"Well, that's easy enough. Just hop on a plane, and I'll pick you up at the airport."

There is silence from the other end, followed by a sigh. "That's just it."

I don't even know what he will say yet, but the way he has framed it, my heart sinks. "What's the trouble?"

"You don't know?"

"Know what?" My mind frantically starts thinking about the details of the day, searching for anything that might answer his riddle.

"The entire Northeast got hammered by a surprise blizzard. It popped up late this afternoon. We've gotten twelve inches of snow in the last six hours, and they have no idea when it's going to let up. *If* it's gonna let up."

"I don't understand."

"I'm snowed in, April. All the planes are grounded, and the winter system has just parked itself over the Baltimore area. They're used to occasional snow here, but not blizzard conditions. Nobody knows when the planes will fly again."

"But before Christmas. Right? They'll surely fly before Christmas."

"I sure hope so. I spent this entire evening racking my brain, trying to think of how I could get back home for Christmas. I really want to see you."

For the first time during the conversation, it dawns on me that he might actually not just be delayed but not even make it home for Christmas. A tidal wave of urgency and anxiety rolls over me. "But you have to make it home. You just have to, Lee."

"I'm trying, April. Believe me, I'm not going to leave any

stone unturned. But at the moment, there are limited options available to me."

"How does this happen?"

Lee laughs. "Well, the temperature drops below thirty-two degrees, and the clouds began to drop their precipitation—"

"Not funny. I meant how does it happen that they kept you up there so long that now you can't come home?"

"Nah, it's not like that, baby. Don't be that way. This is one of those things that happens from time to time. It's just bizarre that it's happening this early in the season and in Baltimore. It's not like we're up in Toronto or something."

I can tell he is trying to make me feel better about it, but there isn't anything short of him coming home that will make this situation alright. I don't like this new feeling. This feeling that if I don't have him close to me soon that I'm actually missing part of *me*. This is a new sensation, and it scares me. Scares me because I might not get to be around him at Christmas, when the whole time he has been gone, I've told myself it's okay that I'm lonely because I will see him at Christmas. But now, if I don't see him at Christmas, I don't know what I'll do. I feel like a bundle of nerves, and I'm suddenly desperately sad.

"Do you not want to come home?" I ask.

I hear him suck in his breath. "How could you ask that? Of course, I want to be home. Even if it wasn't Christmas, I'm missing you terribly. All I could think the whole time I was up here was that I wish you had been able to come with me and stay at the apartment."

"I had to take care of Snow and Associates. Howard was away on vacation."

"Of course, you did. That's why I didn't push any harder about it. I like the fact you want to take care of your commitments. It's how I try to live my life, too. I respect it.

But April, you got to know, I have a big hole in my heart right now because I'm not with you. I'm anxious to get home to you."

I twist a length of my hair around my pointer finger while I talk to him. "Honest?"

"More honest than what you will ever know."

"I don't know what I'll do if you can't make it home for Christmas," I add.

"Don't write me off just yet. Like I said, I'm doing everything I possibly can to find a different way to get down there. But everything is shut down at the moment."

"Okay. I guess I better get some sleep. I have to go in early so that I can leave with Dusty to go on an excursion."

"Hey, I'll be there if there's any way possible. I love you, and I want to see you."

Even hearing him say I love you can't shake me out of the funk. "Love you too. Good night."

The one positive about not having a boyfriend for so long is I was never disappointed. I know to many people that would sound stupid, but nothing rocks me to the core quite like a disappointment. When I count on something and hold it out as a reward—to convince myself to get through a horrible day— only for the prize to disappear? It is a serious gut shot.

I'm now regretting having called Lee. It isn't his fault, and although I did enjoy hearing his voice, I really do not need to know that he might not make it home for Christmas. It is like the anti-joy. It will suck all the happiness out of the decorations and lights around town.

Truthfully, if he doesn't make it home, I do not know how I will cope. I already had this beautiful vision in my head of him hanging out with my family and me. I was hoping that time would give my family a chance to come to love him, too.

It isn't any secret that my brothers aren't exactly warm to the idea of Lee dating me. Actually, I think that Chase, if he weren't the respectful sibling he has always been, would tell me exactly what he thought about Lee if given a chance.

And Lee may have been that man at one time. I'm not discounting the fact that he and Chase were teammates before.

Still, people can change. Heck, look at me. I'm totally different from who I was in high school. If I can change, Lee can change, and Dusty and Chase can change their opinion of him.

But if he doesn't make it home, when will we all spend that kind of time together? The time that would allow them to talk and hang out leisurely? If it was anyone besides Lee, we could do that during the summer. But Lee travels with his team all during the summer and, by March, I will be long gone anyway. Then we wouldn't be in Guntersville except during the off-season to spend time at Lee's lake house.

This is so not what I planned.

I feel so sad. I don't want to cry, but there is a gnawing emptiness in me.

Puppy is snoring at the foot of the bed, and I lay next to him. I knead the soft thick fur around his neck. He stops snoring momentarily and opens one eye. He closes it back as I continue to squeeze his hair in between my hands.

One other thing, snow in December? I thought Baltimore was more south than north. If it's snowing already, that's not cool.

And twelve inches is ridiculous. Lee might have to see if he can be traded to Atlanta or Houston because April Snow does not do snow in December.

Chapter 23

By my clock, I have ten minutes to spare when I drive into my parents' driveway. I must not be as excited as the rest of the team to leave because they are already packed and waiting on me. Dusty, Luis, Chet, and the Early brothers approach me as I get out of my car.

"Do you need a hand with your luggage, April?" Dusty asks as they approach.

"It's just one bag. I have it."

"Are you packed?" Dusty asks.

I turn around and shoot him my best "are you kidding me" glare. He is unphased.

I'm still salty about the call to Lee last night, and I'm spoiling for a fight. Unfortunately, my brother rarely steps on my tail enough to provoke much more than a smart-mouthed comment or a brief mean mug.

"Hey, don't bother looking for your dog," Dusty hollers at me.

"Why not?" I turn and wait for his answer.

"He's riding shotgun with Dad to the grocery store."

"Why?"

Dusty shrugs. "I guess to get groceries for dinner tonight?"

"That doesn't explain why Puppy went with him?"

"Since it's just him and Dad tonight, I guess he's going to let him pick what he wants for dinner."

Ahh! They make me want to scream some days. It would be stupid if it weren't so probable. Everybody messing with my dog. They're probably going to give him diabetes. What then? I'll have to have a full-time veterinary assistant, and everybody will make themselves scarce once he's sick.

Throwing open my apartment door, it hits the wall so hard it reverberates on its hinge as it swings back at me. I'm forced to block it with my forearm.

I snatch up my suitcase, nearly give myself a hernia, think better of it, set it back down, and pull the handle out. It flips over on its side as I bounce it roughly over the threshold.

"You do know y'all are going to kill, Puppy!" I holler at my brother as I march toward the van.

His lips narrow. "I haven't fed that dog anything."

"Meat lover's pizza? Just last night?"

He reaches down to pick up my suitcase. "I meant today. I haven't fed him anything today."

I slap his hand out of the way. "I've got it." I struggle to lift my suitcase onto the bumper and then push it into the back of the van.

"It's not like he's fat," Dusty continues. "He's just thick."

I lift my pointer finger in front of my face. "Hush your mouth. You don't get to do that. He's not your dog."

"All right. But you seemed okay with it last night."

"That was before he wasn't here to say goodbye to me."

Dusty locks eyes with me and grins.

I glare at him and think, *go ahead, say something else. I dare you. I can't wait to kick you in the shin, Dusty Snow.*

Instead, he turns to go around to the driver's side. I take the last seat available on the bench seat. Everyone in the van is perfectly silent. I sense the tension in the air.

But I don't care. I feel onery, and at the moment, I want everyone else to be as miserable as me.

Dusty starts the van and pulls out onto the state highway without a word. Miles is riding shotgun. The Early brothers and Chet are on the back bench seat while Liza and Luis are on the front bench with me.

Luis leans in toward me with his phone. "I gotta show you something, April."

"Not right now, Luis. I just need to think about a few things for a while."

"No, really. You have to see this," Luis insists.

I'm definitely not the wisest person in the world. One of the things I have learned in the nearly thirty years of my existence is that if someone really wants to show you something, you might as well look at it. Because if you don't, they will worry the living daylights out of you until they get the opportunity to show it to you. At least half the time, afterward, you wonder why they thought it was so important you see it. But they're going to get you to see it regardless, so you might as well not fight it.

"All right," I say in a huff.

"Baby goats," Luis says as he pushes his phone under my nose.

The rambunctious little babies are running around the pen, skipping and leaping into the air. They jump on top of the hut the goats use for cover and even jump on the older goats' backs. I immediately began to laugh.

I roll my eyes. Luis is absolutely obsessed now.

He taps his phone. "See that one?"

I sigh and look at the kid. She looks like a smaller version of Maleficent. I smile. "She's so cute," I say.

"I know. They always make me happy. I wish I had a yard big enough for a few of them."

I'm still laughing but explain to Luis that they are incredibly destructive. He would need a farm, not a large yard.

"So, what has you in such a foul mood?" Miles asks in his usual untactful manner.

My initial reaction is to tell him it's none of his beeswax. But the more I consider the point, why hide it? "There's a good chance Lee will not be able to make it down for Christmas." There. Now everybody knows, and I'm not keeping anything back from the team.

"Who's Lee?" Chet asks.

"Her new boyfriend," Liza informs him.

"April has a boyfriend?" Travis asks.

I turn on him faster than a water moccasin. "Do you want to say something smart about it?"

Travis's nose wrinkles. "Congratulations?"

My argument isn't with the team. I need to lighten up and save my bitterness for the correct targets. I wish I knew who that would be—the freak winter storm, Lee's agent?

My argument isn't even with Lee. And given that mother nature is more powerful than anybody I know, being upset with her is just plain silly. Somehow, I'm going to just have to get over it and get on with the Christmas celebrations without Lee. It will be better if he shows up, but I need to plan for Christmas without him.

I'm tired of being the center of the conversation. "Miles, do you have any history on this theater?"

"The Imperial," Miles says.

"Yeah. Whatever. Can you tell us about it?"

"It's a relatively nondescript first-generation theater house. Shelbyville does not have a large population base. The original theater opened up in 1936. It was remodeled in 1939 and then shuttered in 1966. Recently it was scheduled for demolition before a volunteer group raised money to renovate it in the hopes of creating a facility for special events and community plays," Miles says.

"It's been empty for 50 years?" I ask.

"Not exactly. The lobby had been utilized for a retail specialty shop. But all the original theater seating remains, and they are looking into being able to salvage them."

"Yuck. They're gonna need some industrial-grade cleaning for seats that old," Travis interjects.

"And?" I ask.

"Let's just say work by the contractors has ground to a halt," Dusty says. "If you don't mind, I'd like to leave it at that. I don't want to influence Liza's and your readings."

I lean forward to look past Luis to Liza. She grins. Fine, if Bossman wants us to take a reading without any history on the theater, that's exactly what we'll do.

I lean forward to be closer to Dusty's ear. "Did you pack the weapons?"

Dusty cut his eyes to me, then back to the road. "Yes. It is that duffel bag next to your suitcase."

"Okay."

I worked with a professor recently to develop weapons for the team. They are needed because of a couple of close calls with homicidal spirits during some of our excursions.

The professor has set us up with special cartridges that fit a twelve-gauge bullpup as well as Colt 45s. The cartridges he explained to us contain iron and silver shots brushed with anointing oil and garlic juice.

When I first talked to the professor about it at Suwanee University, I had my doubts. But I've already had a live trial and can swear to the effectiveness of the round.

The conscientious objectors of the team, Miles, Luis, and Liza, refuse to carry any weapons. The Early brothers each claimed a shotgun, and Chet and Dusty selected the Colt 45s. I believe in redundant safety features and chose one of each. In truth, it makes sense anyway as the spirits are usually drawn to either Liza or me, and often we are together as a team.

"Any word on when the fifth book is supposed to be published, Dusty?" Liza asks.

Dusty meets Liza's eyes in the rearview mirror. "They're saying February twenty-fifth. They want to coordinate it with the first show of our television series."

I remember Dusty mentioning something about a series, but I don't recall the details. "What series?"

"Good one, April," Miles jokes. He realizes I'm not kidding, and he sobers quickly. "The TV series that we were contracted to do."

"Which is when?" I ask.

Liza leans forward to look in front of Luis. "Remember, it's January third."

"How long does this go on?"

Dusty cuts his eyes to the rearview mirror again. "April, we talked about this two months ago. It lasts for eight weeks."

I lean back on my bench seat and contemplate whether I should let the team in on my long-term plans. No. Because they're just plans right now. Maybe once I actually land the job in Baltimore, I'll let them in. But there's no reason to have them worried this early on.

One thing is for sure. I'm not going to miss being pulled in six different directions every day. When I work for Howard, I'm not just working for him. I work for Lane and countless defendants. Each of them, the most essential thing in their own world each day, and they let me regularly know by pulling me toward what they need.

Then the paranormal gig where I have to manage animism and materialization. One is enough "gifts" for anybody, and I have both.

Lately, even the paranormal with Dusty's team has taken on the multifaceted pull. The excursions have been coming more regularly recently, and now he's talking about eight weeks straight. How am I supposed to get any work done if I am constantly on the road chasing down ghosts? I even had a brief stint where I wrote parts of the fifth book for Dusty.

I'm just getting physically run down and emotionally drained. The constant pull is wearing on me, and now I'm even getting grouchy with my teammates.

Maybe moving is the best for all of us. A clean break without having to worry about hurting anyone's feelings. It's not like the team can be sore with me for quitting since I will be living thirteen hours away?

Besides, maybe it's what everybody needs.

Since my work at the law office is caught up, I didn't bring my laptop. But due to my current antisocial mood, that is a mistake. At least it would act as a buffer if I were busy working on something.

I'm left listening to the Early brothers and Chet talk about bagging a ten-point buck down by old man Waters's farm. Also, some girl Jason Early has begun dating who works at Pizza King in Boaz. I try to remember her name, so I can ask Howard about her.

Luis and Liza are discussing some glassblowing booth they had visited in Huntsville last weekend. It piques my interest that they went somewhere together outside of work. I try to imagine them as a dating couple.

Perhaps there is something more there than a mutual interest in a craft fair. Maybe they are toying with the idea of dating.

No. That pairing doesn't work on a romantic level. Besides, you can go somewhere with someone of the opposite sex and not be *dating* them.

Dusty and Miles are having a discussion below the voices of the rest of the team. I can easily lean forward and join in their conversation.

But I don't join in any of the conversations. Not because they aren't inviting me to, I just don't care.

I don't care about anything other than seeing Lee and moving to Baltimore. It's all I want anymore. Nothing else sparks any interest in me. I couldn't care less who is hunting what, dating whom, or seeing glassblowing demonstrations.

I remain quiet on the bench seat as we make our way to Shelbyville. The drone of my teammates' voices and the vibration of the van tires on the asphalt make me sleepy.

Chapter 24

Waking up with a cramp in my neck, I rub my eyes. "Sorry about that," I tell Luis as I snap my head off his shoulder.

"Don't worry about it. I almost took a nap myself. I'll probably regret not doing so tonight," Luis remarks.

"Are we here?"

"The town square now is in just another mile," Dusty says.

"We're going to drive by the theater and take a look at it, but then we're going to grab something to eat over at the café first," Miles chimes in.

"Our meeting with Heather White is not until three. We have plenty of time to get something to eat before we meet with her," Dusty says.

Usually, that would sound like an excellent plan. But I'm anxious to get this investigation completed and head back to Huntsville. The leisurely pace is not going to play in favor of an early trip home.

We come in from Highway 64 and climb an incline up to the square. A late-1800s courthouse sits in the center and is surrounded by a series of three-story brick buildings. One of the buildings on the west side has a large marquee reading the Imperial.

There is a low thrum in the air. I can feel it vibrating my body and settling in my fillings. I cannot hear it, but every part of me feels the disturbance.

I lean forward and ask Liza, "Do you feel that?"

Her eyebrows draw together as she looks at me. "I don't feel anything."

I nod my head and attempt to explain what I am feeling to her. "It's like a low electrical charge."

"I don't sense anything," she reiterates.

We pull around the old circle and end up in front of a diner. "Well, I hear my stomach growling," Dusty says as he turns off the van.

The thrumming continues as we exit the van and walk into the diner. The bell on the glass door rings as we go inside, and two very tired-looking women at the counter look our way. There is one older couple at a table to our right. Other than them, we are the only customers in the diner.

"Either everybody in this town eats early, or we need to head up 231 and hit one of the fast-food joints," Miles says under his breath.

"It's almost two o'clock. They are probably getting ready to close for the night," Dusty says as he leads us forward.

"Welcome to the Eagles' diner. Our specials for the day are on the board," the woman who looks to be my mother's age says.

We follow her gesture to a large green chalkboard to our left with menu items for the day written out. They have a good selection of my favorites, and the idea of taking time for a meal starts to gain appeal to me.

"Oh man, they've got meatloaf," Chet says. "I haven't meatloaf in forever."

"That sounds good, but I bet that fried chicken would be even better," Luis says.

I'm contemplating the merits of meatloaf versus fried chicken. They both have their strong points, and it is hard to decide. The only other meat selection on the board is hamburger steak.

That's a misnomer. I've tried hamburger steak at enough

diners in my twenty-seven years to know that there is no steak in it. If there is any hamburger, it's questionable. It's usually a barely palatable, dry soybean patty soaked in beef broth.

The seven of us have almost decided on our selection. A round woman in her seventies, with orange-dyed hair, steps up on the stool below the board and starts wiping items with a wet rag.

I watch in dismay as first the meatloaf, then the fried chicken, the okra, the mashed potatoes, black-eyed peas, and turnip greens disappear from the board. The only remaining items are hamburger steak, baby limas, and yellow corn.

"Sorry, it's close to closing time, and it was a busy day," the orange-haired lady says as she steps down from the stool.

Our team, in a half-circle around the board, all exchange looks of dismay.

"Well, that certainly makes the selection easier," Dusty says.

Travis gestures toward the board. "How can that even be a meat and three? To make it a meat and three, I'd have to order limas twice. Limas make me gag."

"Yeah, they kinda make me gag, too," Chet agrees.

"I'm not partial to them myself," Miles adds.

"Why else do you think they're still on the board?" Liza explains.

Dusty steps up to the counter while pulling out his credit card. "I'd like seven plates of the hamburger steak, double corn, and single lima beans."

"Do you want drinks with that?"

"Sure, what do you have?" Dusty asks.

The lady purses her lips, which is not a good sign. "The Coke machine is on the fritz. So, we just have tea today."

"Sweetened?" Dusty's voice almost sounds pleading.

The lady grimaces and taps her fingernail nervously to her teeth. "Out of sugar."

My brother takes a deep breath. "Just seven water cups, please."

The baby lima beans and corn are straight out of a can. The

copious dusting of salt I use livens them up a bit. I was hungrier than I thought. It turns out limas aren't as bad tasting as I remembered. As long as you don't chew them too long before you swallow.

The hamburger steak did not disappoint. It was as tasteless and bland as every other hamburger steak I have ever eaten.

Although the Eagles' diner's version does have a unique quality. I have never encountered it before. It is exceptionally spongy. When I pressed down on it with the side of my fork to cut it, the broth the patty had been soaking in squirted out. Still, as soon as I removed the pressure from the patty, the juice got sucked right back into the pseudo slab of meat. I become obsessed with pressing down on my hamburger, then removing my fork to watch the phenomenon of the spongy hamburger steak when Miles speaks up.

"I'm still not clear on how we are supposed to make the television series work."

Dusty stops cutting his steak. I watch it suck up all the juice on his plate. "How do you mean?"

Miles exchanges looks with the rest of the team as if begging someone else to take the lead. No one does, so he continues. "The books are simple. We go to twenty or thirty locations. We locate, say, ten mildly interesting and then two or three that really scare the dickens out of you.

We take our notes from each excursion and compile them into a story. Then put thirteen of them together, and voilà, we have a book."

"What's your point?" Dusty asks.

Miles favors an abbreviated laugh as his eyebrows rise. "My point? My point is this is like letting the fans see how the sausage is made."

"Or not made," Liza adds pointedly.

Miles gestures toward her. "Exactly. That should be our biggest fear of all. What if we get on site, and it's one of those strikeout nights?"

"Sounds like we better do our homework and make sure that

we're going to an active area," Dusty says.

"But you know as well as I do, even an active site can be quiet some days."

"Miles, as long as you do the research you normally do, we'll be fine."

"Perhaps it would be better if we just did reenactments of prior hauntings. I know, for example, the Sloss Furnaces story would be great for TV."

"Oh, and don't forget that killer clown. That was major scary," Chet interjects.

Dusty shakes his head. "Guys, I know that would be simpler. Believe me, that's what I pressed for, but the network shot it down. They say people just aren't interested in the storytelling shows anymore. They want to be part of it; they want to see it when it happens and feel like they're really one of the team."

"Then they better get the popcorn and settle in for a few hours of boredom on those nights we draw a dud." I look up. Everybody's eyes are on me. Bless it. I must've said that out loud.

"She does have a point, boss. You know, no matter how good the intel and even if we take a preview trip, sometimes we just draw a big zero. It just happens," Miles continues to explain.

Dusty shrugs. "Look, I want it to be a success, but there is only so much we can control. The network sets the parameters. It is the deal they offered, and it is their call."

"I just want the TV series to be a huge success for the production company and us. I wish there was some way we could make them understand that the excursions would be better done as reenactments," Miles continues to explain.

"I'm not disagreeing with you, Miles. What I'm telling you is that they have something very specific they want. Either we deliver it in the format they have requested, or we don't do it all. I happen to think it's worth the risk, and besides, the fact of the matter is, we have been successful without the TV series to this point. If it goes away tomorrow, we will still be successful."

That's the truth. It's hard to miss something you never had. Dusty's statement seems to put an end to at least the verbalized worries about the TV show.

I still have my own concerns about the show. Problems like the knowledge that the show has a much higher probability of succeeding if I am with the team.

As Dusty said the other night, ghosts are attracted to my high level of power. Just like moths to the flame, spirits that hadn't been reported seen in decades all of a sudden appear as if I'm some sort of paranormal catnip.

For the show to succeed, there must be documented paranormal activities that the viewers can see, hear, or be shown with some of Dusty's spectacular high-tech equipment. With a constant flow of paranormal activity, the show will be a smash hit. I'm sure of it.

That's why I'm feeling guilty about leaving town soon after the first show is taped. I would be abandoning the team at the time of their greatest need. I don't want it to, but it weighs heavily on my conscience.

"All right then." Dusty stands and tosses his napkin on his plate. "Let's go look up Ms. Heather White and get the nickel tour of this theater."

As the guys load into the van, Liza grabs my wrist. "Can we talk?"

"Sure." I look over my shoulder and say to my brother, "Dusty, Liza and I are going to walk over."

His eyebrows dip briefly. "Suit yourself. Stay warm."

Chapter 25

Liza and I make to cut across to the courtyard while the boys finish loading up. "What's on your mind?"

"I'm thinking about quitting," Liza says quickly without looking at me.

I suppose I knew she wanted to tell me something that she didn't care for the rest of the team to know, but it never occurred to me she was considering quitting. I walk numbly across the street as we approach the granite-block courthouse.

"Did you hear me?"

"Yeah. I heard you. I'm not sure what I'm supposed to do with that."

"I'm sorry," Liza says.

She still isn't looking at me. "For what?"

"I know how tough it is to be the only one with any true 'gifts' on the team. Everyone looks at you with expectations all the time. It's why I have enjoyed the job a lot more since you started. I hate to end up putting you in that same situation I was in earlier."

"Then what's changed, Liza? I don't want you to quit."

Her eyes cut to me and then quickly away. "I don't want to quit either, but I can't do my job anymore."

"I don't understand."

She grabs my wrist again, and we lock eyes. "I'm scared,

April. This is all getting to be too much for me. At the start, it was just a big hoot. Here are some weird noises, see some odd-shaped mist formation, maybe even smell sulfur or walk through a cold spot. That's what the job consisted of in the early days. But now?" She shakes her head and looks down. "The stuff is too real for me."

"I think you mean unreal," I mumble.

She raises her eyebrows and cocks her head to the left. "That too, I suppose. Either way, I can't do this job afraid."

"Just give it time. It'll get better."

She lets out a long sigh as her shoulders slump. "I hear you, and a year ago, I could've taken that advice. But I swear I feel like I'm someone who enjoys skydiving, and suddenly I'm afraid to jump out of an airplane anymore. I don't want to go into that theater right now. I want to sit in the van and wait for you to finish your investigation. Or better yet, bum a ride back home."

"Then why did you come, Liza?"

Her facial features pinch in as her eyes glisten with the promise of tears. "After all Dusty has done for me? How do I not come?"

There is another reason she felt obligated to travel with us. A more personal explanation than an employer who has treated her fairly. During our first excursion together, I accidentally read Liza's feelings before I learned how to control my "gifts." Her feelings about Dusty.

It has been a few months since then, and her feelings may have changed. Still, given her high level of emotion about leaving the group, I suspect they are only more potent.

I know that nobody else on the team even suspects Liza has romantic feelings for my brother Dusty. Feelings she has never expressed to him, and now that I know her, I doubt she will ever dare to share with him.

As far as her wanting to quit, I can't say I blame her. She has been admitted to the hospital three times in the last six months. The last time when she arrived home, she had an unexpected guest. A possessed doll had followed her home and attempted to murder her in her sleep. By blind luck, I was able to help her fend that attack off.

Liza is no coward. She is one of the bravest people I've ever met. But even brave people lose their edge if they keep getting injured every time they participate in the game.

"Besides, with the skill you have been developing in manifestation, it would be nothing for you to move into expulsion." Her lips narrow before she finishes her thought. "That makes me redundant. I don't really have a role here anymore."

"You're not redundant, Liza. You add more to the team than just your 'gift.' Even if you didn't possess any special 'gifts,' you always help the team remain level-headed and focused on our work."

"It's nice of you to say that." She flashes a brief smile. "But there's no place for me here anymore."

"You can't say that."

"It's the truth. And I'm glad. I'm glad that you're here and I don't have to worry about leaving my adopted family in danger. They're in good hands now."

I'm debating if now would be the appropriate time to drop the bomb that I will be leaving the team in February, March at the latest. It would show her that she is still needed, and she will need to rise above her fear to keep the crew safe after I leave.

My other option is to get involved in her business. She can't leave without letting my brother know her true feelings. I can envision them as a fantastic couple. I would also have the pleasure of making someone I have already come to consider a sister my "real" sister.

She needs to let him know. For both their sakes, she can't let it go unsaid.

"When are you planning on telling Dusty?" I ask.

Liza stops walking and looks away for a moment. "I guess I was sort of hoping you would help with that."

Geez. I would be more inclined to help Liza with informing

Dusty if I wasn't going to have to tell him I was leaving soon, too. No matter Liza's and my friendship, I'm not up to disappointing Dusty twice. "I'll go with you when you decide to talk to him. But I think he needs to hear it directly from you."

"I was afraid you were going to say that." She shoves her hands into her coat. "I just feel so ashamed."

"No. Don't you dare do that. You've got nothing to be ashamed of. We've had several close calls lately, and I get it if your confidence is down a little bit."

"No." Her eyes, now wild and intense, open wide. "It's not just my confidence. I am scared to death to go into that theater tonight."

I point across the street at the long-in-the-tooth marquee. "That old theater? Come on, Liza. The most you probably have to worry about from that theater is stepping in something sticky that wants to pull your tennis shoes off your feet."

"Don't mock me."

"I'm not. I'm just saying that this is a good one for us to have right now. A few noises, a few shadows, but nothing more has been reported." I turn my hands over, showing my palms. "It's just a nice easy one to get back in the saddle."

"I don't need to get back in the saddle. I need to get the heck away."

I don't want to be cruel to Liza, but I don't understand why she came, then. Why didn't she tell Dusty earlier and not make the trip? Why lay this on me?

"I hear you, Liza. I don't know what to tell you. I'd suggest you just talk to Dusty and let him know your decision. I'm sure he'll let you sit in the van if that's what you need to do.

"Or, as you know, we have weapons to protect ourselves now. That makes it different than the other times if things take a turn for the worse. Even though I'm not expecting to need them tonight."

She bites her lower lip and nods her head mutely.

I point toward the theater. "Now, if you don't mind, I've got a job to do. I'd be more than happy for you to team up with me this evening if you want to."

As I start across the street toward the Imperial, I'm surprised to see her pull up even in my peripheral vision. I'm even more surprised when she follows me through the glass doors of the theater.

Chapter 26

Dusty and the rest of the team talk to a tall, heavyset brunette in her late thirties when Liza and I enter the theater.

I'm immediately taken aback by all the black marble covering the floor and walls. The polished brass sconce lights are in brilliant contrast, as are the heavy, red velvet drapes adorning the upper half of the walls.

"Well, this is like a walk back in time," I say.

"I thought they said that it had been a retail store?" Liza comments.

"Maybe the retail store incorporated the original use of the building into their marketing. With a motif like this, I don't know what they could have had in here other than maybe a jewelry store."

"Maybe a gentleman's club," Liza muses.

We exchange a look and burst into laughter. It is good to have the old Liza back. Hopefully, it will last.

Stepping up the three wide, marble stairs, we reach the landing where the guys stand talking. Dusty breaks off his conversation with the woman.

"Heather White, I'd like you to meet the other two members of our team April and Liza."

Heather extends her hand to both of us. "Pleasure to meet you. I was just catching up with the rest of your team on what prompted us to call your organization. We're in the process of remodeling the theater, which includes new wiring as well as plumbing and sound system. Unfortunately, all of our contractors have left the job site, and none of them are willing to return."

"The workers complained of hearing things. Laughter, items falling, and occasionally verbal threats in their ears," Miles adds.

"One of the paint crewmen claims to have seen shadows moving as well," Luis adds.

Heather wrinkles her nose. "Just being fair about it, that painter is known to be a regular user of marijuana."

I don't want to burst Ms. White's theory. Still, all the folks I know who use marijuana don't have issues with seeing hallucinations. Acid tabs and toad lickers, well, that is a different story. The only thing smoking marijuana endangers is every Twinkie and bag of Doritos in a five-mile radius in danger of spontaneous consumption.

"But no apparition sightings, correct?" I ask Heather.

Her brow furrows. "Like a ghost?"

"Yes."

She laughs with a nervous hitch. "Are you serious?"

"You tell me, you're the one who called the paranormal investigators," I say.

Dusty steps forward, breaking the glare between Heather and me. "It sounds as if you might have some residual energies left in the theater. It is not uncommon in a building this old. The best place to start is with the tour."

"Residual energies?" Heather squints her eyes.

"Let's not worry about it just yet. How about you take us around first."

"Okay." Heather exhales loudly.

I can tell she has gotten more than she bargained for when she scheduled a paranormal investigation. It's not uncommon for the person who organizes an investigation to be a non-believer. In fact, that is one of the good things about our service. Sometimes facilities are labeled as haunted when in fact, there is a simple explanation.

Your workers are scared the facility is haunted because they continually hear moaning and won't come into work? We're not going to just check for ghosts. We're also going to check for plumbing vent pipes that are set incorrectly. Or perhaps they hear an odd tapping on the wall and assume someone has been murdered and encased in the wall and their ghost is attempting to get out. We're also going to use a thermal imager to see if maybe some cute little critters have taken up residence inside your wall.

As a rule, people don't like to stay at hotels, shop at stores, or live in homes that are haunted. If we can give the facility a bill of clean health and especially explain where the odd noises and shadows came from, that is more than worth the service fee to most property owners.

If the property is haunted, that's where our group can develop material for our books and soon for the TV series. We also work to help the property owner rid the property of the haunting entity if possible.

There is no mistaking Heather White is not a believer. The only reason she called is to give the theater a quick bill of clean health so she can get her construction crews back in and on the job.

There is a brief moment of hesitation by Heather. One where I feel she might just call the whole thing off.

Her full, coral-painted lips disappear as she sucks on them in thought. Finally, with a dramatic eye roll, she says, "Oh what the heck, let's get this done."

She leads us up to another small landing and through two swinging double doors. The room is dimly lit. Heather reaches to her right, flipping a switch that comes on with a crack that reverberates through the air. Incandescent lighting casts a warm yellow glow across the room.

We are in the center aisle of the ground-level seating. The aged red fabric chairs are mounted on a gradual downward slope leading to a massive stage one hundred feet across. From the stage floor, set back a great distance from the front of the stage, is a screen reaching fifty feet into the air.

"This place is a lot bigger on the inside than what it looks from the outside," Miles says.

"We have four hundred and twenty-four seats on the ground level," Heather says. She points to her left and rotates across the back of the theater. "The side box seats can add another eighty easily. We only open the balcony if we are having a live theater performance or a concert."

Dusty runs his hand over one of the seats. "Are these original?"

"Yes and no. The original theater opened in 1933. There was a small bit of fire damage suffered in 1935, so the seats are from the remodel in 1936," Heather says.

"The ceiling is nothing short of spectacular," Luis says with a dreamy tone of appreciation.

Heather clicks her tongue. "Yes, unfortunately, that has been the bane of the maximization of use of this property over the years."

I look up and am startled to see a highly detailed mural within the theater's domed ceiling. It depicts antebellum plantation homes, horse training stables, riverboats loaded down with bales of cotton, and men hunting whitetail deer and rabbit, all around the lower edge of the dome. The dome's center depicts a large ballroom with women dressed in colorful hoop dresses accompanied by men in smart-fitting suits.

"Because of the detail of the artwork and the artist, Lloyd McCain, who later painted murals of Yosemite and Yellowstone, the building is listed as a historical site. But as you can see, the mural is..." She blows an exacerbated breath out her mouth. "Politically incorrect and makes some guests understandably uncomfortable."

"Yeah, it makes me uncomfortable, too." When Heather glares at me, I realize I said that out loud.

"Yes, that's where we had to reach a compromise with the

historical society. If it were up to me, I would give the historical status back and paint over that mural."

As uncomfortable as the topic of the mural makes me, her comment about painting over it shocks me. Regardless of the subject, there is no disputing that the mural is high art and of what I would consider masterpiece quality. That is before I consider the fact it had to be painted while on scaffolding and how many hundreds of hours it must've taken to create. It is an impressive accomplishment.

"You can't be serious," Miles says. "Regardless, it is a significant historical piece. Not to mention artistic expression."

"And a blight on the property. But no, I am serious, but that is not even an option."

"You mentioned a compromise," Dusty says.

"We've designed a screen system where we can screen off the mural so no one can see it during events. It affects the sound quality of the room a little but saves us the complaints."

Luis points to the mural. "So, you're covering it up after all."

"That's the compromise. The historical society has agreed to it as long as we allow viewings of the mural once a month. The screening can be rolled back during those viewings. Like I said, it would be a lot easier just to paint over it."

Liza points behind us. "How many does that level seat?"

There is another section of seating on the second level that must be directly over the lobby. The seats look to be wider than the ones on the first floor.

"There's another sixty-five seats there, not counting the Ted Barker box in the center."

The thrumming noise I heard earlier washes over me so violently I list to the left. I grab hold of one of the ancient chairs to stabilize myself.

"When Mr. Barker wasn't making films in Hollywood, he would stay for extended periods on a farm he had outside of town. I understand that it was not uncommon for him and his friends to use the box regularly until he died in 1953," Heather adds.

The noise continues to grow in volume and seemingly mutates into more of a hammering noise. Slower than the original thrumming I heard, but even more insistent. The power of the residual energy is making my knees buckle, and it is difficult to concentrate.

"Do you have any information on Mr. Barker's death?" Miles asks. "Everything I could find online was a little ambiguous."

Heather frowns. "That's because he committed suicide, bless his heart. Ted really is a tragic figure. He was raised in the old Catholic orphanage in town. At the age of seventeen, he joined the Marines and was immediately shipped to the Pacific.

There he was wounded while saving his platoon, for which he received the Navy Cross Medal. The government pulled him back to the states to help sell war bonds, and that's when the Ted Barker craze began."

"How's that?" Dusty asks.

The pervasive thrumming sound dies down to the point it is now an occasional weak, thudding noise. The solid residual energy that had knocked my equilibrium off begins to relent.

"My grandma always said that it wasn't that he was *that* good looking. It was just all the men had been shipped overseas for the prior four years." Heather laughs.

The humor transforms her looks completely. She is rather pretty when she laughs. "But I've seen old photos of him in his uniform, and I have to say he was pretty hot for that time period—well, any time."

"Do you have any of those photos here?" Miles asks.

"I'm not sure. I'll have to see if I can find any for you," Heather says as she opens the door to the right of the stage. "The restrooms are back here, as well as the break room, manager's office, and the maintenance room."

The strength of the residual energy has dissipated to just a faint whisper now. Still, one predominant feeling prevails. Fear. It hangs thick in the air like the musty stench of a wet basement.

Something has happened in this old theater. Something horrific. But regardless of the high energy level, I feel from the people and the event, it is one garbled mess. There is no clue offered as to what the event was that is causing the turmoil.

It is unlike any paranormal energy I have felt prior.

Usually, as a spirit reaches out to communicate with me, the voice resonating in my mind maintains their dialect and voice inflection. Also, having waited to be heard for so long, they often have gone OCD. They only have one or two phrases they are insistent on communicating to the living.

If their energy level is weak, it comes across as a faint whisper in my mind. If the spirit's energy level is high, it can sound like a desperate person screaming in my ear. If I am unprepared, it literally makes me jump as it nearly startles me out of my skin.

The high energy level from this spirit should be the latter as if they are yelling at me. Instead, the energy is hitting me like the concussion of a bomb blast making the vocals a garbled cacophony of noise, forcing me to cringe against the blast.

While the new experience is interesting as it promises a fruitful day of work for the team, it is also disconcerting.

I tug on Liza's jacket. "Are you still not getting anything?" I whisper.

"I thought I might've heard something a few minutes ago." She wrinkles her nose. "But it almost sounded like a loud rush of white noise."

"I suppose I should be encouraged that you at least heard that. But it isn't white noise. It is more like twenty TVs blaring at the same time."

Chapter 27

Liza slows her pace. We let the rest of our group move ahead. "Did you see the shadows when we entered the back area?"

My stomach drops. "Uh, no."

She continues to whisper even though the rest of the group is out of earshot. "I couldn't figure out if it was multiple spirits or the same one on a rapid loop."

"I don't understand."

She pulls me in close with her left arm and puts her mouth to my ear. I'm not sure who she thinks is listening. "Human shadows. But about fifteen quickly across the right-hand wall when we first entered the back. Then they scaled the wall, floated across the ceiling, and went out a door."

I pull back so I can look her in the eye. "I didn't see anything."

She shrugs. "And I didn't hear what you heard. And neither of us felt a cold spot."

I can't swear to that. I was so overcome by the power of the thrumming noise maybe it caused me to miss the shadows. Perhaps it distracted me, so I missed feeling a cold spot, too.

"There is something strong here. But I don't feel any malicious intent," Liza says.

Unlike Liza, I've never been able to discern if a spirit has malicious intent or not. People yes, spirits not so much. Consequently, I assume all ghosts are ticked off about not moving to the next plane and are subject to being malicious at any point.

My paradigm makes me uncomfortable. Our team has not unpacked our gear yet, so our weapons are still in the van. "Let's catch up with the rest of them," I say.

"Yeah, that's probably a good idea," Liza agrees as she pulls away from me.

As we catch up with the rest of the group, Dusty raises his eyebrows at me. I give him a brief nod of the head to let him know that yes, we probably have a live subject site.

The hallway makes a U-shape bend behind the screen, and we come out to the other side of the stage. As we walk back up the lower-level seating, Heather explains her position once again.

"The city has recently increased property taxes on commercial buildings. More accurately, they revalued all the properties in the downtown square. My family has owned this building since the thirties. With the increase in taxes, we have to either find a viable business for it or give it back to the city." She exhales loudly. "We're sort of over a barrel right now. I've got $90,000 already dumped into remodeling. If I can't get my crews back in here to finish the job and get this building up and running for the events we have scheduled for the first week of January, I'm done. So, I hope you see that time is of the essence."

"I understand your concern Ms. White," Dusty begins. "I assure you my team will do everything we can to confirm what's happening with your facility. If you don't mind, I need to meet with my team so that we can develop a plan for the investigation."

Heather favors Dusty with a smile. "Thank you."

Dusty calls our group into the old manager's office in the

back. Liza and I explain what we saw, heard, and felt to the best of our ability.

As a team, we bring our gear in from the van. Chet and the Early brothers go to set up the cameras and recorders. Dusty sends Miles and Luis to the city's main library across the square to see if additional information can be found in the city archives.

Liza and I help Dusty set up the manager's office as the command headquarters for the investigation. Dusty is checking the monitors when Travis appears in the doorway.

"We're all set up, boss. Are you getting all the cameras?"

"Yes. The last one just booted into the system. Thank you, Travis."

"No worries. What now?"

"I feel we need to do some floor sweeps for now, given the girls picked up on disturbances already. Have Jason help me on the monitors while Liza and Chet investigate the lower area, and I'd like you to take April up to the second level and investigate."

"Sounds good, Dusty," Travis says.

No. That doesn't sound good at all to me. It seems like we are dividing our group way too thin to me.

I hold my tongue. Unlike most of our excursions, we will be within shouting distance of each other. I suppose at least the rest of the team can hear us being murdered by an angry ghost. I should take comfort in that knowledge.

Travis hands me my bullpup shotgun and my 45 out of one of the carrying satchels the weapons are stored in. I check that the shotgun is loaded, the safety on, and situate it in my backpack, which I sling over my shoulder. I check the clip of my 45, set the safety, and shove it in the back waistband of my jeans.

Chase always complains it's the worst place to carry a handgun. Still, true to form, I was so concerned about securing the weapons for the team I forgot to order myself a holster.

Travis grins as he loads shells into his bullpup shotgun. "I can't wait to get a chance to use this baby."

"I don't think you're going to get an opportunity on this trip," I tell him.

He slides the riot gun into the harness on his back and wiggles his eyebrows. "A man can hope, can't he?"

Yes, and I'm hoping I'm right. The Early brothers and Travis have both proven themselves time and again to be reliable workers on the paranormal excursions. They are accomplished audiovisual technicians. They also have just enough "crazy" in them to never let me be at ease. They are the sort of folks that I always want on my side once the fight starts, but you always have to be concerned that they might be the ones initiating the fight.

"You want to do the lobby first or the box seats?" Travis asks.

I guess he's deferring the leadership role to me. "I suppose since we're down here already, let's run a sweep of the lobby."

As we move further away from the other four team members, it becomes eerily quiet. As we enter the lobby, the only noise is the tapping of Travis's pointed-toe cowboy boots and the squeak of my tennis shoes.

"So, what were you and Liza talking about on your walk over to the theater?" Travis appears to be forcing a nonchalant expression as he asks the question.

"Just girl talk."

"About boyfriends?" Travis asks without looking at me.

I open the door to the ticket booth. It shares a window with the outside wall. "No. We weren't talking about Lee."

"Were you two talking about her boyfriend?"

There it is. Now I know where we are going with this fishing expedition of a conversation. "No, she hasn't mentioned a boyfriend to me lately. I'm not sure if she has one or not."

Travis opens the cabinets behind the ticket booth seat. I'm not sure what sort of ghost he believes he will find in there. A small one, I suppose.

"I've asked her out a couple of times in the past."

"Have you?" I try to keep my tone neutral.

He sighs. "Yeah. She keeps turning me down. I don't know if

she's dating someone or if she's just not interested."

Liza has mentioned on several occasions that Travis gives her the willies and keeps hitting on her. That's the nature of it when one person likes a member of the opposite sex, but the attraction is not mutual. The one who's not interested becomes uncomfortable with the situation.

"Just curious, how many times have you asked her out?" I ask as we walk over to the snack bar.

Travis stops at the waist-high swinging door as his eyes glaze over. I think he might have seen something. No, he's counting how many times he has asked Liza out. This is not a good sign.

"I'm not sure, maybe thirty?"

Oh my, stalker status. Maybe it is time to intervene and help both of them out of the awkward zone. "Travis, why would you ask her out that many times?"

He shrugs his meaty shoulders. "I don't know. I think she's pretty, and I like her."

I can't help but grin at the simplicity of his answer. "Right. I understand that. But thirty times? Don't you get tired of the rejection?"

"Well, I don't mind so much. I mean, if I eventually get a date with her."

There is something both admirable and scary about his persistent attitude on the subject. "But if Liza's telling you no, or she's not interested, maybe you should move on."

"Oh, no." He shakes his head vehemently. "She's just always already got plans. She's never told me that she's not interested."

I start toward the stairs that lead to the box seats and turn back to Travis. "Buddy, has it not struck you odd that she's been busy with something else the thirty times you've asked her out?"

"I don't know. I just guess she's got a lot to do."

Travis is a special kind of simple. I will need to break the current situation down for him as expressly as possible. "Do you mind if I give you some advice about girls, considering I'm a girl?"

His eyes open wider as he flashes his smile. "Sure, that would be great, April."

"If girls like you as a friend and you ask them out, they don't want to hurt your feelings and tell you that they're not interested."

Travis nods his head once and has a look of expectation still on his face. "Okay."

"That's it, Travis. That's the advice."

He still has a blank look on his face. "Okay."

So much for letting him down easy. I will be forced to spell this out. Liza is going to owe me. "Travis, you may ask a girl out, and she's busy. But first off, if she really wants to go out with you, she will try to change her plans. If she can't change her plans, she will tell you to ask again, or she will offer an alternate date."

I'm encouraged because Travis is nodding like a bobblehead doll. "But never *ever* ask a girl out more than three times without getting a date. If you ask a fourth time, she's going to just think you're a creeper."

He is still nodding his head when he asks, "So, do you think she'd go out with me?"

I begin to explain the situation to him again—know what, this is not my issue. "I don't know, Travis. Let's go check out the box seats."

"Okay, boss lady."

I can see where Liza might think Travis is a stalker. For one thing, Liza is an introvert, and I believe before the recent attack at her house, she has always been most comfortable alone. Travis constantly trying to get her to go out with him would absolutely make her uncomfortable.

My impression of Travis is he is harmless. He reminds me of a Rottweiler with half the intelligence of the dog. Still, that makes him an excellent partner to draw when we are on a paranormal excursion.

The stairs are narrower than what I anticipate, and at the

top, they come to a T. "You want to go to the right?" I ask.

"Sure thing."

We walk through a twenty-foot hallway and emerge into the right-side boxes. There are six rows of ten seats, each with a center aisle.

I step down the aisle toward the railing, careful where I place my feet on the worn carpeted stairs. I peer over the edge and see Liza and Chet canvasing the lower level.

Travis comes up alongside me. "Hey, Liza!" he yells. His voice echoes through the theater.

Liza looks up briefly, shakes her head, and turns away, ignoring Travis. Chet waves his 45 at Travis and grins.

I turn and examine the box seats in the area. I'm not sensing any residual energies, but I decide to close my eyes and see if I can feel anything through meditation.

"You okay?" Travis asks.

I hold up a finger as I keep my eyes closed.

"Oh. Right," he says. I sense him lean against the railing beside me.

I drop all mental barriers and push outward toward the seats in front of me. Nothing. Not even a hint of energy. Where is that stupendous force of energy that threatened to bowl me over earlier?

"You ready to check out the center seating?" I ask Travis.

He rolls a shoulder nonchalantly. "If you want to."

Like I said, a loyal Rottweiler who will follow you anywhere you want to go. Not to get into Liza's business, but maybe she should give the guy half a chance. She'd have to feel safer in her apartment.

The center box seats are extravagant. They are the forerunners of the reclining seat theaters that have popped up in the last decade. The seats are wider than average theater seats. There are armrests and adjustable footrests on the seats in the row in front of them.

The view of the screen and stage is also outstanding. With the highly angled floor and the elevation of the balcony, which centers the patrons' view perfectly with the screen, this would be excellent viewing of any movie. It would also be good viewing of any live events. Each chair clears the back of the chair in front of it by at least a foot. This allows for an unobstructed view of the stage, even for the shortest patron.

Travis pumps a shell into his shotgun.

"What are you doing?" I ask as I whip my head in his direction.

Travis leans back against one of the chairs. "I figured we would be hanging out here for a while, and I didn't want anything catching us by surprise."

"Why?"

Travis raises his eyebrows and looks lazily in either direction. "My gut tells me *this* is where the action's at."

I take a few steps toward the banister. "Then your gut is telling you wrong. I think all the action is down by the manager's office."

Travis clicks his tongue. "Different kind."

I freeze and turn on my heels as I get a wild thought. "Travis, how do you know?"

"I can feel the hairs on the back of my neck stand up. There's something here." He frowns. "It might be too chicken to show itself, but it's here."

He is full of it, of course. There isn't any energy in the room. I understand, with the dark drapery and poor lighting, it is a spooky room. But a creepy room can be just that. It does not necessarily portend the appearance of a ghost.

"Well, at least tell me your safety is on."

He cocks his head to one side. "Well, duh."

Hey, it is a reasonable question, and technically I'm downrange from him. I don't want to end up in the hospital with a shot in my butt because Travis thought he saw a ghost and got trigger-happy.

I cruise down to the last row and look out over the lower theater seating. I watch Liza check the planks on the theater floor. Presumably, she's searching for hollow spots or trapdoors.

The Barker box has a low-slung black silk barrier surrounding four seats in the center of the first and second rows. The fabric on those chairs is a soiled golden fabric distinguished from the red material of all the other chairs in the theater.

I turn and admire the view the seats afforded Mr. Barker in his time. With eight seats with the best view in the house and some privacy during the viewing, I imagine he could do a great deal of entertaining at the theater. Celebrity obviously has some perks.

"Travis, do you have the infrared cartographer set up yet?" Dusty's voice comes across the walkie-talkie.

"No sir, not yet."

"Can you get it set up?" There is a pause. "I want to get everybody's stations checked in the next few minutes."

Travis points his shotgun at the box seats I'm standing in front of. "I'd suggest we set up about where you're standing."

"Don't you think we should check out the left side first?"

Travis raises then drops his boots from the back of the chair in front of him, slapping them loudly on the floor. "If you want to. But I think all the action's going to be right here."

There is a reason Travis sets up the equipment, and Liza and I prognosticate the appearance of ghosts.

Travis got the heebie-jeebies like any average person would in an ancient, dark, quiet theater. Me? I'm looking for an actual disruption of the power that might signal a crossing from the veil. There is nothing up here.

"Let's go check the left quickly, and then we'll make a decision." With his mind made up, I half expect him not to follow me, but he does. The left side is totally devoid of any residual feelings, mirroring the center balcony.

"Looks like we drew the quiet rooms, Travis. I hope you brought a good book to read."

He frowns as if he bit into a lemon. "No. I didn't bring a book with me."

I wave him off. "It is just an expression anyway."

Travis points back toward the hallway. "Listen, Dusty is

going to call back any minute and want to know that the equipment is set up. If you don't care, I'm going to set it up in the center balcony."

"Sure, do you need any help?"

Travis shakes his head. "No. I can do this in my sleep."

"Do you mind if I call somebody?"

Travis is near the exit of the left balcony. "No. You can call anybody you want." He disappears through the curtain.

"Thank you!" I holler, not sure if he can still hear me through the blanket-like drapes.

Chapter 28

Sitting down in one of the red chairs, I immediately regret it. The stale scent of old sweat, hairspray, and dust engulfs me as the decades-old air in the cushions puff off the red fabric. I lean forward, but the damage is already done. I scoot to the edge of the seat.

I tap Lee's speed dial number and wait anxiously for him to answer. *Please let him have found a flight home.* I so need him to tell me he will be arriving home soon. Oh no. What if he comes home before me? I hadn't thought about that possibility.

"Hey, I'm glad you called."

His deep, masculine voice has a keen edge to it. He sounds as if he is running out of breath.

"Is something wrong?" I ask.

"No. Well—yes—but not now. We've had another four inches of snow, and the temperature has dropped even more. All the planes are grounded until they can make sure the ice is off their wings and doesn't reaccumulate while taxiing."

None of that sounds good to me. "Lee, I don't want you trying to come home if it's dangerous."

"Oh, no. The FAA wouldn't let them take off if there were any possibility that the ice hadn't been cleared from the wings. But that confirms our worst fears from yesterday. We're not flying out of Baltimore any time before Christmas."

My heart sinks. I knew it was a real possibility that Lee might not be able to make it home for Christmas. I never would have thought that it would make me sad so quickly. It isn't like we aren't able to spend time together regularly. For some reason, though, it is crucial for me to spend this first Christmas together with him. Receiving the bad news immediately deflates my attitude.

"I understand," I whisper.

"What? No. Oh no, April. Wait. Bob Simon and John McAfee are at the airport with me. They both live in Florida, so they are in the same boat. Bob has a four-wheel-drive Bronco, and we are going to find a way back to his house, put chains on it, and head south. With any luck, by the time we hit the Carolinas, the weather will be all clear, and we can hop a flight."

"Are you sure that's safe?" I like the idea of him getting home, but I want him home in one piece.

"Sure, it is. Heck, we probably won't go any faster than a walk until we are out of Maryland anyway. You can't have much of an accident going that slow. Plus, it will be the three of us. We'll be fine."

I can't say I feel great about it. Still, Lee sure sounds confident. "Okay. Promise to call me and give me an update in the morning?"

"You know it. Every step of the way, baby," Lee reassures me.

"I'll hold you to it."

He chuckles. "Don't I know it. Listen, I got to go, but I'm looking forward to seeing you in just a couple days."

"Okay. Be safe!" I holler just before I hear the line disconnect.

He will be able to make it home for Christmas. I'm optimistic about it.

Lee will also be safer driving a four-wheel-drive than flying in a plane that might have ice on its wings. Four-wheel-drives are dependable even in storms. Especially when you put chains on them. Just like he said, they can't be going too fast.

I hear the crackle of the walkie-talkie down the hallway and feel I better join my partner. As I come through the curtain,

Travis's back is to me, but I see he is working with one of the cables.

He moves the walkie-talkie to his face. "Try it now."

"Yeah, that's got it." I hear Dusty's voice.

Travis turns back toward the camera, sees me standing in the doorway, and tilts his head upward in acknowledgment.

He pulls the walkie-talkie back to his mouth. "Anything else you want us to do, boss?"

Dusty's voice comes back through the radio. "Not right now. In a couple hours, I'll have you go back through your areas with a meter. Jason thought he had a reading toward the back of the building a few minutes ago, but it has dissipated since then."

I begin to remind Dusty that Liza had picked up shadows on the wall toward the theater's back. Still, no point in rehashing the common knowledge. Plus, if the energy level had already dissipated on Jason's metering, it could've been a momentary blip. If Jason gets a second reading later, I may suggest that Liza and I investigate the back together.

Travis pulls his iPad out of his backpack. "We can stream the Western Kentucky and UAB bowl game. It starts up in about thirty minutes."

Mystery solved on why Travis doesn't need a book. He has designs on watching a ballgame that has no championship implications. "Thanks. I might, but I probably should unpack my laptop and review my upcoming cases."

"Suit yourself, but Western Kentucky has one of the leading passers in the country."

I sit down on the stairs, thinking they might be marginally cleaner than the ancient chairs. I pull my phone back out and text Liza. *"Well?"*

I read her answer. *"Nothing here."*

Maybe we have hit our first bust in the last months. A few stray shadows and a momentary rupture in the energies present do not constitute a haunting. Interesting, sure. But not a classic haunting.

Yes, there is something here. Yes, people who are highly

sensitive to things that should be on the other side of the veil but have stayed behind will sense them. Still, with no audible noise, movement of physical objects, or visible apparition, there is nothing that should prevent the building from being used for whatever purposes the owner wants.

I unzip my backpack and pull my laptop out. I intend to review my pending cases with Dottie Castle and Rhonda Applewhite to keep them fresh in my mind.

My heart isn't into it. I find myself on the employment board searching for junior partner positions in Baltimore, Maryland, and Washington D.C.

Travis sits down in one of the chairs on my right. He pops in his earbuds and settles in to watch the pregame show of his football game.

Chapter 29

I am surprised when I look at Travis's iPad, and it is halftime. He stands and announces, "I'm going to run a sweep of the areas with my meter."

My job search in the D.C. market is a bust. There are plenty of positions available in the area. The trouble being they all sound sort of boring compared to what I have been working on in Guntersville with Howard.

I start to close my laptop. "Do you need me to go with you?"

He waves his hand. "Nah, this place is dead, like you said. It's more I need to walk around than I'm expecting to find anything."

I have the same idea about the job search in the D.C. area. Dead.

Maybe I need to look in the Baltimore suburbs. Or maybe Annapolis. I've heard it's beautiful there.

"Okay, but send me a text if you need anything," I say.

Travis picks up his shotgun. "Will do. But I should be fine."

As Travis leaves, I go back to the job search. The opportunities looked marginally more interesting in Baltimore. At least the positions in Maryland are not dominated by the internships doing a singular task like the D.C. positions listed. They're still not exactly as diverse as what I have come to enjoy at Snow and Associates.

It isn't like I have to be concerned with earning a king's ransom. If I'm living with Lee, my expenses will be negligible.

Maybe the internship in D.C. would open more doors faster for me in the type of field I want to work. I do have connections in D.C. One of my friends from law school, Martin Culp, has been doing quite well working for a D.C. firm this year.

I could ask him for leads. Who knows, maybe his firm is hiring. It would be fantastic to work with him. We had such a great relationship during law school.

An icy cold chill runs up my spine, taking my attention from the laptop. I hold my breath as I feel a significant drop in the room temperature.

The most frightening and exhilarating second of any paranormal excursion is the moment just before I believe I will have an encounter. Still, an off-chance noise or a random draft can lead my mind to the incorrect assumption that something is near.

That's where the exhilaration lies. Maybe something from the other side of the veil is about to expose itself, or perhaps I have just scared myself. Even if I decide it is the latter, I'll never be one hundred percent sure until I leave the building we are investigating.

Just because the entity does not expose itself right now doesn't mean it won't five minutes or five hours later.

My body tenses as I hear the boot click on the tile surface of the landing directly behind me. I remind myself that Travis has boots on and convince myself he is returning from the meter tests. My logical hypothesis does not squelch my apprehension. I can feel the energy field bulging as if something is pressing through the veil.

There is a faint popping noise. I feel the energy of the room change. It feels like it is pressing on my back as goose pimples rise on my arms, and I shudder. The boot steps, now muffled on the filthy maroon-checked carpet, continue until I feel a presence, invisible, standing next to me.

The black silk curtain encasing the Baxter box seats flutters as if the wind has caught the fabric. It creases, then pulls open momentarily before falling back into place. I clearly hear the click of the boots one more time, but through the three-inch gap left between the silk curtains. I still see no apparition.

It's just the wind, I tell myself, even though my "gifts" are telling me different. It's just an odd draft that cooled my back and forced the curtain to flap open momentarily.

What about the boots clicking, April? That is a little more difficult. Especially since the location of the clicking changed.

I'm still staring through the small gap. I attempt to create a plausible explanation for the clicking of the boots when the seat of the gold fabric chair closest to me in the second row opens and lowers. I stare in shock, my bottom jaw now hanging open.

I want to yell out for the rest of my team. I consider running back into the lobby. I can do neither as I remain in a catatonic state as I watch the improbable happen.

There is no draft brisk enough to make a seat open.

The metal frame of the cushioned seat creaks, and the lower half shifts downward as an impression appears in the center of the back of the chair.

Dizziness comes over me quickly. I might have made it worse since I am panting, which may be causing me to hyperventilate.

Get a hold of yourself, April. There's nothing malicious here. It's just a garden-variety spirit.

For some reason, not being able to see anything is making it worse today. Suppose I could see the spirit in my full Technicolor view. Or heck, even if I could just see a blurry mist being held together loosely in a humanoid shape, it would allow me to get my head around the event.

The chair creaks again as if the invisible occupant is shifting their weight to become more comfortable. Somehow that helps calm me, and I draw a long, deep breath to steady my nerves.

The walkie-talkie is with Travis; otherwise, I would ask

Dusty if he caught the seat's movement with the video equipment. I consider calling him on my phone.

I determine it best to remain calm and not draw attention to myself. At least until I can think of a plan of action.

Many low-power apparitions have traits similar to obsessive-compulsive disorder. They will repeat the same actions repeatedly on their own timetable, not paying attention to anything that has changed in their environment. I'm betting, hoping, the apparition that has sat down in Ted Barker's private box is of that ilk.

Even if it is, I'll need to remain still. There is the possibility something visible may materialize once it settles in and is comfortable in its surroundings. By the crackling swirl of energy in the air, it certainly feels strong enough to emerge.

It occurs to me I need to warn Travis and the rest of the team not to come into the center of the upper deck until I figure out what to do. Fudge nut. That means I'll have to move anyway.

Slowly, I pull my phone out. Travis is the first person I need to warn since he should be coming back after completing his rounds with the meter.

I scroll, hunting for his number. I'm not even sure I have it, as I can't remember ever calling Travis on the phone. Our relationship has revolved strictly around work in the past.

As I continue to search my phone directory for Travis's number, I feel an increase in energy and warmth caressing the right side of my body. Squinting, I look through the small gap in the silk curtain. I'm startled to see the first grainy images of the apparition sitting in the box chairs. Average-to-short height, late thirties, a good tan, and chiseled facial features, including a cleft chin and a prominent, aquiline nose. I'm mesmerized by the classic good looks of the faint vision as it continues to fill in.

The handsome man looks over his left shoulder, smiling broadly. At first, I'm concerned he is smiling at me. I hear the shuffle of leather-soled shoes. A new cold draft chills my back.

Tentatively, I glance over my right shoulder to see what

approaches. A masculine apparition is dressed in blue jeans, a bright white T-shirt, and penny loafers. His face is round and kind, with a full head of thick blonde hair gelled back. He does not look at me as he passes by, sliding down the second row with the grace of a dancer.

The older man stands and embraces his friend before placing a kiss on his lips. Their faces part, staring into each other's eyes for a moment before taking their seat.

The quality of their image is mesmerizing. I have seen more complete apparitions, as they are only fifty percent solid. We have captured on film a ghost so vivid no one would ever believe the movie to be authentic. But I can't recall watching two different spirits carrying on with what looks to be a regular routine. This includes the most minor details, such as taking each other's hands while watching the show on the blank theater screen.

Forget it. I'll never find Travis's number. I've never had a reason to call him before, so it's not surprising I don't have it stored in my phone.

I text Dusty a message asking if he sees the apparitions in the Barker box.

"*Nothing there.*" He texts me.

"*I have two well-formed spirits sitting on the second row.*" I message back to him.

"*Nothing.*"

"*Seats move? You had to see the seats on the second row move.*"

"*Backs of first-row block view. Can't see.*"

I study the video camera Travis mounted on the tripod. I immediately see what Dusty is talking about. Any movement of the seat bottoms on the second row would not be visible due to the angle the camera is set up at.

"*Can you see me?*" I text.

"*Yes. On the steps.*"

Great. This doesn't make a lick of sense. If I can see the apparitions, the camera should be picking them up as well. I have half a mind to walk down, pick up the camera, and see if I can get it working.

"Do you want me to come up there?" Dusty texts.

No. But I want him to warn Travis we have visitors before he comes barging back into the box area. I text Dusty that and let the conversation drop.

The couple laughs at something, and their eyes meet. There is something significant in the look they exchange. I wonder if people see that when Lee and I are together. I sure hope they do.

I have the idea to use my phone's video feature. Travis used the wrong lens on the camera. That is the only explanation for why Dusty is not seeing this.

I aim my phone through the part in the silk curtain and watch the ghosts on my phone as I film.

My heartbeat is racing again as I'm filled with the anticipation of having captured these images. Dusty is going to be thrilled.

After filming thirty seconds, I replay the video. Nothing. I have two golden seats pulled down, but there is nary a ghost in them.

Open seats don't prove squat. It would be straightforward for a fraud to simply put something in the seats to hold them open. My video demonstrates nothing.

There is light tapping of boots again behind me. I wonder if these block seats are typically filled with all of Ted Barker's friends.

The tap on my left shoulder nearly makes me pee myself. I slap the hand away as I turn on my butt and look up. It is Travis. "You scared the pants off me," I hiss.

Travis's brow furrows. "Sorry. What gives? Dusty said you had something."

I point to the box seats and continue to whisper, "I guess I owe you an apology."

Travis looks at the box seats, then back to me. His eyes narrow. "What?"

"There." I point again. "You are right. The activity is in the box seats."

Travis kneels down and moves closer to the opening in the curtain. After a moment's delay, he pulls one of the silk sheets back to afford him a better look.

I grab his left boot, pulling him back. "Don't," I insist.

"There's nothing there, April."

I look around Travis. He is wrong. Both ghosts are glaring at him as if he has interrupted their privacy. Which he has. I hold my breath, waiting to see what the response of the spirits will be.

Travis whips out his EMP meter and toggles it on. Immediately it makes a loud squelching noise and lights up. "Wow! This place is a hotbed."

I pull harder on his boot. "Come out of there."

He looks back at me and squints again. "Why?"

I crook a finger, gesturing for him to come in close. He squats with his ear toward me, and I whisper, "Two ghosts are sitting on the second row."

He pulls away, remaining in a catcher's squat, starts to laugh, and then realizes I'm serious. He sobers.

Dropping onto all fours, he turns and peers through the gap again, taking a few minutes to study it. "Seriously?" he asks as he pulls the curtain open again.

I see the two lovers from my vantage point under Travis's arm. They are not happy with his interruptions, and the air is turning from neutral to negative energy. The younger of the two apparitions stands up. The older tries to grab him by the back of his belt to restrain him.

The bottom half of the seat the younger ghost had been sitting in snaps closed. Travis shakes. "Oh, snap!" he hollers.

"Get back here, Travis," I whisper.

Travis glances over his shoulder at me. His facial features are tight in confusion as his meter continues to wail its high-pitched tone.

The round face of the blonde ghost appears just above Travis's hand, holding the curtain open. There is murder in the blond ghost's eyes. I try to scream, but nothing comes out.

Chapter 30

The handsome spirit's anger crackles in the air. Before I can pull Travis back, the ghost strikes.

Travis slams his hand to his side as the curtains jerk closed.

Hunching over while cradling his hand to his stomach, he yells, "Darn! That smarts!"

Travis's meter continues to sound the alarm of excessive energy forces. Still, I can feel the malice already bleeding out of the power. The lovers are perturbed over being bothered, but lucky for Travis and me, they do not seem to be looking for vengeance.

"What just happened?" Travis asks as he puts his meter in his side pocket while freeing his shotgun from the sling on his back.

"Don't," I say sharply.

He glares back over his shoulder at the now fully closed curtain, exhales, and lowers his weapon.

I gesture with my finger again, and he sits down next to me. "Let me see your hand."

Travis holds out his hand for me as he stares at the curtain. "Was there a loose electrical wire or something in there?"

Travis has four thick stripes across his hand. "I think you got slapped," I tell him.

He turns to face me and makes a nervous laughing noise.

"You're joking, right?"

"No. I saw the ghost knock your hand out of the way." I point toward the silk curtain. "And then shut the curtain."

The color drains from Travis's face as he swallows hard. "That's not cool."

"It could have been worse."

He runs his uninjured hand through his hair. "Dang straight."

We both watch the curtain as if it will do something miraculous. Without a word, I believe we both know what the other is thinking. Was that a spontaneous one-off act of violence by the apparition or the start of a precipitous slide from weird to bad?

An act of violence, even something as small as a frustrated slap, is never good with spirits. Acts of violence have a tendency to grow in severity and proliferate once a spirit crosses the line.

"The camera?" Travis gestures toward it.

"Nothing. I asked Dusty about it just before you got here."

"But you see them?"

I simply nod my head yes.

Travis leans forward, resting his arms on his thighs. "See them, but we can't get any documentation. So, what good is it?"

"I guess you have your EMP meter indication report," I offer.

"I doubt that makes for very good reading for Dusty's fans."

True that. I think that would be a relatively dry read.

"I suppose we could get with Liza and see what we can do to dispel them." I shrug. "Earn our paranormal fee if we can't get any decent material from them."

Travis takes my hand. "Let's clear out of here and talk this over with Dusty."

I think to argue the point with Travis, but I know it is necessary to notify the rest of the team about what we have going on. I don't believe using the walkie-talkies while near the Barker box seats is a wise option.

I follow Travis down the stairs and into the lobby. The clock above the snack counter shows that it has been only two hours since we took our positions upstairs. A lot has happened in two hours, but unfortunately, it is not very productive for the team if we can't get film documentation.

Travis lifts the walkie-talkie to his mouth. "Dusty, do you copy?"

"Go ahead."

Travis explains to Dusty the situation in the center balcony. He takes extra care in describing the physical attack by the younger of the two ghosts.

"That's not good. We'll have to try and remove the spirit if it has progressed to that stage. Are you positive we can't get any physical confirmation of the spirit's existence? I would hate to get rid of them if we can get some material from them."

"I can get a photo of the two seats being down as if someone is sitting in them," Travis offers.

Dusty blows a raspberry. "I don't need a ghost for that. I can do that well with a stick and some duct tape."

"What about the electrical impulse three-dimensional grid."

There is radio silence for a moment before Dusty comes back. "Forget it. I'm not a big fan of that tool. You just hold your places. I'll send Liza and Chet up with some sage and holy water."

Travis lets his radio hand drop to his side. "I should've just gone and gotten the energy scanner. That would've at least given us a sketch of the spirits."

"You don't need that. I can describe them to Liza, and she can sketch them out for us."

"I meant scientific," Travis says.

"The sketch would look better in a book."

Travis turns as if to say something and then grins. "Yeah, those electrical grid points are sometimes like trying to make out things from cloud shapes. Miles or Luis will be like, 'Don't you see the man sitting right there?' And I never see it but finally say that I do just to get them off my case."

"You and Dusty are probably of like mind on that. It is probably why he told you not to worry about it."

Travis puffs out his chest. "If you have to explain to people what they are seeing, that's not very good proof."

"Something like that," I agree.

Travis crosses the bullpup across his stomach as he rubs his hand again. "Man, that smarts. It's tingling like when I have been hunting, and my hands have gotten too cold."

"It might be a concentration of the draft we feel when a spirit enters a room."

Travis's eyes open wide. "You think? It's not like frostbite, is it?"

"It is just a theory," I mumble as I wish Liza would hurry.

"I can't lose my hand. I need my hand," Travis says, his voice moving to a higher pitch.

Oh brother. Me and my big mouth. "Let me see it again."

Travis holds his hand out to me. The red marks have grown together into a giant angry black blob surrounded by a red border. It is remarkable how quickly it is spreading. It is as if Travis's hand has been injected with some sort of poisonous venom.

"What is happening to my hand?" The panic in Travis flows freely to me.

I hold his wrist with one hand and cover the wound with the palm of my other hand. I have no idea if this will work, as my healing "gift" is one of my more random abilities. "Just hold still for a moment."

"What are you doing?" Travis asks.

"Just trust me, Travis." *Since I can't exactly trust myself.* Thankfully, I don't get that many opportunities to use the healing "gift." However, that means I have even less control over it than my other unruly skills. I am genuinely winging it.

Despite Travis's questions and my own doubts, I can visualize his hand perfectly healthy and of full good strength. Something evil drains out of Travis's hand into mine. This surprises me since I have not previously sensed any evil in the room earlier.

The last of the corrupted energy bleeds out of Travis's hand,

and I open my eyes. It takes everything I have to roll my hand off of his to see if anything has been affected. I'm shocked to see his hand looks as good as it did the night before. There are no ill effects left from the attack.

Liza bursts through the doorway. I drop Travis's hand. "Did I interrupt something? I can come back," Liza says with a smirk.

"No. We were just waiting for you. We didn't want to be in such close proximity to the ghosts given how cramped the quarters are in the box area."

"Of course," Liza says as she comes closer to the two of us. "Is there anything you two care to say about your relationship?"

"Nothing is going on here. I was just helping Travis with an injury."

Both Liza and Chet grin as they nod in agreement. Neither of them believes us. Whatever. They're goofballs if they think Travis and I could be a number and not kill each other.

Liza grins while waving her hand that holds the sage in it. "Well, Clara Barton, lead the way to these ghosts no one else can see so we can try to get rid of them."

She obviously thinks she's funny. I gesture with a nod of my head for Travis to lead the way. He racks a shell into his shotgun chamber and starts back up the stairs. The mechanical noise of the gun gives me enough pause to stop following Travis and allow Liza and Chet to go first.

I can smell the sweet scent of the smoldering sage as I enter the center balcony. Liza is wafting the smoke toward the black silk curtains.

Immediately, I notice something is off. I let Liza continue with her ceremony, but the tendril of sage smoke floats directly up with no disruption. Even the sage is not indicating spirits in the Barker box seats.

"I'm really not sensing anything, April," Liza says quietly over her shoulder.

I use what little patience I have to center myself and pull all my energy into a tight ball just below my sternum. When I'm ready, I push out with it, looking for any thoughts coming to me.

I'm equal parts surprised and baffled when nothing returns to me. Throwing caution to the wind, I slide past my three friends and throw open the curtains.

There is nothing inside. No seats held down or semi-opaque beautiful young men. Just eight dusty, old, gold fabric movie chairs in desperate need of being cleaned.

Sometimes when you get exactly what you hope for, you realize you wished for the wrong thing. I was hoping the ghost had just disappeared so we wouldn't have to deal with them.

Sue me, the mean streak in the beautiful blond had me a little apprehensive.

Still, these two could cause some significant injuries on the worksite. We must find them and expel them before we can consider leaving.

"They're not here anymore," I announce.

"That's not good," Liza says as she comes to my side.

"Maybe the sage worked really fast this time," Chet offers.

"These weren't your run-of-the-mill spirits, Chet. They were full-blown apparitions that were aware of their surroundings," I explain.

Liza exhales. "Well, if it makes you feel any better, I don't feel any negativity."

"That's just it. I didn't either, but Travis still ended up with a nasty wound on his hand where one of them struck him."

"Ow." Liza turns to Travis. "Let me see."

Travis holds his hand out to Liza. "It's gone now. April healed it."

Liza shoots me a look full of accusation.

"I have no clue how," I tell her.

"You're a healer?" she asks.

"Sorta—kinda—maybe."

Liza gives me a scorching, disgusted look. "You know you really are a waste of good talent."

Wow, that is harsh. "Thank you for being so supportive."

"Darn, April. With just a little bit of effort, there is no telling how effective you could be for the team."

"Hey. I pull my weight around here," I say.

"Lay off, Liza," Travis interjects.

"Yeah. You're being sort of mean," Chet adds.

Liza points at both of them. "You two don't know what we are talking about, so you need to stay out of it."

Now I'm getting mad. She can pick on me if she feels the need, but Chet and Travis were just trying to help.

Besides, I know darn well this is just her attitude going negative because she plans to tell Dusty she is leaving the team soon. Forget that.

"You think I'm not pulling my weight because I'm not honing my skills as sharply as you would?"

Her lips thin and she nods her head. "More or less that's what I am saying," Liza says.

"That's awfully rich coming from someone who is going to leave the team high and dry without an expeller."

Liza's jaw drops open. "I don't believe you!"

"I just made it easier for you. You have to tell them some time. Why not now?" I say.

"You're leaving us?" Chet asks.

"I thought you liked working with our team," Travis adds.

Liza's eyes narrow as she glowers at me. "That was a private conversation."

"Oops," I say as I push past them. "I'm going to check the left side. I would appreciate it if one of you could check the right box seats before we go back downstairs."

"I am just contemplating my future," I hear Liza explain to the boys as I walk the hallway to the box seats on the right.

It was wrong of me to blow Liza up like that in front of the guys. It was also bad for her to admonish me for a skill that is random at best.

A few months back, the only skills I thought I had were the ability to read people's thoughts and see a random spirit or two. I have significantly underestimated the extent of my "gifts." It seems like I may never know the full breadth of them.

There is nothing in the right wing. The same as earlier.

I didn't believe the spirits had fled to either of the wings. If I had to bet, they crossed to the other side of the veil or changed location and time matrix altogether. They were powerful spirits and would have ample options available to them.

Something I don't have right now. Options.

It will take considerably more effort than I planned to land a job in Baltimore or D.C. I'll need to start calling prospective companies in earnest on Wednesday and beg for an interview.

"I'm good with that. It's time to move on with my life. Lord knows I have been itching to do this for months. That probably was a contributing factor to why I snapped at Liza."

I reenter the center balcony. It is empty. "Liza?" I call out. "Chet? Travis?"

Nobody answers me. I walk toward the left balcony hallway.

Someone steps into the hallway from the other direction. My heart jumps into my throat.

"Travis!" I clasp my hands to my chest. "You spooked the daylights out of me again."

"You've been jumpy today."

"Yeah. I suppose I have been." I gesture toward him. "Anything on the left side."

"All quiet. Not a single blip on the meter."

"All quiet on the right, too. Where's Liza and Chet?"

Travis shrugs. "I think you sort of ticked Liza off. They went back to watching the lower level."

I nod my head. "I suppose we should get back to the center and relocate the camera."

"No. Dusty wants us behind the stage. He just called and said that Jason keeps hearing things, and he would like you to look into it."

"Okay. I have a feeling the two we scared off won't be back anytime soon."

"We can always run another check in a couple of hours," Travis offers.

That is solid thinking. The theater is not that large, but the cut-up nature makes it very difficult for a team our size to watch every area around the clock.

Besides, watching a specific area is where the boredom often comes from on a paranormal excursion.

As we walk down the sloped walkway of the theater's first floor, I see Chet and Liza standing in front of the stage. Liza seems to work extra hard not to make eye contact with us. I guess I really did tick her off this time.

We check in with Dusty at the manager's office. He explains what Jason claims to have heard. He asks us to do at least three sweeps of the area behind the stage.

I feel it's sort of lame given that I am now in complete agreement with Travis. All the action is on the second floor. If we can just figure out how to capture the image with our equipment.

Still, Dusty pays our checks. So, if he wants us to waste our time chasing some noise Jason feels he heard, who am I to argue.

Chapter 31

We make our second circuit around the U-shaped hallway behind the stage. The heat doesn't work very well in the hallway, so it's naturally cold.

Not cold enough to ignore the draft that blows by us, dropping the temperature at least another ten degrees. I don't need to ask Travis if he felt it as he crossed his arms across his chest in response, too.

I wonder if he feels the evil crackling on the air or if he smells the overpowering scent of fear and burning plastic as I do.

I instinctively crouch to escape the nonexistent smoke as the voice speaks in my mind.

"Exit the building!"

Barely able to breathe, I make eye contact with Travis. "Did you hear that?" I ask.

"I was about to ask you," Travis says, his eyes becoming more prominent by the second.

Without warning, an invisible force drives me toward the back of the building. I fall over onto all fours while the pressure continues to build. I look to Travis for help, but he has fallen to his knees, too. I feel his hand on my shoulder as I struggle to my knees.

"Are you okay?" he asks.

"I think so."

Travis points toward the wall. "What is that?"

Following the direction he is pointing, I get a chill. I see the blur of dark shadows on the hallway wall, much like Liza described earlier.

They are humanoid in appearance, except floating, not walking, toward the back exit.

The thrumming I heard earlier in the day picks up again in my brain. It is a rapid succession of noise.

My stomach churns and my mouth waters as if I am about to projectile vomit. The world is spinning.

Travis pulls me to him and holds me to his chest. "Hey, there. Stay with me, April. Don't go anywhere."

Visions roll across my mind's eye with such rapid velocity it compounds my queasiness. I can't discern who or what in the quick glances of another reality is essential.

Still, I get an overwhelming sense of sadness. These are innocents caught up in something traumatic. Something catastrophic.

"Exit the building." The invisible commanding voice reverberates off the walls. Icey tentacles of fear run across my skin.

The thrumming noise intensifies in rapidity and volume. The scent of heavy, putrid smoke carries through the hallway, choking and blinding me as I sputter and cough.

My panic intensifies as the burning sensation from smoke inhalation threatens to sear my lungs closed. I can't breathe. My vision dims as the smoke suffocates the last of the light.

"April! Stay with me." I feel a tapping on my face, and I force my eyes open.

Travis hovers over me. He continues tapping my face lightly with the palm of his hand. His expression is full of concern.

The thrumming grows to an incredible crescendo, then decreases in intensity and rapidity.

I manage to pull in a breath as the noise slows to *thump, thump*.

The pervasive noise stops all at once.

It is silent. Except for Travis's heavy breathing and the beating of my heart, which seems to have taken up residence in my ears.

"What was that?" Travis asks as he continues to support my head in his lap."

I struggle to pull myself up to a seated position. "I'm not sure, but it is an eleven on the volume scale."

Travis flashes a surprised grin. He takes a breath so deep his chest visibly rises.

"It is full of emotion, too," I say.

"Full of something," Travis says as he pulls his meter out and toggles it on. The display on the meter goes completely red. The alarm did not sound nearly as loud as earlier.

Travis rolls the volume down. "I need to give my eardrums a rest."

That's when I realize I'm not alone. "You heard it, too!"

Travis frowns. He stands and offers me a helping hand. "Something."

"Did you smell the smoke?" I ask.

"I don't know, April. I think I smelled something like burned bacon." He shoves his meter back in his backpack. "But that's just weird. Maybe someone burnt their breakfast this morning."

I catch his eye as I put my hands on my hips. "Seriously. There's nobody cooking breakfast in here."

He fidgets from one boot to the other. "I don't know what to tell you, April. I just know I didn't see anything."

"But *you* heard it and smelled it."

The walkie-talkie beeps, and Travis appears mightily relieved as he answers. "Go ahead."

"Come eat. Miles and Luis are back from the library," Dusty says.

"You don't have to tell me twice," Travis says. He gestures for me to follow him. "Let's get there before the guys wipe it out."

"We're not done here," I say.

Travis raises his eyebrows. "I am. I don't know what that

was, but I don't have to be a psychic to know it had ill intent."

"So, we'll get the rest of the team and the equipment—"

Travis raises his hand and shakes his head. "I wouldn't know how to explain it to the rest of the team. I'm also not in the mood to have anyone else on the team experience that."

I get it. The big bad boy who is scared of nothing just met fear for the first time. Still, we have a job to do. "That's not your call, Travis."

His jaw sets as he growls, "You don't think I know that? I'm not saying we're not going to bring the rest of the team in on it —" He shakes his head. "I'm just saying let me get some food in my stomach and try to get my head around it before I tell your brother.

"You know darn well that if we tell him right now, we'll have the whole team back here immediately. Just let me think about it first."

It's not going anywhere, and there's no reason to ruin everyone's dinner. "Alright. But we tell Dusty after dinner, and he makes the decision."

Travis rolls his eyes. "Geez, woman. That's what I've been trying to tell you."

Chapter 32

At eight o'clock, Miles and Luis bring us several large pizzas and some Cokes for dinner.

Strangely enough, I'm not hungry. I want to investigate what took place in the hallway. When the aroma of pepperoni carries from Liza's plate, my stomach changes my mind for me.

"Did you find anything new on Ted Barker?" I ask Miles.

He holds up a finger to me. "Yes, but let's come back around to that. Did it ever seem odd to you that the theater had to be remodeled just three years after it initially opened?"

No. But now that Miles brings it to my attention, it does seem odd. "A little."

"It wasn't a voluntary decision." Miles pauses.

Miles has a bad habit of drawing things out when he knows he has information the rest of us are interested in. I think his dream job would be a game show host. "And now for one million dollars, our contestant will open their secret envelope ... After five minutes of commercials."

"And?" Liza says.

"In 1939, there was a fire that required the entire theater to be refurbished," Miles reports.

Dusty scoffs. "Is that the minor damage Heather referred to?"

"It seems so," Miles says.

My thoughts go to the detailed mural on the ceiling, "The soot didn't destroy the painting?"

"The painting wasn't commissioned until 1940 and completed in 1941 for the fifth anniversary of the theater," Luis adds.

"It's important to understand the theater was used for all sorts of events during its heyday. Not only was it used for movies and plays, but it was also utilized for high school graduations. A few city meetings of high interest that were open to the public were even held here," Miles explains.

"Mostly everything except for weddings," Luis adds.

"So, in essence, the owners are attempting to return it to its original use," Dusty says.

"Sure." Miles nods his head thoughtfully. "But the spirits from the 1936 fire persisted. Eventually, the only events that could be scheduled in the theater were the movies. The entire city considered the building to be haunted and bad luck."

"The theater limped along for a few decades, the new owner keeping it open mostly as a matter of pride until he died in 1966," Luis finishes the report.

Luis buried the lead. "New owner?" I ask.

"Yes. The original owner didn't have enough insurance to cover the damage done to the theater by the fire, much less pay out the settlements to the families. The Reed family, who originally owned the property, filed for bankruptcy, and the local bank foreclosed on the property. It was later transferred to a local city council member and farmland owner named Austin Tate. He ordered the remodeling and reopening as well as commissioned the painting, which was done during off-hours. At the same time, the theater continued to run," Miles says as he reaches for another piece of pizza.

"What about the scaffolding," Dusty asks.

"Took it down each afternoon before the movies showed and were back in early in the morning to put it back up," Miles explains.

The painting would've been difficult enough if the scaffolding were left up year-round. I can only imagine the army that would have been required to put it up and take it down each day. That doesn't make sense to me.

"Tate seems to have been an influential player during the '40s and '50s. He dumped a small fortune into this property, and I'm sure he would never have wanted it to be known that it was losing money," Luis adds.

"What can you tell us about the fire in 1939?" Liza asks.

Miles winces. "Just that it was tragic. The fire broke out on the first floor near the stage. Inexplicably, thirty-two people tried to exit through the back door rather than the front and got caught in the hallway."

Travis and I lock eyes. The room seems to swoon as I am touched by vertigo.

It is precisely what we experienced. It was a panicked crush of people headed toward the back exit, and we were caught up in it.

"They were most likely confused by the fire. Once there is smoke in the air, and folks begin to panic, logic can leave people really quick. A couple of people break toward the back exit—" Luis shrugs. "The next thing you know, a large group follows them to their doom."

"It doesn't make any sense. An exit is an exit," Chet observes.

Miles frowns. "True. But, on top of bad timing, the theater had received a shipment of popcorn, soda, and oil that afternoon, and it was left at the back door.

"For some reason, the delivery man had placed the crates directly in front of the door. The weight prevented the door from being opened. At least that's what the newspaper reported the fire marshal determined."

"And the cause?" I ask as my curiosity is fully piqued.

"They thought it might've been a cigar left unattended, but nothing was ever conclusive."

I had felt the panic of the crowd. I panicked when I was pushed to the ground and felt the pressure of the group moving toward the blocked exit and their death. I feel at one with them and am overcome with sorrow.

How awful. To come to enjoy some entertainment with a friend or family member and end up burned alive because of a few careless mistakes made by others. An unattended cigar and a misplaced shipment of refreshments, who would think that could culminate in a fiery death?

Miles's research, as usual, is quite enlightening. It confirms that we have two spiritual events transpiring in the theater, not just one. The thirty-two lost souls attempting to escape the theater with their lives and the two lovers in Ted Barker's box seats.

Miles gestures toward me. "Regarding Mr. Barker, his celebrity was generated from his appearance in fourteen B-list movies. His good looks gave him a high level of notoriety in the community. Basically, it sounds like everybody loved Ted Barker, and everyone had a crush on him.

That's one of the reasons Mr. Tate had given Barker the eight box seats. It was good for business as people would come to see a movie and possibly get a glance of Ted Barker as well."

"So, he didn't pay for his box seats?" Travis asks.

Luis grins as he shakes his head. "One of the many perks of being a celebrity. People try to curry favor by giving you stuff for free."

Daddy used to say that wealthy people didn't have to spend the same amount as the rest of us because people were constantly giving them things to get in their good graces. I suppose the same can be said for celebrities.

"It obviously wasn't all roses," Miles continued. "Ultimately, Ted and a close friend of his, Ross McQueen, hung themselves on that large oak tree just outside the courthouse in 1953."

I am dumbfounded as that news settles in on me. How tragic.

"Who first?" Liza asks.

"On the same night," Miles answers.

That can't be right. "Miles, are you sure about that? I've never heard of a double suicide."

"Maybe suicide pacts aren't such a recent occurrence, April." Miles lifts his cup to his lip and pauses. "I don't make the news. I just report it."

That isn't like Miles to be so flippant about a factoid so illogical. If what he says is true, it would be like one of the first double suicides by hanging ever reported in the history of mankind. Something isn't ringing true.

"Why?" I ask.

Luis rubs the stubble on his chin. "It's all sort of spotty after that. There is at least one comment that he may have fallen on some hard financial times, but after his death, it was as if Ted never existed."

Now *that* rings true. I have noticed in my life that the moment anyone enjoys a modest amount of success, the very people who cheered them on tend to try to discredit and ruin them.

I have my suspicions that Ted Barker was one of the two spirits we saw in the box seats upstairs. I'll need to confirm that if I can. My bet is also that the other spirit will turn out to be Ross McQueen.

"Miles, did you have any pictures of Ted Barker or Ross McQueen?"

"There's plenty of pictures on the search engines for Ted Barker. Ross McQueen moved here from Hollywood only a few weeks before he committed suicide. There are no pictures of him in the papers."

"You remember Ted Barker," Dusty adds. "The movie I was watching the other day downstairs. That's why I was watching it. It was a Ted Barker movie."

Why is it everyone always assumes I commit everything I see and do to complete memory recall? I remember Dusty watching a movie that looked like a cheesy black-and-white. He mentioned that it was research for the upcoming paranormal excursion. Outside of that, I can't remember anything about the movie. Possibly I would have, if I had been warned there would be a pop quiz later.

"Oh, yeah," I say.

I can look up a picture on my phone in a few minutes.

"So, what's the plan, boss? I need us to get this wrapped up so I can make it to my aunt's house tomorrow evening," Chet says.

Dusty pulls at his red beard. "Given you and Jason were unable to raise an image with the infrared cartographer—"

My back straightens in surprise. I had no idea that the rest of the team was attempting to document the Barker box ghosts. I'm equally surprised that Dusty's cutting-edge expensive equipment failed to pick up an energy field to map.

Unless the ghosts became perturbed and left.

"And because April and Travis weren't able to confirm the noise Jason heard, we'll have Liza and Luis bless everything and call it a night," Dusty says.

I cut my eyes to Travis.

He shakes his head and mouths the word no.

Sorry, Travis.

"That's not true, Dusty. Travis and I felt something in the back hallway before you called us to dinner."

Dust squints, obviously wondering why we had not mentioned this sooner. "Travis felt it, too?" He turns his attention to Travis.

Travis nods. "Something. I'm not sure what."

"It must be strong, then," Dusty ponders.

"Very," I confirm. "The emotion signature is off the chart."

Dusty swallows hard. "The guests who didn't make it out."

"I suspect so," I whisper.

"There's something else, too, Dusty. Something wicked," Travis interjects.

"What did you experience, April?"

I meet his stare. "I can't be for certain, Dusty. It is sort of like being in a cemetery where everyone is trying to talk to me at once. Only, they weren't. Trying to talk to me. They were just panicked, and it was just one big sea of screams and hollering. I didn't see anything, though."

"I did earlier," Liza interrupts. "Remember when we first

went in the hallway. You felt something, but if you remember, I told you I saw a mass of human-shaped shadows flowing across the wall."

My mind must be on vacation. I had already forgotten about seeing the shadows before the smoke took my breath. "That's right. Shadows, Dusty."

Dusty looks to Luis. "What do you think?"

Luis clasps his hands in front of him. "I think it would be worth the effort to set up video and audio in the hallway. That much activity, we might be able to salvage something."

"What about up in the balcony?" Travis asks. "The ghost up there struck me."

"There's nothing in the balcony to film or record," Liza says. "Like Dusty said, while you were investigating the back hallway, Jason and Chet ran the equipment, and I searched too. It's clean."

"No. There is something not right up there, too." Travis insists.

I can see Travis's panic build. I've seen it before. Heck, I feel it regularly. Still, he needs to get control of it before he cracks. I try to make eye contact with him in hopes of calming him down, but his eyes have taken on a wild look as he begins to look around the manager's office.

"If there was anything, it's gone now," Liza insists. "The best thing we can do up there is bless the area and cover the box seats with holy water."

"We need to burn those box seats!" Travis's words shock me.

"Travis, really?" Dusty scolds.

Like I'm in kindergarten or something, I raise my hand and clear my throat.

Dusty turns his ire from Travis to me. "Yes?"

I don't want to go into it, but since Travis already broached the subject… "If the goal is to cleanse the theater of spirits, holy water and blessing aren't going to take care of the upstairs boxes."

"Why is that?" Dusty asks.

"Hmm … I'm pretty sure there is a considerable amount of cell remnants on the seats from Barker and McQueen. The only way to cleanse totally would be to get rid of the cushions." I gesture toward Travis. "To Travis's point, burn the seats."

Miles snort. "I find it highly unlikely that fifty years later, we'll find hair remnants from anyone who sat in those chairs."

"I'm not talking about hair, Miles." He remains confused. "Something sort of sticky and a whole lot more personal than hair."

Miles's eyes open wide as his mouth forms an "O." "I see," he says.

"I'm never going to the movies again," Liza says.

"I'll have to check with Heather White before we burn them. I'm not sure how strict the historical society is going to be about such things," Miles says.

"That's why it's better we just go ahead and do it and tell her about it later. There's no reason to make her go through all the red tape. If we just do it, it's done."

"April's right." Liza backs me up. "There are certain things that need to just be done. One of the two apparitions struck Travis. That means it already knows that it can cross the veil and affect the physical on this side. If they plan on having people in this facility in the future, it can go bad quick."

Dusty is rocking his chair as he contemplates our options. "I'm afraid you're right. This is the plan. Travis, take Chet and Jason with you.

"I want you three to dismantle the seats from the box area and burn them in the alley. Miles and Luis, I want y'all to focus all the AV equipment within the next hour on the hallway where April and Liza reported the shadow figures.

"Liza and April, I need you to set up watch in the hallway." Dusty gestures toward me. "April, you have your weapons?"

"I do." I'm not exactly excited about being put into a position where I might need to use them. Still, I do have them.

"All right, folks. Everybody has their assignments. I'd like to get this wrapped up as quickly as possible, as it's now nine o'clock."

Chapter 33

Within the hour, Luis and Miles have all the audiovisual equipment trained on the hallway. Liza and I sit on lawn chairs close to the back exit. I have my bullpup shotgun across my lap.

"When do you think will be the right time?" I ask Liza.

Her brow wrinkles as if she is in deep thought. "I have a suspicion that this is on a time loop of some sort. But so far, we've only had it occur twice in the seven hours we've been here. It would make more sense if it were hourly or daily." She shakes her head. "Your guess is as good as mine as to when the next show will be."

"I was talking about when you think it will be the right time to tell Dusty that you're leaving."

Liza's head jerks in my direction as her eyes narrow. She put a finger to her lips. "Audio equipment. We'll talk tonight in our room."

Yep. There is definitely a room in the lovely town of Shelbyville, Tennessee, on my agenda for tonight. I think the first moment I saw Ted Barker's beautiful face, I knew we would not be leaving Shelbyville tonight.

Hopefully, with any luck, the boys will get the box seats out the door and get them burned. I also hope the hallway ghosts are "on a loop," as Liza says, and are about to make an appearance. I am ready for bed.

I pull my phone out to see if I have received any text messages from Lee. I'm thoroughly disappointed when I see the only text message I have is from Chase asking if it is okay if he feeds Puppy a cupcake.

I tell him yes and remind Chase that Puppy cannot have chocolate. Initially I want to respond that Puppy does not need any sweets. Despite my aggravation, I am sort of impressed that Chase is asking for a change. I'm content with that win.

"My stomach is kind of queasy," Liza announces. "I wonder if something was wrong with that pizza."

"That's why I never eat sausage on a pizza."

"I didn't have anything but the cheese and pepperoni pizza," Liza says.

"I had a piece of that, too, but I don't feel anything. Do you want me to ask Dusty if he has any antacids?"

The features of Liza's face pinch.

"What's the matter? Is it that bad?" I ask.

"Do you not smell that?"

I'm not sure what Liza could have possibly gotten a hold of to give her food poisoning. I'm grateful I don't have it. She is turning green and looks as if she is in pain. "Let me go see if we have anything for you to take."

Liza grabs my wrist before I can stand.

"No, stay here with me."

I feel the anxiety coursing through her body as she squeezes my wrist tight. "Well, let me at least call Dusty and see if he can bring us something."

"Something's happening. Do you not feel it?"

It takes me a moment to catch up with the conversation. I thought we were still talking about spoiled sausage on pizzas, and Liza has changed the subject to an energy force disruption. This is particularly disconcerting because when Liza senses something, and I don't, it typically means we are dealing with things of a Biblical nature.

Demons and angels are her specialty, not mine.

"I'm sorry, I don't," I say.

"Use your other skills, April." Liza's eyes open wider as sweat beads up on her forehead. "This is not good."

"But I felt the disruption's in the hallway both times earlier. Why am I not feeling it now?"

Liza closes her eyes and lolls her head from left to right. "Don't know," she grunts as she appears to be fighting the urge to vomit.

My hand finds the ornate cross Liza gave me early in our relationship. I pull it from under my shirt and chant a simple protection blessing as I stroke the sterling silver cross with my thumb.

I'm not very accomplished with these skills. It is only recently that I knew I had any skills in the same realm as Liza. But my granny has been working hard to teach me a few methods to harness the spiritual energy.

I stand chanting the blessing even louder as I clear my mind and visualize the hallway clear and void of all supernatural energies.

Something tugs on my back jean pockets. Turning, I see the greenness has left Liza's skin.

"It's gone," Liza says.

"What's gone?"

She squeezes her eyes tight and gasps a breath. "I have no idea. Big and nasty, though."

"The crowd?"

"No. That had nothing to do with the crowd." She lifts her shoulders. "Maybe it does, but it wasn't present when I saw the shadows earlier."

It could've been present when I felt the crowd right before dinner. It would be impossible for me to know. "But you're better now?"

"Yes. It's past."

I don't feel much like sitting after that excitement, but since she is sitting, I sit.

Peaches. For a simple, quick paranormal excursion, this trip is getting more complicated by the minute. "But you still haven't seen any shadows?"

"Sorry, no."

"Are you girls all right?" Dusty's voice comes across the walkie-talkie that Liza carries.

She presses the side button. "Yeah, we're fine. We had some sort of entity passing, but there won't be any audiovisual on it."

"Ten-four. I'll send some more team members as soon as we finish with the seats."

"No rush," Liza says.

"You sure about that," I grumble.

Liza smiles at me.

"What?"

"Manifestation of cleansing light prayer, I'm impressed," Liza says.

"What's that?"

Liza gestures toward me. "The prayer you were reciting. That's a difficult one. Your granny is very ambitious, or she senses you have a tremendous amount of skill."

I let a laugh escape me. "If I know Granny, she's probably just reckless."

Liza grins and looks away. "Just keeping it in the family, I suppose."

When I move to D.C. and become a senior partner at a prestigious law firm, I will not miss Guntersville the least bit. If I want to go for a boat ride, I'll just own a house on the Potomac and drop a boat in the water. There's no difference. The homes just cost a lot more in D.C.

But I'd be lying if I said I'm not going to miss the paranormal excursions. I know it makes no sense. The pay is pretty good, but there's no future in it.

There is for Dusty, with his book deals and TV series deals, but for the Early brothers, Chet, and to a lesser degree Miles and Luis, it is a tread water sort of job. You can make some good money and do something interesting, but you aren't building anything in the end.

It had been a long time since I felt like I was contributing to a team for a common goal. In some odd fashion, the paranormal team has given me that. Something I didn't even know I needed.

It is bittersweet to think that it is coming to an end. It makes me more than a little sad.

I hear the voices. So clearly that at first, I believe it is the boys bringing the box seats through the hallway.

Still, the level of angst and fear riding on the energy flowing to me lets me know it is the thirty-two perpetually lost souls. "We've got company," I whisper to Liza.

"Yes. I caught a glimpse of a shadow a second ago."

I lock eyes with her. "A shadow?"

She shrugs. "So far."

When your partner is recovering from turning seafoam green because something evil passed by you, and you are waiting on a group of thirty-two panicked ghosts, the last thing you want to hear is that you have a *single* shadow being cast by a spirit coming down the hall. It could be the first of the pack of panicked ghosts. Still, my mind goes to probabilities much more sinister.

I see the single shadow. It disappears as the voices in my head grow in complexity and volume. There are multiple tenors, and the disconcerted nature leads me to believe numerous entities are coming toward me.

"There they are," Liza whispers.

The voices grow even louder. So loud it is difficult for me to concentrate. Still, I do not see any shadows. "Where?"

Liza raises her arm. Her hand crosses my face, and I follow the trajectory of her finger.

No wonder. I was expecting to see human silhouettes on the wall again. I had visualized a replay of the night they met their doom and seeing the shadows they cast.

Instead, inky humanoid shapes slither across the hallway's ceiling. It is hard to see how many, but it would not be difficult to believe there are thirty-two.

The unnatural side-to-side motion of the dark splotches reminds me of snakes in the grass, causing the hair on the back of my neck to stand up.

We are silent as they make their way down the hallway, collecting in front of the exit door. I feel their presence pushing down on me, crushing me against the wall as they push to open the door that will never open for them.

The *thud, thud* noise on the door is maddeningly loud and threatens my sanity.

I struggle for my next breath. My chest is so compressed, I cannot pull one in. I grab Liza's forearm, and she seems to understand. She holds her hands palm out, imploring me to be patient and not to panic.

The ink spots dissipate. The voices fade away, and the horrific *thud, thud, thud* on the door decreases until there are only three shadows left beating on the door.

The pressure on my chest releases. I draw in a ragged breath, leading to a coughing bout brought on by the hot, smoky air I pull into my lungs.

As I panic, the beating ceases. The last inky shadow disappears.

They are gone. I draw a breath, finding it to be smoke-free and full of oxygen.

"Are you okay?" Liza asks.

"I am now. It's like I'm there with them."

Liza smirks. "Then whatever you do, don't time travel and end up in this hallway."

"Good idea."

Liza puckers her lips as she examines the location of the cameras. "As long as Luis has those in the right spot, I think he might've gotten some fantastic footage."

"I hope so. Lord knows those were some spooky-looking visions."

"Yes." Liza sits back and stretches. "But thankfully benign. We should be able to clear these out relatively easily, and the workers can be back in here and finish the remodel. As long as burning the seats clears out Mr. Barker and his friend that you saw, we should be done."

"What about what you felt earlier? That wasn't the thirty-two movie patrons."

The door at the far end of the hallway opens. Chet comes through with the first of the gold chairs from the box area. "These babies did *not* want to come loose."

"What was the problem?"

Chet laughs as he carries the seat, that he has upside down, by the footers. "I don't know, maybe the bolts didn't like the fifty years' worth of Cokes spilled on them."

"I would've thought the spilled butter would've evened it out," I joke.

Chet chuckles, and I notice him straining to keep his balance. "Don't make me laugh. How about you make yourself useful and get that door?"

The Early brothers come through the far door as I open the exit and hold it open for Chet. "How much longer before you get the other five loose?"

"No. We got all eight of them out. We just have to carry the rest down now," Chet says as he passes through the door.

"You need help carrying them down?" I ask.

"No offense, but they're a little heavy. Just let us get them. If y'all will, keep both doors open. It would be a huge help," Travis says as he approaches the exit door, huffing for breath.

I'm not as big as the Early brothers or Chet, but I'm confident that I could be almost as strong if I need to. Still, I think holding the door sounds like a much better job.

Chapter 34

We circle around the pile as Jason throws some paint thinner he found on the gold chairs the boys have stacked in the alley. He sets one corner of the stack of seats on fire.

The flame initially struggles against the cold December wind. Still, eventually, it finds the pile's interior and catches fire in earnest. As the flames lick toward the stars, I notice no less than seven long, silver streaks fly up the orange flames.

Liza nudges me. "Did you catch that?"

"Yep."

"Good call," she says.

"Thank you." Even when making the right call is about something bizarre that most people can't even comprehend, it still feels good to be right.

The fire loses some of its intensity, so we leave Jason in charge of managing the fire. He is sort of our assigned arsonist.

Liza and I go about the chore of cleansing and blessing the hallway. We take particular care with the exit door.

I seriously doubt it is the original door from the night of the fire, but I still bless it. Liza marks it with a peculiar rune that she says will allow it to be a portal across the veil for any spirit that comes to it.

Hopefully, the rune is a one-way ticket.

It feels good to cleanse the property. We are allowing

troubled spirits to be at rest. At the same time, we are helping with the revitalization of the historic building. Now the crews can come and finish their work.

Dusty and Luis rave about the film footage they have of the ghosts in the hallway. I'm happy for them—us. They had not expected much from this quick trip, and it's always nice when they can score another story unexpectedly.

The boys break down the equipment while Liza and I run one more scan of the theater. We decide to sweep with the EMF meters as well as our natural skills.

There are no residual energy disruptions in the balcony area. The lobby is clear, too, as are the first-floor seats of the theater.

We walk the U-shaped hallway behind the stage, and the meter remains silent. Despite the meters, I have the eerie feeling of being watched.

"What do you think?" I ask Liza.

She wrinkles her nose. "I don't sense anything." She puts her hands in front of her stomach. "But something is making me queasy again."

"Yeah, me too. Maybe residual energies from all the spirits? I mean, thirty-two is a lot."

"Maybe." She looks uneasy. "Still, the cleansing should've taken care of that."

I want to get into bed. I'm exhausted. "Do you want to cleanse it a second time?"

She gives an eager nod. "I think we better since we're here."

That's the one bad thing about paranormal. It's not like accounting or being an attorney. There is no set task-completed process.

There are no manuals or work procedures. Perhaps the blessing we are using is only half effective and we should use a different one. Or maybe these particular spirits would react more favorably to smoldering sage than holy water.

Paranormal is always a guessing game, which means knowing when you are done is anyone's best guess.

I'm not particularly happy about having to make more rounds with Liza. But I suck it up and try to be positive and supportive. We even double up our effort. As she blesses the hallway, I cast a clearing spell. One of them is bound to work.

The boys pull the van around to the back alley and load up the gear. I see Jason through the open door, poking at the smoldering metal remnants of the gold chairs.

We stop at the door. Liza adds one more blessing to the rune she has drawn. She stands straight and takes a deep breath.

I freeze, waiting intently for her judgment, praying for her "all clear" signal.

"I think we're good," she says.

That's good enough for me. "Cool," I say as I sling my backpack over my shoulder. "Let's go get a room."

"Done?" Dusty asks just outside the door.

"A clean bill of health." Liza steps past him.

"Good." Dusty steps in and inserts a key into the push bar.

I get an uneasy feeling and wish Dusty had waited until I was in the alley. As I stand in the hallway watching him secure the door to lock when we exit, I believe I feel a minute energy pulse. I get the sense something is attempting to hide. It is gleeful we are preparing to leave, and highly impatient.

I glance over my shoulder down the long hallway. The energy disruption evaporates immediately.

It is probably something residual. We just cleansed the hallway. Some things take time to dissipate totally.

Dusty straightens his back and opens the door wide. "How about we go get us some shut-eye, Tink. I think we'd all like to head home early in the morning."

"You don't have to tell me twice," I say as I walk past him.

As soon as my butt hits the van seat, I can't help myself and text Lee again. It is getting late, and I hope for an update from him.

"Have you got anything back from him yet?"

I notice Liza craning her neck to see who I'm texting. "No. I don't know if I'm supposed to be worried or not."

Her eyes soften as she favors me a smile. "Lee said the snow was bad. He could be driving. You won't want him distracted if he is."

"I know. I'm just not good with not knowing if he's okay."

"I'm sure he's fine. He's a big boy. Maybe you should just let him take care of himself."

I know Liza is correct, but I can't ignore the uneasy feeling in my gut. Nana would tell me not to borrow trouble. That is worrying about something that hasn't taken place yet. No one has called to inform me Lee is in the hospital from an accident. Therefore, I shouldn't worry about it. Nana is wired that way. I'm not.

I worry about everything.

The van stops in front of a motel that has a giant neon stallion sign. The circa-1950 motel is done up in 1970s motif and color selection. Lots of oranges, yellows, and earth tones.

Dusty gives Liza and me a key to room seventeen, and we lug our backpacks to the room. Liza sets her backpack next to the bed furthest from the door and collapses on her bed.

"The shower is all yours if you want it. I'm going to travel sticky tomorrow," Liza announces.

"Yeah, I think it's going to be a ponytail and ballcap sort of day," I say as I sit down on my bed.

Liza shifts her body so she can look at me. She grabs at the back of her head. "Speak for yourself about the ponytail," she teases before turning her back to me.

Her body language speaks louder than any words possibly could. I know she does not want to talk about leaving Dusty. But I'm about to explode. I need to find out how she plans to tell him and when she is going. Then I must let her know I'm leaving for Baltimore in February. We will have this discussion no matter how badly both of us would prefer to ignore it.

"So, when did you plan on telling Dusty?"

She drapes her arm over her head, her nose buried in the crook of her elbow. "Do we really have to have this conversation right now, April?"

"If not now, when?"

"I don't know, just not now. What's the rush anyway?"

"I'm leaving for Baltimore in February." Sometimes it's best to just let it all run out at once. I held my secret much longer than usual. I feel a release of pressure already.

Liza sits up and stares at me. Her eyebrows draw together. She's looking at me as if I have lost my mind.

"It's true. Lee's team is based in Baltimore, and I have a friend who works for a law office in D.C. I can't pass up on that sort of opportunity." I try to sound like I have thought this all out thoroughly.

Liza's upper lip curls back. "But you can't."

I so despise it when people tell me what I can and can't do. "I need this. It may sound weak to someone like you, but I like having a guy in my life, and in particular, I like Lee. Plus, it meets the criteria that I set for myself. A large town with enormous opportunities. I can't turn this down, Liza."

"But your uncle and your brother?"

I understand how she would have a hard time understanding how I could leave *family*. "They were both doing fine before I showed up this year. I'm sure they'll do fine after I leave."

"Well, sure, before they got used to your help. You have pretty much ruined both of them now."

That doesn't make a bit of sense. "I'm sure Dusty and Howard can find their way back to how they used to do their jobs."

Liza gestures in my direction. "And what about the training on your skills? Without your two grandmothers, who can teach you that?"

I don't mean to, but I let a laugh escape. "I don't want training in my skills. The only skill I want to get better at now is litigation. I don't know if you ever check the papers, but there's not a bunch of listings for clairvoyants or expellers."

"Wow." Liza looks down her nose at me. "Some people can't appreciate anything."

That flips my switch. "How dare you. After all we've been through together, and you're gonna sit in judgment of me?"

"I'm not sitting in judgment of you. I'm just stating the facts. You are a classic case of having your cake and eating it too, and *now* you don't even want to pay for it."

I shake my head in confusion. "What does that even mean?"

"Nothing. Someone like *you* would never understand."

"Someone like me? Oh, that's real rich coming from you, Ms. I can't handle this anymore, I'll have to quit."

"I'm shaking half the time I'm on these excursions, April. I'm not doing anybody any good if I can't do my job."

"I think that's just a made-up story to cover for the real reason you're leaving. I saw you working today. You are as steady, if not more unwavering, as ever. You always have a handle on the situation. It's me who is freaking out all the time. So, no. I don't buy your phony reason. Why don't you just own up to what this is really about?"

Her jaw sets as we glare at one another. "I don't know what you're talking about," Liza says.

I almost believe her until her pupils dilate and her eyes tick briefly to the left.

"You should tell him how you feel rather than run away from it."

Liza's mouth opens and closes twice as if she is going to say something and then stops. Her shoulders are shaking. "That's just wrong, April," she croaks.

I know I hurt her, and I try to regain control of my emotions. It's not my intention to be ugly to her. I just want her to be honest with herself and not do something she'll later regret.

"Listen, I don't want to argue with you. I was just trying to bring up the point that we're both leaving Dusty at a critical time, and we need to give him as much time as possible to find our replacement."

"Forget this," Liza says as she picks up her backpack and stomps toward the door.

"Where are you going?"

"Out for a walk and then to bed." Her eyes bore into me with hostility.

"Okay, I'll leave the chain undone for you."

Her upper lip curls back again. "Don't bother. I'll room with Miles and Luis."

She slams the door before I can get another word in.

I think to chase her down. But to what end?

There is no good solution to both of us wanting to move along at the same time. Whether we talk about it for five days or not, the end result is the same. We will be leaving Dusty in a lurch.

I recheck my phone. Still nothing from Lee. I resist the temptation to send him another text. He doesn't need me badgering him.

Man, this just bites. This is what I get for trying to be honest with people. Everybody gets their feelings hurt and starts acting like it's my fault.

It isn't my fault that Liza has a crush on my brother and is too chicken to tell him. It isn't my fault that Master, Lloyd, and Johnson were a bunch of crooks, and my dream job dissipated the first day I was in Atlanta. It also isn't my fault that I have done an admirable job for both Dusty and Howard while I worked for them.

I have been transparent with *everybody* from day one. Since I moved back to Guntersville, I've been telling *everyone* I would be leaving as soon as I got the right opportunity.

And why am I feeling guilty? Why do I care that Liza got her feelings hurt?

I need to talk with somebody before I go nuckin' futs. Unfortunately, my boyfriend is MIA in a snowstorm. My best friend from middle school is acting like a jerk, and my best friend since I got back to Guntersville just stomped out of my motel room.

As Grandpa Snow used to say, if everybody's angry with you, maybe it's not them; perhaps it's you.

I just wish I knew what I was doing wrong. Whatever it is, I'm batting a thousand at pissing the stew out of everyone I come in contact with.

I am so desperate I almost call Mama. I decide against it. I don't need any more harsh, truthful coaching.

Exhaling, I take the offramp from my emotional highway. I'm just tired. I need sleep, and in the morning, everything will be right as rain.

I strip down to my bra and panties then shuffle to the bathroom vanity, trying not to think about the stickiness of the carpet on the soles of my feet. I wash the little bit of makeup remaining on my face and brush my teeth.

I feel better and enjoy a few minutes of surfing the web on my phone. Still, I become perturbed as the preponderance of good news posted by my overly happy friends makes me question why I'm such a dysfunctional freak.

They are all posting about their dreamy lives, with their flawless husbands and their perfect children. Meanwhile, I sit all alone in a seventy-year-old motel in Shelbyville, Tennessee.

It is effortless to feel sorry for myself right now. And I'm doing an excellent job of it.

With resignation, I turn out the lights and lie back on my pillows, staring at the ceiling with the small horizontal line of light the top of the blinds lets in. It is going to be a long night.

Chapter 35

It's odd how when my mind slows, it will allow some of the most obscure images to bubble to the surface. As I wait for sleep to overcome me, I have a vision of Toby Graves playing kickball in third grade.

I was still shy in third grade. I had a significant crush on Toby and not a clue on how to let him know.

He was taller than most boys our age, and I remember how he had a bridge of freckles across his upturned nose. He could make the entire class laugh by wiggling his ears. Toby was fun, loud, and had unparalleled athletic abilities in our PE class at the age of nine.

At the time, he was the ideal boy—man to me.

I haven't thought of Toby in many years. But whenever I do, I always smile as I remember he was the first boy I was ever going to marry.

He didn't know it, and I didn't have a clue how to let him in on my secret.

It was an overcast day toward the end of our third-grade year. I was playing second base on the kickball team that was playing Toby's team. It was Toby's team because Toby was always the player picked first regardless of who the team captain was.

This was a day that became a part of student mythology at

LBJ Elementary School. It was brought up in select circles as late as my senior year in high school.

Toby came up to kick six times that day, and all six turns were grand slams. He was also the pitcher that day and rolled a perfect game with all six innings, my team going three and out.

Even those of us on the losing team were in awe as he strung the perfect game together. I've never seen such total domination since, and I'm an Alabama football fan.

***

I feel the cool air whipping my loose hair against my cheeks. I push the more unruly strands back from my face.

There is a collective groan from most of my team as Toby comes off the sideline and trots to home plate. If he had thought to look at me standing to the left of second base, I'm sure he would think I am a loon. I am in complete admiration of his short-cropped strawberry blonde hair, standing upright in the wind, and his cocky smile.

Becky Bucktooth, our pitcher on the mound, turns and instructs everyone to back up. I take three steps back, knowing that in all likelihood, it will not matter.

Becky turns and rolls the ball quickly. As it comes toward Toby, it hits a rock and begins to skip and bounce wildly. Toby, undeterred by the bounce and wild roll of the ball, steps forward, planting his left foot just past the ball before swinging his right leg, toe pointed down, at the ball. His foot disappears behind the ball. *Thwank!* The red ball soars off his foot as the rubber band sound reaches my ears.

"That one's gone!" Richard Travis says as he crosses in front of me, trotting to second base. The ball continues to gain altitude long after it went directly over my head.

I can't help but admire the flight of it as our centerfielder first backpedals, then turns and runs as fast as he can toward the woods. Seconds later, you can hear the rubber ball crashing through pine tree limbs as it works its way down the branches.

I turn back to the field just in time to see Toby rounding first. He isn't smiling like he usually does. He has a very stoic expression for any nine-year-old.

Toby breaks from the baseline, jogs, and then slows to a walk as he comes toward me. "I haven't seen you in ages, Maple."

Both the forgotten nickname and the fact Toby is talking to me in my dream shake me. "Yeah," I reply most eloquently.

One of my girlfriends that year, I forget who now, maybe Erin Beverly, was kidding me about my name, saying she would call me May April instead of April May. Then she thought May April sounded like Maple. Luckily it only stuck during third grade.

"Did you forget?"

Toby still has the same effect on me. I find it hard to breathe and nearly impossible to talk. He is so handsome it is painful.

"The appointment," he prods.

Still, I'm staring at him with my mouth slightly open.

"Your grandpa told you I would be coming to visit. Remember? I'm the Ghost of Christmas Spent."

My stomach flips. Sweat trickles from my underarms in a rush as reality tries to shake me from my adolescent lust.

This can't be happening. This is just a dream. I've been concerned about what my grandpa said, and now I'm dreaming it.

Toby extends his hand toward me. "We probably should be getting started. We don't have all night." He grins and wiggles his ears. "Actually, we have all the time in the world."

I'm in full panic mode now. Every alarm in my body is going off. I know I am in trouble. If I am time-traveling again, I must wake up and stop this madness.

"Wake up, April. Wake up, April. Wake up, April!" I chant.

Toby tilts his head and chuckles. "Don't worry. I won't get you caught in the void if that's what you're worried about."

No. This is a dream. I'm asleep. I'm twenty-seven years old, and I'm just having a dream, or maybe a sleeping memory of a past event. I almost convince myself until I look down and see my flat chest and battleship-sized feet I have not grown into yet.

This is getting way too real for me.

"You can trust me," Toby tries to assure me.

I've had enough bad experiences with boys who used that exact phrase before, so it doesn't exactly calm my nerves. Even if that were not the case, my fear of the void is real.

The idea of spending eternity caught between two times with no sensory input for all eternity petrifies me. I get bored having to wait fifteen minutes past my nail appointment at the beauty college, and there are magazines to flip through there.

"This can be a blessing if you treat it that way."

I lose myself in Toby's beautiful hazel eyes.

This isn't a dream. Or at least I begin to believe it isn't a dream.

The cold breeze at my back blowing my hair forward feels too natural and familiar. I can hear old man Wilson running the tractor in front of the school, mowing the grass. I can even smell the scent of fresh-cut clover in the wind. I've had vivid dreams before, but never ones that took such care of the smallest detail.

And, of course, there is Toby. Toby, in all his youthful masculinity, balances on edge between handsome and cute. The gold standard for elementary alpha males with good looks ... before the end.

It had been a brutal end. Not just for Toby, but for all of us at the elementary school.

His parents had sought to save us all by allowing him to stay at home. It would've been best for him. It would be easier for him to have rested during the day.

Toby was too much of a fighter for that. He refused to be treated differently than anyone else. He insisted that he would get better, and he did not want to get behind in his school work.

From the start of his diagnosis of bone cancer, two weeks before Halloween of our fourth-grade year, he was locked in an epic battle with the disease.

Cancer would have him in a death hold for weeks on end, and by the time Christmas break neared, we all feared we would not see our friend in the new year. But to our surprise, the last three days before Christmas break, he was on top of the disease and kicking its butt. For those three days, he was the old smiling Toby, minus a few pounds.

He returned to us at the start of the year, and the battle continued. Each time, the disease would win for more extended periods. Still, Toby would always make a recovery for a day or two, and the entertaining young man we all knew him to be would return to us.

March 15, the ides of March, Toby missed his first day of school. The date didn't mean anything to me at the time. It was not until my freshman year in high school, as I read Julius Caesar, that the betrayal of that day stuck in my mind like a bullet too close to my heart to ever be removed. March 15 was the day Toby's body ultimately betrayed him.

He never was able to come back to school. And on Good Friday, he passed. I cried that entire Easter weekend.

Daddy took me to Toby's funeral over Mama's objection. She had told Daddy I was too young.

He disagreed and said that if I wanted to, I should pay my respects. Mama was right. The little boy in the casket looked like a little old man.

I barely recognized him.

I knew at that moment that we had all lost something special.

Now, here he is in front of me the way I always wanted to remember him. I reach out and take his hand. I don't know what I was expecting, but it is warm and human and fits my hand perfectly like I always knew it would.

Toby favors me with a lopsided grin and looks down toward the ground when he says, "You might want to hold onto more than my hand for the journey. I wouldn't want you to get separated."

I have waited two decades to hug him, and I will not let the opportunity pass. I place my hip to his and wrap both arms around him. It feels like we are spinning the next moment, and I hear his familiar laugh in the wind.

Our destination, the school lunchroom, is quite anti-climactic. I release my death grip on Toby as soon as my head quits spinning.

"You know where we are?" Toby asks.

"Our cafeteria."

He wiggles his ears. "Friday. Pizza day. My personal favorite."

"It wasn't bad," I comment as I follow him down the aisle of what seems like too-short tables. I hear the din of talk and laughter, but it is as if it is muted just enough that Toby and I can have a civil conversation.

Toby stops at the end of the aisle and points toward a skinny, blonde-headed little girl sitting on her knees, talking excitedly. "Recognize her?"

I've seen her in the mirror every morning of my life. "That would be me." I'm getting a sick feeling in my gut as to where this is headed.

I am having a discussion with Jackie Rains and Leslie Pater. Whatever I'm saying seems to be much more important than what the other two girls are saying. I appear to be the leader of the group.

Funny, that's not how I remember it.

"Why are we here, Toby?"

He glances at me and grins. "Have a little patience, April."

I notice the nickname is gone now. That makes me sad.

To my horror, I see Becky Gray coming toward our table. I hang my head and look at the floor. I don't think I can watch this train wreck.

"Hi, April. Is that seat taken?" Becky's familiar voice is unmistakable, and it draws my eyes up from the floor.

"You bet it's taken," I watch myself tell Becky.

Becky blinks hard and then forces another smile as she points to the open seat next to Jackie but still directs her question toward me. "What about that seat?"

"Uh, no. Taken," I say with my hands on my hip.

Becky's face falters, but she recovers quickly. "Who's sitting there?"

"None of your beeswax," Leslie kicks in.

I watch in horror as I shake my head and say, "Truth is, Becky, we're all afraid that buck teeth might be contagious."

I feel sick as my words come back to haunt me. Mean words spoken by a mean girl to someone she now works with regularly.

Leslie immediately bursts into laughter, and a pleased smile blooms across my young face as I greedily take in the extra attention.

Becky stands in front of us with her mouth open. She is too shocked to move.

"Close your mouth and go somewhere else, loser," Leslie chides Becky.

Becky's chin tucks against her chest, and her lower lip trembles. She turns to leave, and her milk tumbles off of her tray. As she crouches to pick it up, the contents of her tray almost fall to the floor.

"That was mean, guys," Jackie scolds us as soon as Becky is out of earshot.

"She's just some loser, Jackie," Leslie says.

I roll my eyes. "Nobody likes her, Jackie."

"That doesn't mean you get to be mean to her."

My eyes bulge. "So, I should let her sit with us?"

"I don't know." Jackie crosses her arms. "It just doesn't feel right."

No. It doesn't. I did enjoy Leslie's laughter, but it was short-lived.

Later that day, I *did* feel bad about what I had said to Becky. Not that she couldn't sit with us, but the comment about her buck teeth. It's not like she'd made herself buck-toothed. She couldn't help that.

I'm so wrapped up in my thoughts of that day I miss that Toby is moving toward the cafeteria exit. I have to jog to catch up with him. "Where are you going?"

"We've got a few more stops."

I follow him in silence. When the silence isn't working for

me any longer, I ask, "So, are you in heaven, Toby?"

"Something like that," he says as he winks at me.

Toby walks toward the bathroom. The entryway Ys. Boys to the left, girls to the right. Toby turns to the right.

"Did you forget how to read?" I tease him.

"No one can see us."

"Yeah, but you can still see, which makes you a peeping Tom."

"Or, more accurately, a peeping Toby?"

I take in his smile and think that he is having way too much fun with this. Me? I'm feeling like a schmuck. But I suppose I earned it.

The cry of a wounded animal shakes me from my thoughts. I follow Toby to the last stall in the girls' bathroom, which appears to be the origin of the sound.

Toby makes eye contact with me. He raises a hand to the stall door, which lightens in color. A slight circular mist appears in the center that dissipates, leaving a transparent porthole into the private area.

I see the dark chestnut hair cropped just above the ears of Becky Gray as she sits on the commode. Her shoulders shake with each sob, and I feel the guilt tear through me.

"Becky, I'm sorry."

Toby glances over his shoulder at me and exhales. "You can talk to her if you wish, but she can't hear you."

I wonder if maybe she can feel my presence like I experience when a ghost is in the room. Am I a ghost?

No. I don't want to go down that tangent. Besides, if Becky could sense my presence, it probably wouldn't be while she's sobbing her eyes out.

"I was young. I was just trying to fit in, myself."

Toby holds up a hand to stop me as he shrinks back from me. "This isn't about me, April. I'm not on this plane anymore. This is for your benefit. Nobody is judging you here."

That isn't entirely true. I'm judging myself, and I find my old self quite lacking. Why did I think I could hide my insecurities of not being included by making someone else feel insecure and excluded? There is no logic to it.

"I think I get the point. I think we're done here."

"Are you sure?" Toby asks.

I can only nod my head. My empathy for Becky is kicking in. If I stay any longer, I will be sobbing along with her.

Toby turns to me and grasps my shoulders. Without warning, we are spinning in the air again. Color smears like oil paint on a palette, and the smell of ozone fills the air.

When we land, I feel that I have been spun on my heels for hundreds of rotations and my body lists to the left. I spread my legs wide and grab at the sofa in front of me as I wait to regain my balance.

There is nothing familiar about the small living room. I have never been here before.

The apartment is decorated in eclectic pastels with small animal figurines on almost every flat surface. From our vantage point from behind the sofa, I can see into a small kitchen with pots and pans hanging from the ceiling and a small two-chair dinette next to a window lit by the early-morning sun.

I like the apartment a lot. It is very homey and makes me want to smile

"Where are we?" I ask Toby.

He holds up a finger advising me to wait. I suppose Toby's done preaching the patience is a virtue thing to me.

"Don't be obtuse about this, Randy," I hear the feminine voice from the hallway to our right.

A chill runs through my body, and I feel ill. My jaw clenches as I glower at Toby. "Why would you bring me here?"

His brow wrinkles. "Because you need to know."

I can't possibly imagine what I need to know about Jackie Rains, the backstabbing, steal your boyfriend out from under you, fake friend. I know everything there is to know about Jackie Rains.

So, this is her apartment. No wonder there are so many stupid little dog and kitty cat figurines littered everywhere like some old granny's knickknack antique store.

I suppose it's her idea of fashionable since she's a veterinarian from Auburn University. The *cow* college.

She obviously doesn't have any home-making sense either. Anybody in their right mind would have put slatted blinds up so they wouldn't have their vision permanently impaired by the sun.

And what's with all the pots and pans hanging from the ceiling? Like I'm so sure she cooks.

My nemesis appears from the hallway, and momentarily I'm concerned she might see me as she looks toward the sofa. She moves toward me, every hair of her long, chocolate-colored hair pulled back expertly into a perfect ponytail accented with a yellow bow.

"I'm not being—whatever you called me." Randy appears from the hallway. "It's just she's been both our friend."

Jackie turns the TV on and selects a channel. Soft classic rock begins to play.

Jackie is ignoring Randy.

"Jackie." Randy tilts his head.

Jackie slams a hand to her hip. "What?"

"She's a friend," he insists.

"No, Randy. She's your ex-girlfriend and my former friend. *Not* friend."

Randy walks over to her and takes her hands in his. Jackie's shoulders slump as she blows a puff of exacerbated breath.

"Come on, Jackie. Weddings are about new beginnings. Can't we just start over? Everybody deserves a second chance."

Jackie pulls a hand free and pinches the bridge of her nose. "Randy, I hear you, baby. But do you think I like not being able to talk to the person that used to be my best friend? Do you think I like the way she always acts like I've done something wrong by falling in love with you when you two weren't even dating anymore?"

Randy shrugs. "You know April. She just likes the drama."

Jackie pulls her other hand loose as she laughs. "Maybe your idea of drama is really messed up. I mean, I told you. When she brought that cute keeshond in last week. I swear I thought she was going to punch me in the face."

"You know that's not true. April just has that way of looking at people kind of—"

"Like she wants to stab you in the eye."

Randy put his hands in his pockets. "Well, yeah. But she's never done anything like that."

"I don't care to be her first victim."

Randy moves close again and takes her hands in his. "Now who's being the drama queen?"

"You'll be awfully sorry if I come back from work and I've got an eye poked out."

Randy wraps his arms around the small of her back and puts his nose inches from hers. "You're too fast to let that happen." He gives Jackie a peck on the lips.

"I might be distracted and move out of the way too late," she pouts.

"Hmm. Not my warrior princess. Nobody ever gets the drop on you."

Randy kisses her on the lips, and I can feel the sexual tension in the air. I clear my throat as I begin to feel like some sort of sick sexual voyeur.

"Okay. You win. I'll send April an invitation," Jackie says.

"See, now doesn't that feel better. It's always better to forgive people."

"I'm doing it for you, *not her*." Jackie pushes his hands off of her waist as she turns for the kitchen. "Besides, I have no doubt she will throw the invitation away without even opening the envelope."

I feel the heat of embarrassment flash across my face. I hang my head in disgrace as Jackie is correct. One worse, I had torn the unread invitation into twenty pieces *before* I threw it away.

The happy couple walks into the kitchen. To be fair, Jackie seems to like Randy a lot more than I ever did. I always found him to be sort of underfoot and underwhelming in the intelligence department. It doesn't seem to bother Jackie.

Man. Jackie really needs to put some blinds up in their kitchen. The morning sun is coming through, and I have to hold my hand up as a visor not to go blind.

"Hey, are you hungry?"

That seems like an odd thing for a ghost to be asking me. I struggle to get the sun out of my eyes.

"April, wake up. Dusty's not going to wait all morning for us. You don't want to make the trip on an empty stomach."

"Liza?"

"You know it's not Prince Charming because I didn't give you a big wet kiss on the lips. Frankly, after last night you're lucky I don't smack you upside your head."

I sit up, struggling to shake the cobwebs from my mind. "Did you sleep here?"

She huffs. "No. I told you I was going to room with Luis and Miles last night."

"What time is it?"

Liza yanks the covers away from me. "Time for you to get up." She claps her hands twice. "Chop, chop."

Blessedly, Liza leaves the room after prodding me to get up. I go to the vanity and check my reflection in the mirror.

Sigh of relief. I'm the twenty-seven-year-old April Snow version.

I don't know what I expected, but the ghost visit was not as bad as I anticipated. In some small way, it was nice to see the Toby I fell in love with when I was in elementary school.

Reality hits me like a cold shower.

Everybody hates me. I'm an awful person.

This has to be the most uncomfortable revelation of my life. Sure, I know I'm no saint, but I never considered myself cruel and despised.

I mean, for heaven's sake, the only person taking up for me is an ex-boyfriend with an extremely low IQ. *Darn it!* I just did it again.

How do you fix something like that? I don't like being judgmental, and I don't like being petty, but it just comes so easily to me. It's like I'm sort of hardwired that way. How can I change a natural tendency?

"Thank you, Grandpa Hirsch. I really appreciate you making me feel like dirt," I yell.

"Are you okay, April?" My brother Dusty is standing in my doorway.

"Yeah. Sure. Why do you ask?"

Dusty scratches the back of his head. "Liza said you were acting funny this morning, and you two had an argument last night."

I favor him one of my fake beauty pageant smiles. "Nothing to see here. Thank you for your concern, though, dear brother..."

Dusty's eyebrows pull together as he nods. "Okay, good." He gestures over his shoulder. "We'll be leaving in five."

"I'll be there with bells on." I favor him with another award-winning smile.

Chapter 36

I pull my ponytail through the back of a ball cap and brush my teeth. That will have to do for today. Besides, we're just catching breakfast, then riding home anyway.

As we pile into the van, I pray Dusty has found someplace to eat besides the café we ate at for lunch yesterday. My prayers are answered as he tells us we'll stop in Fayetteville to eat breakfast at a pancake restaurant.

I text Lee right after getting in the van. After fifteen minutes, I decide he has had plenty of time to answer me, and it is time to make it real.

I dial his number. The phone goes to voicemail. "Hey, baby. Just really concerned about you. When you get a chance, please give me a call and let me know that everything's okay."

"Still no word from him?" Liza asks.

"Nope, and don't tell me he's probably still driving."

Liza crosses her arms and looks away from me.

Yeah. I've got a lot to work on.

I replay Toby's visit from last night. In many ways, I feel cheated. Toby only showed me the terrible things I have done. I know I've done some good things in my life, too. Why wouldn't he show me those?

Because it would take a whole lot of good to make up for the way I treated Becky Gray in elementary school or how I turned on Jackie Rains our last year in high school. He could've shown me, but it wouldn't have evened the scales.

I have so many issues to work through that it takes me a while to realize that the rest of the crew is way too quiet. "Is there something wrong?"

Dusty glances at me in the rearview mirror as Miles turns and looks at me with a tight frown.

"Luis," Dusty says.

Luis leans forward to talk in front of Liza on the bench seat. "I couldn't sleep last night."

Glad to know I'm not the only one who isn't sleeping these days. I wonder if Luis's ghost let him relive all the times he helped old ladies cross the street when he was in the Scouts.

"So, I decided to go back over the audiovisual," he continues.

"Please tell me the visuals from the hallway are good," I say as my gut sinks.

His face lights up. "Oh. They're more than good. They're spectacular."

I make a point of looking at everyone in turn. "And that's a bad thing?"

"Oh, no," Luis says. "The video saved the entire trip. This won't be a lead story, but it can easily be a number two or three now."

Luis has been hanging around Miles too long. He seems to be working the suspense factor subconsciously.

"The audio is the problem."

I shrug. "The audio is not so important for the books. If this was one of the film sessions coming up, it would be a big deal, but for the books, it's not as critical." Everyone is still somber-faced. I laugh nervously. "Did I miss a punch line?"

"We have perfect audio, April. Of an entity stringing to-gether expletives that I didn't even know could be combined as adjectives and adverbs. A very loose translation would be, 'Get out or die.'"

I swoon as Luis tells me what the entity had been saying. Still, I don't understand the long faces. "But that's cool, we expelled him or her."

Nobody says anything as I look to each of the team members. They all look away from me. "Bless it. What aren't y'all telling me?"

"Timing up the audio with the video, the cursing and threats were while Liza was expelling the ghost the first time *and* during the second blessing."

I knew I felt something nasty breathing down my neck. It kept hiding in the shadows, and I never could get a direct bead on it. If I could have just been sure last night, we could have—"Hey. Wait, why are we leaving? We need to go back to the theater and clear it out."

"We have done everything we can do," Dusty says.

I snort a laugh. "Seriously? We left an angry entity in the theater waiting to pounce on the next unsuspecting person it crosses paths with."

"Perhaps. But Liza is our expeller, and she blessed the entire site. If she wasn't able to clear it out, we're out of cards to play. We'll have to suggest Heather White employ a priest for cleansing the building."

Butterflies take flight in my stomach. I'm grateful that Dusty is unaware that Granny thinks I have a tremendous ability to be an expeller. First, I don't want the responsibility. Second, I can barely control the "gifts" I have already been working on with Nana. I can only imagine how bad I can mess up an exorcism. Third, I'm not long for this ghost-hunting gig.

Still, if Liza's skill set doesn't cover *everything* that we may run into, I might have to rethink my decision.

"I'll contact the local dioceses on Monday and see if we can set something up for Heather. Then I'll call her and bring her up to speed on the situation and the solution," Dusty says.

"Well. I don't want to rain on your parade. Still, that woman is gonna be upset when she realizes you burned eight historically significant theater seats and failed to expel the evil spirit."

"Hey, for a top-shelf story for the next book, I'll deal with an upset property owner and gladly pay for a priest and some new chairs."

"Amen to that," Miles says.

I wish I could be so cavalier about it. But I know that what I felt is both powerful, old, and sneaky. It knew when to hide and when to come out.

I hope the church sends a cardinal rather than a priest.

Chapter 37

Dusty pulls our van into the truck parking at Jeffrey's Giant Flapjacks. I'm too hungry to be overly concerned about the taste of the food. Still, the parking lot is filled to capacity, including people parking on the grass, which I take as a good sign.

As we walk in, I know Dusty has found a diamond in the rough. The smell of crispy bacon and flapjacks floats in the air, engulfing me as if giving me a warm hug.

I sure hope they have blueberry syrup. That would make it perfect.

My phone vibrates. I look down and see Lee's name on caller ID, and my heart skips. "Hello?" I hold my hand to my other ear and duck away from my team.

"Hey, baby. I was just checking in." Lee sounds out of breath. I can hear the wind whistling past him.

"Where are you? I've been worried."

"Sorry, babe." I hear him pant. "We're south of Millersville now."

"Why does it sound like you're winded? And outside?"

He laughs and then pulls in a labored breath. "Because we are."

I tense as I feel tears welling in my eyes. "What do you mean, Lee? What's going on? Why aren't you in the Bronco, Lee?"

"Slow down, baby. The highways are a mess from all the eighteen-wheelers that flipped over, so we decided to take some country backroads to get around the traffic. The snow is coming down really hard, so it is nearly impossible to make out where the road ends, and the shoulder begins."

My anxiety builds. I just need answers. "What happened?"

"The right side of the truck caught a ditch. We sort of rolled the Bronco."

"Oh lord, Lee! Are you okay?"

"Sure. All three of us are fine. We probably could use a change of shorts. The truck is a total loss."

"It's got to be freezing outside. How long before the police are there to help you?"

Lee laughs and then struggles to catch his breath. "I'd say about a week."

"A week?" I must've misunderstood him.

"Baby, it's like the wild, wild West out here right now. Half the state is out of power, the highways have all been closed, and first responders aren't even braving the weather just yet. Everybody is on their own."

"But, Lee. You don't have a car. You guys can't go traipsing around in a snowstorm. You got to get help."

"Baby, don't worry. It's just like going hunting without a gun. We'll be fine."

The line crackles. I fear I will lose connection with Lee. "Can I call somebody?"

"No, baby. If there was somebody to call, I would've already done that. Just chill. We've got this."

I hear one of Lee's companions say something. It is garbled in the wind and the lousy cell line.

"Hey. Listen, Bob thinks he sees a barn up ahead. We're going to go check it out and get out of the snow for a while. I'll give you a call a little later."

The line is dropping in and out. "Lee, just keep me on the line, so I know if you make it to the barn."

"I love you too, baby."

"Lee!" The line goes dead. It takes all the discipline I have not to redial his cell phone number.

I can see the headlines later this week. Three key Baltimore professional baseball team players were found frozen to death in a snowbank from the freak winter storm.

Get that out of your head, April. Granny would tell you that if you think it, you'll manifest it.

I've had several boyfriends in the last six months and lost all of them to circumstances beyond my control. I sure don't want to start having them dying in snowstorms. And I especially don't want to help by bringing on the tragedy.

He's going to make it home. Lee will be home safe to celebrate Christmas with me. I close my eyes and chant the two simple, short sentences repeatedly in my mind. If I drill it into my head long enough, I will believe it and give strength to his chances of coming home safe.

I can't do it. I am worried sick that I may have just had the last conversation I'll ever have with Lee Darby. It would kill me. I'll simply die if something happens to him.

Life can't be this cruel. It's one thing not to have something. It's entirely different to experience the joy only to have it ripped away from you. What I feel for Lee is real. I have already begun to build my future on the bedrock that is our relationship.

I can't start over now. I don't have the energy.

My eyes are dry. I'm too sad and heartbroken to even cry. The only thing I can think to do is back myself into a corner, slide to the floor, and curl up into a ball.

I just want the world to go away.

Get a hold of yourself, April. You're just being melodramatic.

Lee and his friends are accomplished athletes and hunters. They'll be fine.

It's you that is in danger of driving yourself crazy over something you can't affect. All the worry in the world won't melt one snowflake in Maryland.

Okay, I can do this. I cross my arms and rock to and fro. I must stay busy and not think about what Lee is doing. Stay active, keep my mind occupied, and don't worry.

I start back to join my team and take a detour to the ladies' room. I stare into the large mirror as the door shuts behind me.

A thought crosses my mind. It is risky, and Nana would disapprove, but I check the two stalls to ensure no one else is in the bathroom.

Once I'm convinced I'm alone, I rummage in my purse and extract the golf-ball-sized crystal sphere Nana gave me to practice viewings.

Of course, I dropped it in my purse the day she gave it to me and have totally forgotten about it until now. But to be fair, she did instruct me that I should only use it in extreme circumstances. I knew Nana, and I would have a difference of opinion over this event being extreme, but I must know where Lee is and how they are faring.

I cup the small milky-white crystal in my left hand as I visualize Lee's face and direct as much energy as I can muster in my sad state toward the crystal. The opaque white swirls, becoming a bright white.

I continue to watch, waiting for the vision to clarify. The realization comes slowly for me. The image is as coherent as it will become. It is of a white-out blizzard.

My gut clenches with fear as I see firsthand how dire the weather conditions are in Maryland. This snowstorm looks like something that belongs in Alaska, not Maryland.

I move the crystal left and then to the right to adjust the point of view. There is a small, dark shadow in the distance, and I move toward it with the large clumping snowflakes now blowing directly toward me.

It is a barn. The old gray planks curl outward at the edges, and the barn has a distinct list to the right by several degrees. A fair amount of snow has already accumulated on its A-shaped roofline.

My point of view floats through the large double doors. A two-by-six bars the door from inside. The barn houses several pieces of farm equipment in varying degrees of disassembly. The floor is hard mud frozen to the point that small spikes of frozen soil rise up.

I notice a ladder leading to the loft and adjust the crystal view up the ladder. The loft is full of loose hay and nothing else.

My spirits are falling quickly. My hope was that this was the barn Lee had talked about from the road. Is it possible that it *is* the barn, and they didn't make it? Could they be in a snowbank further out from the barn?

A voice that I don't recognize speaks in my mind. "These pillows sure are good for warming my hands."

"Those aren't pillows." Another voice I don't recognize says.

"How about them Bears?" That voice I do recognize clearly as I rush toward the middle of the loft. Looking down into a large indention, I find three grown men lying in a triple-spoon position. They are laughing as if at summer camp and telling the best joke ever.

On the one hand, I'm greatly relieved to see they have found cover. But it doesn't alleviate my fear in the least.

I have seen what awaits them outside, and without any help, there is no telling how long they will be stranded in the barn. How long can they last without food and heat?

I am grateful they are in good spirits, but it also could be false bravado. The situation looks dire, and there is nothing I can do to help them.

It is almost impossible, but I tear myself away from looking at the crystal. Nana had warned me of its addictive nature. She may have understated the danger. If I'm being truthful, I would love to settle in and watch over Lee and his teammates until they back home safely.

I drop the crystal back into its velvet bag and replace it in my purse. I nearly pull it out a second time to see if I can locate a street address but manage to leave it in my purse.

What good is knowing the street address if the first responders can't get out to help in the storm? Until the storm clears, there is nothing to be done.

Plus, I can't hide out in the ladies' bathroom of Jeffrey's Giant Flapjacks forever. That would be too weird even for me.

I force myself out of the ladies' room and trudge back to my team. I'm surprised to see my teammates are almost done eating breakfast. I sit down heavily next to Liza.

"Is everything okay?" she asks.

I start to say something and choke on the words. I shake my head no and lower my eyes.

Liza puts her arm around my shoulder. "Eat some pancakes. It'll cheer you up."

I'm not hungry. I'm too sad to eat.

Chapter 38

Once we're home, I know better than to let myself sulk in my apartment. I go to my parents' house and find Daddy watching old Christmas movies.

After the second one ends, he makes us some sandwiches. Puppy and I curl up together on the loveseat.

I wake up disoriented. Loud voices are coming from the kitchen.

It crosses my mind that possibly the next Christmas ghost has made their appearance and not introduced themself to me.

As I pad into the kitchen, I have to wipe my eyes to make sure I see Barbara Elliott talking to Chase and Daddy. Puppy is by their side, looking at Barbara with the same adoration as the two men.

"Barbara?"

She turns her head and smiles. "Oh, April. I'm sorry. Did I wake you?"

"No. I was—"

She surprises me with a full hug.

"It's so good to see you. It's been a while since I saw you at Rex's."

Barbara was my idol when I was in middle school. She is who I wanted to grow up and be like.

She still has her dancer's body and her beautiful smile. What sets Barbara apart from every other woman is her ability to make you feel like you are standing in the sunshine when she is near.

Some days I hate my brother for having screwed up their relationship. I'm not sure what he did to run her off, but she should be my sister-in-law.

"I've been a little overly busy lately."

"I know. Chase tells me you're burning the candle at both ends. Working for Dusty and for your uncle, I don't see how you keep up."

I gesture toward the sofa. "I guess that's why I pass out like an old lady in front of the TV. Not much of a social life, I'm afraid."

Barbara smirks. "That's not what I hear. Chase tells me that you and Lee Darby are getting along together really well." She wiggles her eyebrows.

"Yeah. He's stuck in a snowstorm up in Baltimore right now."

"I heard about that storm. There's a lot of people without power. I'm sure he'll be fine."

If it had been anyone other than Barbara, it would irk me that she assumes Lee will be alright. People say stuff like that all the time without really knowing if it is true. But for some reason, when Barbara says it, it has a calming influence on my troubled mind.

"What brings you out here?" I ask.

She rolls her eyes playfully. "I was out doing some last-minute Christmas shopping, and my car battery died. I'm not sure if I left the light on or if it's just a bad call. Lo and behold, guess who pulls up next to me as I'm popping the hood to check the battery connections." She gestures toward Chase. "My knight in shining armor."

"It was all some elaborate hoax on Barbara's part to let me play the handy mechanic friend for her," Chase says.

She laughs. "Right. Because I just knew you would be pulling in at Anna's Accessories Attic."

"A man can't have too many hairbands," Chase jokes.

"I was wondering," I drawl.

"I'm still trying to find some stocking stuffers for Mama. She's getting harder and harder to buy for each Christmas," Chase explains.

"Those homemade Christmas cards with construction paper aren't working for you anymore?" Barbara asks.

He shakes his head and feigns dejection. "They don't get the reaction they used to."

"Imagine that."

Watching the two interact drives me crazy. Barbara and Chase could virtually set a room on fire in high school, and the chemistry has *never* diminished.

They just ignore it now, and they are the only two who can ignore it. Every time I see them together, I want to scream, "What's wrong with you two? Just get married and have a bunch of uber-cute and sweet babies already!"

"I was about to put together some chicken Alfredo for dinner, Barbara. Why don't you stay?" Daddy asked.

"I don't know, Mr. Snow." Barbara looks to Chase.

He sobers somewhat and shrugs. "That's up to you, Barbara."

I feel it is time for me to intervene. Number one, because I still hold out hope that one day these two numbskulls will realize their love is too rare to throw away. Number two, before Barbara showed up, Daddy hadn't even mentioned cooking dinner.

Chicken Alfredo is one of my favorite dishes. I suspect the only reason he offered is that he knows it is one of Barbara's favorite dishes.

"Come on, Barbara. It's been ages since you ate dinner with us. Besides, it's Christmas. It gives us all a chance to catch up." I hope I don't sound too desperate.

"Are you sure it's not any trouble, Mr. Snow? I don't want to impose." She tucks her chin slightly as she asks.

"No trouble at all. But you have to stay in the kitchen and keep me company."

"Deal," Barbara says.

Chase gestures toward the door. "I'm gonna go check the alternator and test the battery while Dad's cooking."

Barbara's smile loses some of its shine. "Okay. Thank you, Chase."

"Don't mention it."

As Barbara settles in at the sink while Daddy pulls ingredients from the refrigerator and Chase leaves out the side door, I'm torn about which direction I want to go. I would like to stay in the sunny spot and hang out with Daddy and Barbara while they catch up and cook dinner, but I also want to go to the mechanic shed and bounce a large wrench off my brother's hard skull. For the good of all romance in the world, I roll my eyes as I open the sliding glass door and march toward the shed.

Chase's long legs have already carried him to the shed's door. "Hey. Wait up," I yell.

He rolls up the overhead door. I catch up with him as he walks toward Barbara's car in the driveway.

"What do you need?" he asks as he walks by me.

"What's that about?"

"What are you talking about?" he says as he gets into her car.

Shaking my head, I walk back up to the shed and wait. He pulls her car into the bay. As he gets out, I pick up the conversation. "Why did you leave?"

"I didn't leave. I need to check Barbara's car over and make sure she doesn't have anything more serious than having maybe left her lights on."

"Well, you seem like you got perturbed that she is staying for dinner."

His eyes narrow. "I'm not perturbed. Barbara can do whatever she wants to do. She doesn't need my permission for anything."

I let out an unladylike grunt. "Y'all were getting along so well in there."

"Because we are friends."

"You know you two are more than that."

Chase glares at me. "No. We are not, April. Don't you have enough going on in your relationship to butt out of mine?"

"Well, I do have a lot happening in my relationship. Thank you for asking. But I still think it necessary to take the time to make sure that my boneheaded brother doesn't screw up his life."

Chase's expression contorts into a severe frown. "Who are you?" He pops the hood. The driver's door slams shut.

I follow him to the overhead door as he pulls it shut. "I'm your sister, and I love you so much that I'm willing to get into your business."

The door strikes the pavement and rattles. Chase turns and points his finger at me. "You shouldn't get into business that you don't know anything about, April."

I throw my arms up. "How am I supposed to know when it's been some huge secret for the last eleven years, Chase? I mean, Barbara was in my life, our family's lives, every day for years, and then all of a sudden … nothing. No Barbara, no explanation, nothing, and you think that that's okay?"

Chase's shoulders rise to his ears as his mouth opens. At first, I expect he is about to scream, then he relaxes. "Do you understand that Barbara was dating *me* and not you or our family? If you want to date her, I suggest you let Mr. *Lee Darby* know and then take it up with Barbara."

I didn't think it possible, but my ire raises another notch. "And that's another thing. What's with your condescending attitude toward Lee?"

"What are you talking about now?"

"What do you have against Lee?"

Chase opens the hood of Barbara's car as he grabs a wire brush. "I don't know what you're yammering about. You're just acting crazy, April."

I march toward him, pointing my finger at him this time. "No. You don't get to do that. You don't get to dismiss me by calling me crazy."

He cuts his eyes up toward me from under the hood. "Then tell me how I can get rid of you. I'm working here."

"You're not working. You're doing your ex-girlfriend a favor. You get paid for work."

"I'd pay you twenty dollars right now to leave me alone," he grumbles.

"You're unbelievable. I don't know why I even try."

"Me either. But I wish you *wouldn't*."

I can't help it. I just can't stay mad at Chase long enough to affect any positive change. I hate myself for it, but I burst into laughter.

Chase stops scrubbing on the battery terminal with the wire brush as his shoulders shake. He can't hold it any longer and laughs with me.

"Lord, you are impossible," I tell him.

"It's not exactly rainbows and free fishing lures being your brother, either."

I sigh. "You really don't feel anything for Barbara anymore?"

Chase winces. "I feel a lot. She's a great friend, I've got a lot of good memories of our time together, and I hope every day that she's happy."

"I guess I meant there's no chance for you two."

Chase frowns as he goes back to work cleaning the corrosion off Barbara's terminals. "Sometimes, no matter how good of friends people are, they're not compatible. It's best to know these things before you end up getting married and bringing a lot of kids into the situation."

Saying Chase and Barbara are not compatible is like saying Mama and Daddy don't have a successful marriage. I know Chase is not always the most brilliant guy in the world, but I still will never understand how he can be so blind. Still, I can tell by his body language he has allowed me as much latitude on the subject as he plans to, and I need to draw the conversation to an end.

"So, what's your problem with Lee?"

"I never said I have a problem with Lee."

"You don't have to. Everyone can see how you react when he's around."

"I think you're mistaken."

"Just tell me. I won't say anything to him."

Chase sets the wire brush down and stands straight. "You won't say anything to him because I'm not gonna say anything. A teachable moment here ... this is how you don't get into somebody else's business." He picks up the wire brush and begins scrubbing again.

This will be a more extended conversation than I initially intended. "Do you have any beer in the fridge out here?"

"Nope." His ears turn the color of radishes. I know he's lying.

One thing you must know about Chase, he's the mule in the family. He'll carry a lot of burdens and not complain about them. Still, once he decides he's not going to do something, Chase will dig in his hindquarters by gosh, and he is not going anywhere. I don't want to admit it, but the conversation is over whether I want it to be or not.

"Well, I guess I'll go up and help Daddy and Barbara with dinner."

"Okay."

"Are you at least coming up for dinner once it's ready?"

"As soon as I get her car checked out and know it's safe to drive."

I exit the standard-sized door to the side of the overhead door. The crisp December night air immediately steals all my body heat.

I stand in the driveway halfway between the mechanic shop and the lake house and look up between the oak trees into the night sky. I follow the stars of Orion as I did when I was a little girl.

Truthfully, I don't feel much different than what I did then.

It was Chase who pointed out Orion to me the first time. I think I was eight.

I huff in exasperation and watch as the condensation forms a puff of smoke. I don't know what I am going to do about Lee and Chase.

In one sense, I want to say Chase just has to get over it. I haven't seen where Lee has done anything to Chase. But if they don't work it out, it would make me incredibly sad to lose the closeness I have always enjoyed with my brother.

I haven't broached the subject yet with Lee. There's a possibility that if I did, Lee could explain what has transpired between them in the past. But it just seems so—awkward. It would be so much easier if Chase would tell me what his problem is with Lee.

Whatever. The boys will have to work it out amongst themselves. I'm going to spend some time with my daddy and the sister-in-law that was robbed from me.

Chapter 39

Chase finishes with Barbara's car, and Mama makes it home in time for dinner. We have a wonderful time catching up with Barbara.

She still works at Rex's, as well as part-time at the dance studio. She mentioned that she has been saving up lately and is considering opening her own dance studio in the next year or two.

She asks jokingly if I might want a third job as a cheerleading coach. I tell her I would prefer to take on a job as a target holder at the firing range.

I tell myself I will have to let it go, but there are practically sparks flying across the table between Chase and Barbara during the meal. It is as if the two were originally one. Their electrons are trying desperately to pull the two bodies back together.

Don't get me wrong, I feel a lot of heat when Lee walks into the room. But I'm not talking about soulmate type stuff. If there is such a thing, Barbara and Chase are strong candidates.

After dinner, Puppy escorts me back to my apartment. I'm a bit surprised since Daddy and Mama had settled in for the second half of the Christmas movie marathon. Daddy has about ten favorite Christmas movies he likes to watch each year, not counting the cartoons.

My takeaway is that Puppy isn't much into Christmas movies.

I'm thankful tomorrow is Sunday. I'm looking forward to sleeping in. Still, I will be forced to get up in time to brave the malls to collect some Christmas gifts.

Even with express delivery, which I can't afford, ordering online is officially out. I can't believe tomorrow is already Christmas Eve.

I'm ashamed I have procrastinated this long. I wish Christmas were a few more days away to give Lee time to get home and me more time to shop for Christmas.

I recheck my phone for about the twentieth time in the last hour. Still no text from Lee and no voicemail. I hit speed dial again as I sit on my bed and get the already familiar "The person you are trying to call—"

I'm holding it together by a fragile thread.

The itch to pull out my vision crystal is a real struggle. Nana had been right about it from the start. I can tell that it is a monkey that wants to get on my back. I know that if I were to pull it out now in the comfort of my own apartment, I wouldn't get any sleep or any gifts bought until Lee arrives home safely. Besides, I used it this morning, and I know they are holed up in a barn, relatively safe from the elements, waiting for the storm to pass.

But what about the phone? Why isn't his phone working?

That is easy. Either the battery died, or Lee has turned his phone off to save the battery until the weather clears so he will have enough power to call someone for help.

Or possibly the roof of the barn collapsed on them, and they're dead. There was a lot of snow on top of that barn. It didn't look like the sturdiest barn in the world. Or maybe they went to sleep and froze together in their triple-spoon position.

Stop it. Stop it right this instant. If I'm going to do anything, I'm going to have a positive image of Lee.

I try to visualize him at his lake house with me. But I can't hold the vision. I'm in too much of a funk. Finally, to help, I pull out my laptop and begin to search for a Christmas nightie.

Two things are inevitable right now. First, I need some solid visualization to knock me out of the blues to hold a positive image of Lee being home. Second, the next time I have the opportunity, no more of this play-it-coy, good-girl stuff.

I need to get me some love before the opportunity goes to waste.

Yes, I still have that one percent "off" feeling about Lee that I can't put my finger on. Still, I am one hundred percent sure I can use some stress-relieving sex. It has been so long I can't even really remember how it feels to be sexually satiated.

Puppy hops up on the bed and lays his muzzle across my thigh as we surf the web for the perfect Christmas nightie.

I want it to be sexy, classy, and not *too* naughty, but naughty enough that Lee can't resist. Although, truthfully, Lee seems to get turned on by old sweatpants and worn-out Crimson Tide T-shirts. Well, the nightie will be a slightly different shade of red.

I find one I like. It also has a sleek matching silk robe that I can wear until the moment of reveal. I like that because it gives me the last-minute opportunity to back out if I lose my nerve.

I order it and splurge for the next-day delivery because I'm feeling decadent and optimistic that it might arrive tomorrow and not at Easter. Pleased with myself, I snap my laptop shut and give Puppy a vigorous rub between his ears.

"Good night, buddy."

Despite the long nap I'd had while watching Christmas movies with Daddy, I know as soon as my head hits the pillow, that sleep will come quickly.

Chapter 40

Puppy's low, grumbling growl wakes me from a profoundly deep sleep. The scent of stale beer, pine, and campfire tickles my nose.

I open one eye, then close it in despair after seeing the pale gray light in my apartment. I had forgotten about tonight's ghost visitor.

"Ms. April?"

Puppy's growl intensifies.

If I just play like I'm asleep, maybe he will go away. Perhaps he will come back tomorrow. When I am better rested, I'll be more inclined to see what he has to show me then.

"Ms. April. You need to get up."

No. I don't. I need to stay in bed and get some rest. I close my eyelids even tighter.

I must've closed them too tight because suddenly, this blinding light is behind my eyelids, and everything is white. I open my eyes and am forced to shield them with my hand. The artificial light source dims considerably as I wake.

"Sorry about that. We have a schedule to keep."

As the light continues to dim, I'm able to make out the outline of the man standing in my kitchenette. The light dims a little more, and I can see his features. I can't help but grin. "Jethro?"

He smiles as the light increases quickly. I shield my eyes again.

"You did remember me. Your grandpa said you would, but I told him there was no way you would remember me."

Jethro Mullins was a client of mine a few months back. He was a basically good guy who had been taken advantage of by a woman who didn't appreciate him. He took out his anger on his next-door neighbor.

One thing led to another, Jethro lost two teeth, and then Jethro lost his house to a Molotov cocktail he tried to throw at his neighbor's home.

I had done my job and gotten him a reduced sentence for his stupidity. It was a lenient deal considering the circumstances.

I think Jethro was prepared to accept it, but then he found out that his wife, Ruth, was done with him for good. It was more than Jethro could deal with, and he managed to hang himself in his cell that same night.

No, I would never forget Jethro. As a matter of fact, it took six weeks of sulking for me to get past the point I was unable to save him.

"I wouldn't forget you, Jethro."

"Man, am I glad to see you," he says.

"I wish I could say the same, Jethro."

He grins again, but this time he can control the light level and not blind me. "I understand. But I'm sure when we're done, you'll be glad."

"I hope you're right."

He moves toward me. It may be morbid of me, but I look for the scar on his neck. Thankfully there is no sign of it.

"Will you take my hand?" he asks.

Puppy stands and barks. I place my hands in Jethro's. The room fades out as if I am passing out. As my knees collapse, Jethro pulls me closer to him.

Seconds later, I'm in a familiar apartment. An apartment I used to visit regularly.

"Why are we here?" I ask Jethro.

He turns his hands over, showing his palms. "Beats me, April. Your grandpa gave me an agenda, told me I'm the Ghost of Christmas Now and to get after it. I'm just following orders."

"He didn't tell you?"

"I'm not sure," Jethro continues, "but I believe *you* have to come up with the reason."

Of all the places I would have thought the Ghost of Christmas Now would take me, the apartment of my best friend Jacob Hurley has never crossed my mind.

Jacob's home is eerily silent.

"This is right now?" I ask Jethro.

"Yes, ma'am."

"What time is it?" I ask.

Jethro grins as if it is a silly question. "A few minutes after midnight, of course."

I rotate slowly, taking in the apartment that I believe to be familiar. The overstuffed L-shaped sofa looks to be older than Jacob. I'm sure it is a hand-me-down, and it has a couple of tears on it that are leaking stuffing. The drapes are dingy from cigarette smoke. Obviously, from the last tenant, as I know Jacob does not smoke. The walls need painting, and there is a sad three-foot-tall Christmas tree in the corner with some clip-on cardinals and a lopsided star on it for decorations. There is one gift under the tree.

I walk into the kitchen, being my usual nosy self. It is as clean as it can get with its chipped enamel sink and Formica counter that looks like a dog has chewed the edge.

"Is he in his bedroom?" I'm not sure what I'm supposed to do. Looking in on my sleeping friend without his knowledge seems wrong.

Jethro frowns as he shrugs his shoulders.

"Fine time for the cat to get your tongue, Jethro," I comment as I walk toward the sad little Christmas tree. "It doesn't seem like having a guide does me much good if y'all can't contribute some basic information."

I bend down and flip the card open on the present. I'm not

sure what I was expecting, but I sure wasn't expecting to see "Merry Christmas, April." I have a momentary case of the dizzies and rock backward on my heels, nearly losing my balance. It's all I can do not to fall onto my butt.

Tears well in my eyes, my nose runs, and I can't catch my breath. I stand as a small gasp escapes me.

"Are you okay?" Jethro asks, his voice full of concern.

No. I'm not. The only happy thing in this entire tiny apartment is a gift, and my friend is giving it to me. "Yeah, I'm fine," I say as tears stream down my face.

"Are you sure?" Jethro cocks his head to the side. "You don't look so fine."

Of all the people to be stuck with as a guide, I have to draw Jethro Mullins. Jethro, who killed himself because his wife didn't appreciate him. Jacob and I certainly aren't married, but it cuts to the bone to think that our relationship is obviously more important to him than it is to me.

Who am I kidding? What relationship *is* important to me? I mean, if someone asked, I could tick off fifteen or twenty relationships and tell you that they were vital to me.

But how many gifts do I have under the sad little Christmas tree in my apartment? I'll tell you how many—I don't even have a Christmas tree up. That's how many.

How bad do I suck?

The tears fall quicker, and I start to feel like I'm hyperventilating. I begin to ask Jethro to take me to the next destination when the front door unlocks and swings open.

There is Jacob, my big, beautiful lug of a best friend, looking exhausted in his blue officer uniform. He locks the door behind him and trudges to his bedroom.

I follow him and watch as he lays his service pistol to the side of his bed with his hat. He starts to unbutton his shirt, and I'm going to step out of the room when his phone rings.

"Hey, Mom."

He stops unbuttoning his shirt and walks past me on the way to the living room. "No. It's fine. I'm off duty now."

He reaches the kitchen and opens the pantry. I look over his shoulder at the collection of canned soups, chili, and packs of ramen noodles.

"No. I don't want you to worry about me. Grandma needs your help, and it's been a couple of years since you've been able to take a visit up there." He selects chili and works the can opener as he holds the phone against his shoulder. "No. I'm not going to be sitting around moping at Christmas. There are always some of the guys with families who need somebody to work their shift. I'll just swap out and then have a couple days after Christmas off to myself. Maybe I'll go hunting then."

I didn't believe I could feel any lower, but I'm wrong. I hadn't touched base with Jacob in the last few days because of the "weirdness" that cropped up when Lee and I began dating. It had not even occurred to me to ask him what his plans were for the holiday.

"I'll be fine. Honest. Yes, ma'am. I'll call you if I need to talk. Call me when you get there. I love you."

I watch Jacob put the chili into a bowl and shove it into the microwave. I don't know if I have ever seen someone in such need of a hug. My heart breaks for Jacob as he leans against the counter, watching the yellow ceramic bowl turn slowly in the microwave.

I ache to give him one. I know who will be first on my shopping list in the morning.

"Jethro, I have to get out of here."

"Are you sure?"

I give him my famous "don't try my patience" look, and he understands. He holds his hands out toward me and smiles.

I take hold of his hands, this time prepared for the swirling motion, and I keep my legs. The journey seems much shorter this time. Still, it could be that I'm getting used to it.

It seems odd to me to end up in the living room of the lake house. It's not like it required a magical journey. I could've simply walked up the pathway and slid open the glass door for this excursion.

Mama and Daddy are lying on the sofa. Daddy faces the TV with Mama sprawled across his chest. This has been normal for them for as long as I can remember. It doesn't even feel awkward to me anymore.

"Are you sure?" Daddy asks.

"I think it would be best. And it's just this year."

"But I think the rest of the family prefers to open gifts on Christmas morning."

Mama is tracing a figure eight on Daddy's Charlie Brown Christmas sweater. "Yes, Ralph. But I would like April to open her gifts here with the rest of the family, and you know she's going to be over at Lee's Christmas morning."

"Well, I'll just tell her she has to spend the night here." Daddy juts out his lower lip as if he were laying down the law.

"Are you prepared to have Lee spend the night?" Mama asks as she raises her eyebrows.

"What is the deal between him and the boys."

"I have no idea. I've never seen either one of them act this way about someone she's dating."

Daddy shakes his head. "I wish they would quit complaining to me about Lee and take it up with her."

Mama starts to laugh and pokes at Daddy's chest. "And who was it that beat it into their head not to get into other people's business and to let everybody have enough room to live their own lives?"

"Well, it works most of the time," Daddy grumbles.

Mama lays her head back on Daddy's chest. "I just wish I had known. There's no way I would have invited him into our home if I had known our boys felt this way about Lee. He seems like such a nice young man."

"He still seems like a nice young man to me. Until those boys can come clean with what their issue is with him, it's going to be hard for me to say otherwise."

"So, open up gifts tomorrow night?"

Daddy's eyes squint. "No. Wait a minute. We might still be getting an early Christmas gift."

"How's that?"

"I think Lee and a couple of his friends are stuck in that blizzard up in Maryland right now. He may not get home until after Christmas."

Mama raises up. "That would work. We certainly want him to get home safe." She shakes her head. "Because I sure can't handle the drama if, heaven forbid, something happened to him."

"Right. Sure. We just don't want him getting home before Christmas," Daddy says conspiratorially.

"So, play it by ear tomorrow?" Mama asks.

"That's all we can do. Hope for the best, plan for the worst."

Mama drops her head back onto Daddy's chest. "How in the world did it come to this?"

"I don't know, but I sure did like it better when they were all little. Remember when we could tell them what they were going to do."

"It is a shame they had to grow up."

"Yes. Babies and younger children were fun." Daddy huffs. "And with these losers, Viv, we might never have any more babies in this house."

Mama props up on one arm. "We could always try to make some more."

"That's not possible."

"No, but it would be fun to try," Mama says with a giggle.

Daddy lets out a guttural laugh as he pulls her tight against him. "I like your thinking, Viv."

I quickly turn my back before my parents permanently scar my retinas with parent porn. Only then am I aware that my lower jaw is hanging open.

I knew Chase had an issue with Lee. I certainly didn't realize that Dusty did, too. Never in my wildest dreams did I think my parents were altering the Christmas festivities around my relationship with Lee.

I'm not sure how to process all this. Should I feel glad that my parents would adjust their plans to make everyone comfortable? Or horrified that they have such a low opinion of the love of my life? It is all just too much.

"What is all this supposed to mean?" I turn on Jethro.

"That your brothers don't like your boyfriend?" he says with a shrug.

That one's on me. I know Jethro's not precisely Mensa material.

I'm racking my brain trying to think of what Lee might have possibly done to offend my brothers. It can't be while we've been dating because he's been nothing but a perfect gentleman to me. I know I haven't complained about anything, and during the few times that he's been around them, he's been nothing but polite and courteous.

It has to be something from before we dated. Something personal on the part of my brothers.

Well, again, that isn't my problem. If they had a disagreement in the past, that's their issue. My brothers will have to get over it. I'm not sure which one of them he ticked off, but it always has been this way. If one of them has an issue with somebody, they both do.

Twins.

Oh my gosh. Vander warned me about Lee, too. I don't know how inclined I am to trust somebody who can't even be honest with me about what he does for a living, but it isn't just a twin-brother thing.

"Are you okay, April?" Jethro asks.

"Why do you keep asking me that, Jethro?"

He flinches. I immediately feel bad for blowing up on him. "Because you look like you have indigestion?"

Great. Now ghosts are calling me out for having gas. This is going to be just a wonderful Christmas.

My boyfriend is stuck in a barn in Maryland in a snowstorm. If he makes it home in time for Christmas, my family has rearranged Christmas specifically because my brothers don't like him and want to kick his butt. Wow, this is awesome.

I notice Jethro is looking over my shoulder toward the sofa. I thump him on the chest. "Stop that."

"Sorry about that." He shakes his head as his face reddens. "Are you ready for the next step?"

"Are you kidding me? What do I get, the baker's dozen tonight?"

Jethro's mouth hangs open. "I don't understand."

"Toby only took me to two places last night."

Jethro holds up a finger. "I've got one more. Your grandpa gave me an—"

"Agenda. I know. I gotta talk to Grandpa about his planning. I could walk out the glass door and be at my apartment without all this magical flying around."

Jethro frowns. "Well, really no. You're not on this plane right now."

"I know that, Jethro. I just mean it would've made more sense—" I blow an exasperated breath and hold out my hands. "Never mind. Come on, let's get this over with. I have some shopping to do in the morning."

He takes my hands, and the colors swirl until they turn white. A freezing wind cuts through my clothes. It's pitch dark while thick clumps of snow pelt my face.

Chapter 41

"Where are we, Jethro?"

"Uh, I may have missed by a few yards."

"Missed what?"

"There is supposed to be a barn here."

Another thick, wet clump of snow splashes across my face. "Why am I *feeling* the snow?"

Jethro runs both hands through his hair. "I think we're on this plane."

"Like traveled, traveled?"

He grimaces. "Maybe? I may have messed up."

"Who gave you your license for this?"

"Here, give me your hands again."

Against my better judgment, I give Jethro my hands and pray I don't end up in the void with him. The only thing I can think of as worse than being stuck in the void for all eternity is possibly being stuck here with Jethro.

I experience the same swirling vertigo and, seconds later, pitch dark with large cold, wet clumps striking my face. "Jethro?"

"Darn it. This storm must be messing with my ability to locate the barn." He reaches out for my hand again, and I pull back.

I can feel him. It's difficult to explain, but I can feel Lee. I start trudging through the snow to the left of Jethro. My feet sink to my knees with each step.

"Where are you going?" Jethro hollers against the raging wind.

"To the barn." Thankfully Jethro doesn't ask any questions and follows me.

I'm encouraged that I can feel Lee. At least I know he is alive.

According to Jethro, that would mean right now, at this moment, he is safe. After fifty yards of laboring through the heavy snow, I begin to doubt myself. How do I know that it is actually him?

Still, I push on. Magically, the snow parts as my hand touches the rough, grainy surface of the barn.

As I work my hands along the boards in search of the door, Jethro comes up behind me and yells, "You found it. Great job."

"I need to find the door," I holler back over the screaming wind.

Jethro puts his hands on my shoulders, and there is a pop in my eardrums. We are inside the barn.

"A little easier to hear you in here," Jethro says.

The biting cold is gone, and I know that Jethro has gotten us off the actual plane of existence Lee is on. *Great, if he had left well enough alone, I could have talked to Lee.*

"Where is he?" I ask.

Jethro points up the ladder. "He's in the loft. If you don't care, I have a bit of a fear about heights."

Jethro has a fear of heights? Never mind spatial displacement and the possibility of getting caught in the void for all eternity. Let's worry about falling out of a hayloft. Whatever.

I work my way up the ladder, and from my previous visit via my crystal, I know exactly where to look in the hay. The three of them are lounging in a circle formation in the hay. They have covered themselves with hay from the waist down.

"Sheila was okay before we got married. But if I'd known she was going to be half the ballbuster she is, I would've just kept living with her. I swear ever since I said 'I do,' she only says 'I want.'"

Hector shakes his head. "That's how all three of my wives were. It drove me crazy."

"Darn, Hector, three wives?" Lee asks. "You don't look old enough for that many."

Hector purses his lips. "What you talking about? I'm twenty-two."

Lee chuckles. "I guess different strokes for different folks. I'm looking at it from the standpoint of a twenty-eight-year-old who still hasn't asked anybody to marry them."

"What about that Amy girl you were talking about?" Bob asks.

Lee rolls a shoulder. "April. Maybe. I mean, she's hot and everything. You never know. It could happen."

"Maybe you're not into girls," Hector offers.

Lee looks shocked. "What are you talking about, Hector?"

Hector raises a hand. "No. It's okay if you're not. It's just my cousin Michel. He kept waiting to get married, and then one day he realized he liked guys."

"I assure you, Hector, I am into girls," Lee says.

Hector rolls his hands over. "I didn't mean to offend you. It's just that you've got a really nice butt."

Lee's brow furrows as he laughs. "Okay. Thanks? So, what is that supposed to mean?"

Hector appears flustered. "It's just that most of the guys I know who like guys have a really nice butt."

Bob starts laughing so hard he falls backward into the hay. "He's got a point, Lee. You do have a nice butt."

"Well, I appreciate the compliments, but I'm currently off the market. If anything happens, I'll let you know."

Hector has a blank stare. "No one can ever understand how Michel likes boys. I didn't understand it." Hector shrugs. "But earlier, when we were trying to stay warm, and your butt fit so perfect right here, I couldn't help but catch wood."

Bob begins to howl with laughter, rolling over in the hay.

Lee shakes his head as he laughs. "Hector, do you really have a cousin named Michel? Or is there something you're trying to tell me?"

"No. I really have a cousin. I was just saying I get it now."

Bob begins to sober and sits upright. "Hector, this guy is, like, one hundred percent girl lover. As a matter of fact, I told him one time that he should open an online course. He can teach men how to pick up beautiful women and have sex with them without them ever even asking their name."

"Knock it off, Bob," Lee says.

"Don't let him kid you, Hector. We used to lay bets on how quickly he could convince some cute ball fan to have sex with him while her boyfriend went to get popcorn."

Hector leans in toward Lee. "Is this true, Lee?"

Lee rubs the palm of his hand against his eye. "I had some wild years. Not like Bob's exaggerations, but that's all changed now anyway."

"You only go after the single ones now?" Bob jokes.

"I only go after one now," Lee says.

"Amy." Bob's interest seems to be growing as he leans forward.

"April. And yeah, there's something there. I'm not sure what yet, but I want to give it some time and see what develops."

"Whatever you do, don't let her move in with you. That just starts the slippery slope toward marriage. Then it's a life of no sex, no money, and no pride." Bob crosses his arms as if to dare Lee to disagree.

Hector nods in agreement. "It's true. There's no sex like sex with the woman trying to get you to ask them to marry you. After that—not so much."

Lee bundles some hay behind him and lies back on it. "I appreciate your concern, and I will take it under advisement, but this is something I'm going to have to find out for myself."

"In your case, you better make sure that all the steak knives are out of the apartment." Lee rotates his head to look at Bob, who then flashes a grin. "If you were to slip up and revert back to your old ways, I wouldn't want her to Bobbitt you."

"I'm not going to slip up." Lee rolls over, resting his head on his arm with his back toward Bob and Hector.

I wait a few more minutes and watch the three men fall into their separate periods of sleep. I'm happy to at least know the three of them have each other and are out of the storm.

I'm still concerned about what they will do for food, but I also know that the three of them are very resourceful. I have no doubt they will be okay.

I think it best to get home now. I climb down the ladder and walk over to where Jethro inspects one of the old disassembled combines.

If Grandpa thought that this would be some sort of a revelation for me, he was mistaken. I've known for years that some men talk crass. Not the men in my family or my friends, but I knew it existed. Besides, it wasn't Lee who was being vulgar. It was Bob.

Sure. I realize Bob is referring to the past exploits of Lee. They may or may not be accurate. But even if they are, am I supposed to judge Lee on his past transgressions? If he has done anything that Bob is talking about, what does that have to do with me? It was long before he came back to town. Plus, he even said that he was done being that guy.

Shouldn't we all get the opportunity to remake ourselves? To evolve into a better person?

No, Grandpa was sorely off-target if he thought that this was going to be a meaningful excursion. I heard that Lee is so much in love with me that he is working on becoming a better man. What more can I want of my man?

I turn to Jethro and raise my hands. "Are we done?"

He appears genuinely surprised. "Oh. Are you ready to go?"

Let's see, I was tired before Jethro showed up. I now comfortably know that Lee is—at least for the moment—safe, and I have a lot of Christmas gifts I need to buy tomorrow to prove to the world I'm not a sorry friend, sister, or daughter. "Yes. I am very ready to go."

Jethro approaches me with his hands out. "Well, we'll go

then. Before we do, though, Ms. April. I want to tell you how good it is to see you, and I need you to know how much I appreciate you."

"For what, Jethro?"

"For making me feel human when everyone else made me feel like a piece of garbage."

Jethro clasps my elbows, and the barn spins before I can respond.

Chapter 42

Something is tickling my face.

I swat at my face, and my hand lands on Puppy's mane. Opening my eyes, his muzzle is nearly touching my nose. We are eye to eye. "What?"

He lets out a brief whine.

I notice that it is very bright in my apartment. I flip over in search of my phone. "Fudge!" It's almost noon.

Throwing back my covers, I run into my bathroom for a quick shower. I towel dry and rip the brush through my wet hair. "You know you could've gotten me up earlier," I scold Puppy.

I hear plastic striking rubber and crane my head around the doorjamb of the bathroom. The dog door is still swinging from where Puppy has exited. I guess that is his way of telling me this one is on me.

I start my car and head out for Huntsville. That's one of the things about living in Guntersville. If you need to shop for groceries or household items, there's plenty of stores. There's also a plethora of antique stores and odds-and-ends stores.

But there are no *real* shopping stores. So, suppose you're looking for some quick last-minute Christmas gifts. In that case, because you procrastinated too long, you're forced to drive into Huntsville.

That was sweet, what Jethro told me last night. Regardless of what he says, I still wish I had been able to save him. Still, I do feel better knowing Jethro understands I did everything in my power. The fact of the matter is that he had so many things go wrong by the time I got to him; he already had one foot on the way out of this world.

I feel better about Lee, too. So much so, I decide not to call him again to leave more voicemails. I think 119 messages are probably enough anyway. I can wait for him to call me once he can.

I'm coming to accept that I will not see him for a few days in all likelihood. But that is okay. Just putting things into perspective, he's alive, and it sounds like he's in love with me.

That's going to be just as crucial on December twenty-sixth or December twenty-seventh as it would be on Christmas day. It doesn't make it any less of a gift. I can speak from experience about what it's like not to have love in your life, and love is definitely a gift. A gift that should be cherished 365 days a year, not only on Christmas.

Besides, it will make it easier on Mama and Daddy. I don't know what my brothers' issue is. I've thought about confronting them on it, but really it's their issue, not mine. If things continue to go right with Lee and me, the boys will come to terms, I'm sure. Besides, with me living in Baltimore, surely, with time, they'll get over whatever happened between them and Lee.

One image I saw last night that I can't get out of my mind is the little Christmas tree in Jacob's apartment. Sad doesn't even begin to explain how it makes me feel. Realizing the only gift under the tree is for me still shames me.

I have known Jacob most of my life, and if I ever have a problem I can't work out, he is always the first person outside of my family I would talk to. He is always there for me, and here I haven't even thought about him since—well, really since Lee and I started dating.

I pick up my phone and speed-dial Jacob.

"What's up, Snow?" Jacob's voice is uncharacteristically clipped.

"Are you on duty?"

"Lunch break."

"You at the doughnut shop?"

"Yeah, I'm running my tongue along the edge of a red velvet right now."

That shocks me into a laugh. "Send me a picture when you get a chance. I'd like to see that."

"FCC would block it." He deadpans.

I'm suddenly nervous, which is weird since this is Jacob. Maybe it is because I haven't asked Mama, or perhaps it is because I'm dating Lee. "What are you doing for Christmas dinner tomorrow?"

"I don't know, Snow. I'm working Jeff Briar's shift tomorrow morning so he can open gifts with his boys. After that, I'll probably just grab something to eat and take a nap."

"How about you come to my parents' for dinner. It's at two."

He pauses before answering. "Do you want me to?"

"Well, yeah. And it's Christmas. You're supposed to get together with your friends and family."

"What does Lee think about it?"

I know Jacob is just being respectful, but for some reason is stokes my ire. "What do you mean, what does Lee think about it?"

"Simple enough question. Does he know that you're inviting me? Did it bother him?"

"He wouldn't care. Besides, right now, he's stuck in a snowstorm up in Maryland."

"So, he doesn't know."

I'm quickly starting to regret calling Jacob. "No. And it's not like I can call him right now. His phone is dead."

"Calm down."

"Well, you make it sound like I am hiding something from Lee by being nice and inviting you over."

"No. Nothing of the sort. I couldn't care less what Lee thinks about me. I was wanting to make sure that your inviting me isn't going to cause trouble between you two."

"It won't," I snap.

"Okay." He laughs with a mocking tone. "I would love to eat dinner with you and your family. Thank you for the invite, and I'll see you tomorrow at two."

I guess it is too late to rescind the invite due to his insolence. "Okay. Have a safe shift, and I'll see you tomorrow."

Chapter 43

My family treats credit like it's heroin. It's the gateway drug to bankruptcy and homelessness.

Whether it is Nana, "You should always live below your means," Daddy, "There's a big difference between wants and needs," or Grandpa Snow who pulled no punches, "Credit is the nectar of the devil," everyone in my family believes in saving up and paying cash.

They are so old school. I mean, there's no way I would be able to buy all the Christmas gifts I need to buy today if it weren't for the new credit card that came in the mail last month.

Besides, I will have to be flying back and forth between D.C. and Huntsville before too long. Two percent of everything I buy today goes toward free airline tickets. *Boom.* That's what you call working the system.

It's not like I don't *want* to pay cash for the Christmas gifts. It's all those stupid student loans I've got hanging over me that keep my cash flow in the negative.

I'm feeling pretty good about myself. I have gotten everyone in my family something. Also, a few gifts for Lee, including a pair of Christmas boxer briefs with mistletoe on his package pocket, and for Liza a lithograph of a fairy garden. When I transported into her apartment a month ago, I noticed that she didn't have any paintings on the wall. Just crucifixes, lots of crucifixes.

And the best gift of all, I dropped two hundred dollars for a refurbished first-generation home gaming console for Jacob. He had one back in middle school. We used to play it for hours.

I figured it would be something good for him to remember me by once I leave for D.C. It probably is odd that I even care if he remembers me. Before last night it had never even occurred to me whether he would or would not miss me. I sort of assumed things would always keep going like they were going.

In the same way, I thought things would just continue going on the same way for perpetuity when I went to Alabama. Because nothing ever changes in a small town. Right?

I realize now everything changes. When you leave, you pull away from the friends and family you love. They still love you, but you have lost some of the adhesive that held you together. Just like duct tape, I wonder how many times I can pull away and come back before all the stickiness is gone from the relationship?

Jacob is still friendly when I call, but he has been short with me. A little less jocular. Is our stickiness wearing off?

I hope not. It would be a sad day if I no longer had Jacob in my life.

He's going to marry some cute little country girl, and they're going to have, like, a zillion kids, so I know we won't always be the same way we are now. But I like having him in my life. What happens to the relationship when I leave town?

That nostalgic feeling that is my enemy starts to creep in on me again. It is a significant reason I never wanted to come back to Guntersville once I completed my law degree. I would switch over immediately from law school and head up to the big city, in a perfect world.

It was all arranged. I had worked my tail off to get the coveted appointment as a junior associate at one of the most prestigious law firms in the Southeast. It wasn't my fault that the owners were a bunch of crooks and I never even got to clock the first hour of pay.

Now, every day I stay in Guntersville is making it that much more difficult to leave. It was hard enough to leave family and friends behind when I went down to Tuscaloosa for college.

Sure, I played it up and made it seem like I couldn't wait to get out of town, and don't get me wrong, I was excited. Still, I also remember crying myself to sleep for the first two weeks because I was homesick and didn't want to tell anybody. It's hard to be the cool new girl with runny mascara.

This time I'm afraid it is going to be even worse. Because I know what the reality of the situation is. When I left for Tuscaloosa, I had it in my mind that it would be like living at home. Just with no curfew and nobody getting into your business, but I'd still maintain my friendships and relationships. I kept telling myself that Tuscaloosa was only three hours from Guntersville. I would be home at least every other weekend.

Every other weekend? I did well to make it home two times a semester, not counting holiday breaks. That was being only three hours away.

I refuse to kid myself. D.C. is a thirteen-hour drive away. Or, if I am flush with cash, half a day boarding a flight to catch a ride from the airport to my parents'. I am down to visiting *possibly* three times a year Christmas, Easter, and Fourth of July. That is only if I manage to arrange the time off from my new high-powered job.

Returning home has strengthened my bonds with my family. My brothers aren't just amusement anymore. I actually understand them and appreciate them. I now am in awe of Mama and Daddy's long-term love affair. I now have to be on guard not to let the fact their relationship has lasted for more than thirty-five years make me feel like a loser. It's not fair that I struggle to keep relationships together for thirty-five days.

Then there are the magical things I have learned about myself through my grandmothers. I roll my right hand off of the steering wheel and snap my finger. A small blue flame appears in the palm of my hand.

It still just tickles the living daylights out of me that I can do that. Sure, it's not useful unless I'm lighting a candle, and I can't bring it up and show my friends at a party. Still, it is fantastic to know that whenever I want to create a flame, I just have to snap my fingers and concentrate on it.

Maybe the detour back home had a purpose. I'm starting to be of the impression if I had started immediately in Atlanta, I never would've really understood where I came from and why I am who I am.

Maybe, as daddy has said, I was meant to be here for now.

I know I would not have met the love of my life if I had not come home. That's one immutable fact that has come out of my return home. Even if Lee were the only reason, it was worth spending the last six months at home.

I check my phone, still no text and no voicemail. I'm going to keep my word and not call him. But I will check the crystal when I get home. I didn't make any promises about the crystal.

Chapter 44

The top two gifts I'm balancing almost fall to the porch as I try to open the glass door. I tap the door with my toe and see Dusty wiping off his hands with a kitchen towel before he opens the door.

"You know there are no rules against making more than one trip." Dusty turns back to the kitchen island where he is working on scalloped potatoes.

"Don't push me. I've got two paper cuts on my thumb and one on my tongue. I'm not in the mood for you picking on me."

Chase looks up from the onions he is chopping, "How'd you get one on your tongue?"

I break left toward the living room and the family Christmas tree. "Don't ask."

As I lay out the gifts I wrapped, I'm somewhat disappointed. When I was purchasing them, I visualized them in perfectly wrapped colorful paper, tight with no seams showing, and big beautiful bows. Basically, I thought they would look like the gifts Mama wraps. Several of mine look like I had put them in the center of the wrapping paper, wadded it up around them, and then just circled tape around the ball of wrapping. How are you supposed to wrap boxer briefs, anyway?

What's done is done. At least everybody has something from me.

I pad back into the kitchen where my brothers and Daddy are preparing all the casserole dishes today that they will put in the oven tomorrow. Luckily, if I decide to do the Rice Krispies Treats, they're best done the same day.

"Have you gotten an update on Lee?" Daddy asks.

Here, Daddy, let me put some rock salt in your hand so you can rub it in my open wound. "No, sir."

"Well, I don't want to give up hope. But that storm has done a number on the mid-Atlantic. If he hasn't made it here by now, he may not make it home until after Christmas." Daddy looks genuinely troubled. "I know that's disappointing."

No, disappointing is getting a green hoodie for Christmas when you were hoping for a pink one. Lee not making it home is leaving a hollow spot in my gut. "At this stage, as long as he makes it home safe, I don't care when he gets home."

Dusty stops cutting the boiled potatoes. "That's a really mature way to look at it, April."

"Besides, that lump of coal Santa leaves in Lee's stocking isn't going to go bad," Chase says as he continues chopping onions.

"And that would be the antithesis of mature." Dusty glares at Chase.

Chase scrapes the chopped onions into the skillet and throws a stick of butter in with it. "Whatever."

"You hungry?" Daddy doesn't look up from the cheese he is cubing.

"I probably could eat in a little while." I pull out my phone. "Good, Lord. Is it already eight?"

"Your mama went to get dinner at the Smiling Dragon. She should be back shortly."

Daddy must have made it to *The Christmas Story* in his movie marathon if it is Chinese night.

The first year I watched the movie with him, I begged Daddy for a BB gun and to let us have roast duck for Christmas dinner. Things have always been a negotiation with Daddy. He agreed that we could try roast duck on Christmas Eve, but Christmas dinner would still be roast ham and the usual fixings.

He also got me a BB gun, but I was required to wear the nerdy safety goggles he purchased whenever I shot targets.

After I went through two boxes of BBs, I bummed a 22 caliber off Grandpa Snow and never bought any more BBs. The Chinese duck, Christmas Eve dinner, stuck around. I don't know what happened to the BB gun.

"Did she order some sushi?" Chase asks.

"She got that Nigiri dish she likes." Daddy pops the cheese into the microwave.

"You know that stuffs raw, don't you?" Chase says as he stirs his onions.

"Duh." I favor him with a pronounced eye roll.

"I'm just saying in most circles it's called bait. I can go down to the boat dock and get you what you need to make a catfish roll."

My face wrinkles. "Are you already drinking?"

Dusty shakes his head. "Dad got us some craft beer, but he won't let us have any until we get the casseroles made and put in the fridge."

I pull out one of the barstools and sit down to watch. They have been doing this same menu for so long they barely even glance at their recipes.

"That beer would probably go really well with those catfish rolls." Chase laughs.

Sometimes with Chase, you have to push back before he leaves you alone. "So, is Barbara coming over for Christmas dinner? Since Lee can't make it, we'll definitely have an empty seat."

Chase looks at me out of the side of his eye. "She did say she would try to make it by for dinner tomorrow."

I have to grab the counter, so I don't slide off the barstool and embarrass myself. I was not expecting that revelation. Welcomed? Yes. But totally unexpected. "She knows you're cooking?"

"It's not her first rodeo. I used to cook casseroles when we were in high school, too," Chase says as he blanches the broccoli.

The pungent smell of the broccoli rises, competing with the onions sautéing in butter. My stomach rumbles. I'm hungrier than I thought.

"When's Mama supposed to be home?"

Like magic, the glass door slides open, and Mama enters with a bag in either arm. I hop off the barstool and take one of the bags from her.

"There's another one out in my car if you don't mind, April."

The air has cooled considerably since I got home from Huntsville. As I walk to Mama's car, I see the silhouette of Puppy down on the dock. He is sitting at the very edge, looking out over the dark, inky water.

It dawns on me I have not even considered how the move will impact Puppy. If we live downtown, he will be a latchkey puppy that will only get out once or twice a day for a leash walk. That will be a significant decrease in his quality of life. It has never occurred to me.

As I pick up the last bag from the Chinese restaurant, I mull over why everything has to be so difficult. Why does your life load up with so much inertia when you stay somewhere for just a little while? Why can't it be easier to move around and experience different things than just stay in the same town your entire life?

Oh, get over it. April. I suppose anything worth doing is challenging. Puppy will end up enjoying D.C. or Baltimore just as much as he does the lake house. He's a dog. It doesn't take much to make him happy.

I set the bag down next to the two Mama is unpacking. "I got my shopping done today," I announce.

"Awesome. And you have nearly twelve hours to spare. What will you do with all that extra time?" Mama continues setting the table.

I ignore her sarcasm. I'm not going to let her knock the shine off my accomplishment. "Are both Nana and Granny coming tomorrow?"

"Your Granny is a definite yes. Nana says she plans on it, but she has a tremendous backlog of orders she has to fill." Mama stops setting the table. Her eyes narrow. "What do you know about the products she is selling online?"

"Me?" I yelp. "Uh, not much."

Mama crosses her arms as she angles her head. I am such a lousy liar.

"You don't believe she'll get herself into any legal trouble, do you, Counselor? I worry the tonics don't work as she's advertising them." She sighs. "I also worry they *will* work as advertised."

I know of one potion I sure hope works as advertised. A dab of Nana's "Make My Monster Grow" and my sexy-yet-cute Christmas nightie should break the April sexual drought.

I'm preoccupied during our traditional Christmas Eve Chinese dinner. My use of the looking crystal this afternoon has brought a severe mental itch into my life. Nana warned me against it. I wish I had taken her a little more seriously.

When I checked in on Lee and his two teammates this afternoon, things were pretty much the same as they had been. They had improvised and melted snow for drinking water, but they still had no food, and the snow was still falling in heavy clumps, though the worst of the whipping, frigid wind had ceased.

As Puppy escorts me to our apartment, I'm enumerating in my mind all the reasons why I can't pull the crystal out and check on Lee again. In addition to all the addictive reasons I should leave it alone, there is still one immutable fact that remains. If something is wrong in Maryland—what in the world can I do to help Lee? Nothing.

Despite the danger, as soon as I shut my apartment door, I fish the blue velvet drawstring bag I keep the crystal in from my purse. I open the bag and roll the milky-white stone into my hand.

It is warm and releases pleasing dopamine to my brain.

Maybe if I just hold it and don't use it. Perhaps that would be enough to scratch the itch.

Puppy sits on his haunches with his head cocked to the side. He is watching me intently.

"Don't judge me. I don't need you to judge me," I tell him.

He continues to stare me down.

Bless it. I almost forgot about the amulet that started this whole resurgence of my "gifts." I hadn't thought about it in its safe place for months. I know I should store the looking crystal in the same manner.

Oh, wow. Imagine if I combined the amulet's power with the looking stone. There's no telling what I could—no. Nope, I'm not going to risk it.

Puppy whines at me.

"Fine. I'm not going to do anything stupid." I stand and stomp to my kitchenette, where I pull a plastic cup from the cupboard. "I'll be sorry I did this if I have an emergency," I grumble.

I fill the plastic cup half full of tap water and drop the crystal in it. I place the cup in the freezer next to the Tupperware bowl I know holds my aunt's amulet. "Happy now?"

Puppy quits staring me down. He hops up on the bed, circling twice before lying down.

I feel a powerful pull back toward the freezer. I can still get the crystal out now, and it won't be frozen in the ice.

No. I'm stronger than that, I tell myself.

I strip off my clothes and get under the covers in bed as quickly as possible. If I can just fall asleep, I won't have to deal with the itch. The desire to just sit and watch what the crystal will show me.

Chapter 45

The sound of a hundred wind chimes in a thunderstorm wakes me. As my eyes focus, I see a woman close to my age in a business suit. I realize, quickly enough, she is the third Christmas ghost. Still, I'm mildly surprised and pleased to see a female since the other spirits had been male.

She stops talking on her phone and slips it into her large leather bag. "Are you ready to go?"

"Go where?"

The blonde businesswoman rolls her eyes as she huffs.

She's good. She must have been practicing that for years as she has the eye roll down to a fine art.

"I declare. For some reason, I remembered you as being smart."

"Remembered?" I ask.

She waves her hand dismissively. "If you don't mind, your grandpa gave me a *huge* to-do list. So, we better get busy."

The ghost points to her chest with two fingers. "In case you're not as smart as I remember, I'm the Ghost of Christmas Promised, or if you prefer, Forthcoming."

"That's sort of a mouthful. Do you have a name?"

My question seems to have caught her off guard. She smirks and says, "Call me Amy."

"Okay, Amy."

As I say her name, the wind chimes clatter loudly again. Their clanging transforms into a multitude of telephones ringing.

Amy pulls her silver phone from her bag, checks it, then pulls out a purple phone. Her chin drops to her chest as her eyes close.

"Is everything okay?" I ask.

She sighs. "It's just I'm getting hammered. Everybody demands something right now."

"Do you need to take care of your business and maybe come back tomorrow?" I'm becoming hopeful that I may be able to slide out of the third ghost appointment.

"No. No. It doesn't work like that. Listen, we're going to have to blow through this as quickly as possible, so I can get back to my clients. I mean, I know this is about you, and you're the most important person in your world." She shakes her hands above her shoulders in a mocking gesture. "But I've got important things to do."

Wow. Am I being disrespected by my own Ghost of Christmas Promised? How rude.

Amy extends her hands, and as I go to take hold, she pulls them back. "Careful of the manicure. I got them done today."

I don't care to get separated during the spatial displacement, so I clutch her wrist. She does not object.

My room spins, and I feel a touch of seasickness coming on. As the spinning stops, I can tell we are in a vast city. I can't see all its glory, but I can smell the water nearby. The day is crisp and cold.

"Where are we, Amy?"

She is rechecking her phone. She looks up and appears startled when she sees me staring at her. "Oh. Alexandria, Virginia."

My heart skips several beats with the realization. I made it; I'm working in the D.C. area as a lawyer. "Is this where I live?"

Amy slips on a pair of Ray-Ban sunglasses. "Don't be silly. You live near the waterfront of Old Town. This is just where your annex office is located."

"Annex?"

Amy rolls her eyes again. "There's no reason to fight the traffic on George Washington Memorial if you don't have an appointment in D.C. The firm's staff is based in D.C., but two of your three assistants work out of this office."

I'm getting my head around the thought of having three assistants when I step up on the curb to avoid being hit by a sleek yellow sports car. The woman in the sports car stands up and straightens her expensive business suit. It is tasteful and tailored like a glove. The ensemble screams "get out of my way, or I will mess you up," except for her really excellent strapped heels.

I think I like the heels more than I do the sports car.

"Let's just follow her in so we don't have to do that whole door thing," Amy says as she waves her phone at the front door of the law office.

I can't help but point. "Is that me?"

"In all your glory, baby."

How awesome is this? Most people have to operate on faith that their hard work will pay off. I do not take for granted what a blessing it is to know that if I stay the course, I will meet my goals and be the big-time law partner I always dreamed of becoming. It will be so much easier to weather bad days, knowing all my dreams are destined to be fulfilled.

I eagerly follow my future self through the massive mahogany doors of the office.

Look at that figure. I must work out in the gym twice a day. *I'm hot.*

"Jennifer!"

I jump when the future me yells out the girl's name. The assistant at the first desk, I assume Jennifer, nearly comes out of her skin, too.

"Yes, ma'am?"

Future me towers over the young girl as she looks up from her chair. "Didn't I ask you to put my dry-cleaning in my downstairs changing room?"

"Yes, ma'am. I did."

The future me looks like I'm about to have an aneurysm. "Then where is my cream georgette blouse."

Jennifer licks her lips before answering. "Remember, it had that small stain." She points at her chest; her finger is trembling. "The cleaners are having to try different chemicals to lift it."

"There was no stain on that blouse."

"Yes, ma'am, from the Taft lunch?"

The future me raises her perfectly sculpted eyebrows. "No, Jennifer. You are mistaken. But I want you to understand something, I don't pay you to argue with me or fail to do the simple task I give you. It's okay if you're not capable of the job. But I would rather you resign than force me to fire you if you can't handle it. Do I make myself clear?"

"Yes, ma'am."

I follow her to a huge office with a ten-foot mahogany desk that appears to be manufactured from the same wood as the office front doors. A few paintings of sailboats and frigates are placed strategically on the walls to create a mariner feeling. It is an attractive room, although it has a cold sense that I can't put my finger on. Maybe it is because I'm feeling disoriented about what I witnessed between her and her assistant.

I mean, my assistant and me.

It could be Jennifer and I have a long work history where she has always been incompetent, and I have reached the end of my patience. If not—I'm a really mean lady with excellent heels and a firm tush.

Yeah, that won't balance out being a mean person.

The future me pulls out her phone and dials a number.

Amy taps me on the shoulder. "Are you ready to get out of here?"

I point toward me, dialing the phone. "Didn't we just get here?"

Amy waves her hand dismissively. "You have seen one queen

bee, you have seen them all."

"That's it?"

"Oh, good gosh no. We have a couple more stops. But seriously, I'm running behind, so if you don't mind."

After Toby and Jethro, Amy is a horrible guide. Still, the sooner we get this tour over with, the sooner I'm done with the whole excursion Grandpa planned for me. I grab hold of Amy's wrist, and we have a speedy spinning motion before we stop.

I look out over my balcony at the river before me. The sky is clear, the temperature crisp, and the sun reflects off the river, giving it a metallic look. It is reminiscent of our Lake Guntersville during December.

The voice of the men behind me startles me. They are in their late thirties, wearing long-sleeved sweatshirts stained with salsa as they drink a beer.

"Then leave her. Life's too short to be married to a woman that makes you miserable," says the darker-haired of the two men.

The blond, who looks pregnant due to the extra weight he carries in his stomach, purses his lips. "I can't. Everything is hers. I would be flat broke."

"You still get your retirement from the league."

"Oh, please. That would barely pay for my beer tab each month."

The dark-haired man laughs. "Sounds like you got a beer problem more than a wife problem."

"Yuck it up. Not all of us are lucky enough to have a rich dad die."

The dark-haired man takes a long sip of his beer. "I worked for that one. I didn't think that old geezer was ever going to kick the bucket."

"Yeah, well, I actually kind of liked your dad."

The dark-haired man leans forward, one elbow on his thigh. "Liked? I loved my dad. But I needed his money."

The blond finishes his beer. "Some days, I wonder how I ended up here." He peers out over the water with a thousand-yard stare.

"I don't know about you, but I drove." The dark-haired man laughs at his own joke.

"We better cut this short before she shows up. Unless you like getting lectures." The blond man stands.

"No. I don't. But I am inclined to hang around and hit her over the head while you grab her purse."

The blond man's face contorts into a frown. "Why in the world would we want to do that?"

"So you can steal your balls back. She keeps them in her change purse, doesn't she?"

The blond shakes his head. "Yeah. You got to go."

The two men enter the house. I turn and take another look out over the river expecting Amy to pressure me to leave.

I feel her come up along my side. "It sure is beautiful, isn't it?" she says.

That is the first civil thing she has said to me so far, and it surprises me. "Yes. Sure."

"The water always has a calming effect on me."

She says it as if it is a unique circumstance for her. Almost everybody I know feels that way. We stand in silent companionship while we continue to watch the river.

A loud commotion from inside the house breaks my tranquility. I stare at the glass door as if I can see what is going on inside.

Amy grins. "Game on."

"What's up?" I ask.

She crooks a finger as she walks for the door. "Come with me."

Like I have any choice in the matter. Amy is my ride home.

As the glass door opens, I hear screaming. "You're a sad, worthless little man."

I don't have to see her face to know that is the future me. I'm not going to jump to conclusions. I don't know the circumstance of her marriage to the blond pregnant-looking guy. From the sounds of it, the relationship has been on thin ice for a while.

"My brothers warned me that you were worthless. Do I listen to them? No. I've got to find out for myself."

"Well. It's not all rainbows and ice cream cones living with you either, woman. You're a tough one to be around."

"How would you know? Anytime you see me, you run off to the bar."

"Sure, I do. Nobody at the bar makes me feel unimportant."

"Nobody makes you feel unimportant. You are unimportant. You decided to be unimportant. You don't have to be, but *you* decided to be."

The dark-haired man taps the blond on the shoulder. "Hey man, this is sort of a personal conversation. I'm going to head out."

"Hold up." The blond man turns back to the future me. "You know, I may not be the rock-star lawyer you are—and my career may have ended a lot sooner than what I ever believed it would—but I don't need your approval to make my life complete. I know who I am, and I'm okay with that. It's you who's got to make a decision."

"You know who you are? I know who you are, too. You're a drunk," future me says.

"Yeah. Sure, whatever you say. But you know what I know?"

"Not much."

The blond favors her with a sardonic smile. "I know that your issue isn't really with me. Your issue is with you. You're not happy with your decisions. I can't help you with that."

"You're crazy. Any time we try to have a conversation, all you do is talk in a circle." The future me is twirling her index finger next to her temple.

Blond man begins to walk away, turns back to her, and raises his finger. "Let me simplify it for you. At the rate you're going, you will die alone a bitter, old woman."

"Really?" She laughs, but it sounds hollow. "Well, you're going to die a drunk at the bar."

He shrugs. "But at least there will be people around me." He gestures with his hand toward his buddy. "You want to take this party to McClary's?"

The dark-haired man nods his head enthusiastically. "I thought you'd never ask."

I watch the two men leave through the front door. I expect the future me to go ballistic. Instead, she appears to remain calm. She pulls out her phone and climbs the stairs.

"Are you ready for the last stop?" Amy asks.

"I don't know. This is all too depressing. Is this like fate? Like I can't change any of this?"

Amy makes a sour expression as she holds up her hands. "Whoa. That's a taboo question. First off, I don't know, and second, if I did know, I couldn't tell you. The way they explained it to me is it's all one of those 'you have to figure it out for yourself' things."

"I have to hope I can change it."

Amy nods her head. "I feel you, girl. This life seems to kind of suck."

Amy stretches her hands toward me, and I retake a hold of her wrist. The spin is longer, and when we stop, I feel winded and tired.

"I don't feel so good," I say.

"You don't look so good, either." Amy points at the coffin.

I feel dizzy as I examine the metallic gray coffin at the end of the aisle. I can just make out my forehead and nose peeping above the rim. I'm forced to grab hold of one of the folding chairs to steady my balance.

Amy scratches her head. "I asked him if this was necessary. You understand, it's orders. Nothing personal."

"Sure." Something she said sounds odd to me. "Why would it be personal?"

Amy's brow furrows. "Did I say personal? I didn't mean that."

I look around the room. The funeral director is giving a canned speech to three men in tailored suits. One of them checks the time on his Rolex. Nobody else is at the funeral.

"It's not like I think I am the president lying in state or anything, but where is everyone?"

Amy points at the three men. "All three of your partners are here."

"Family? Friends?" I ask.

Amy bites her lower lip. "Yeah. About that."

The blond drunk pregnant guy is right. I seem to die with nobody. "Amy, I'm ready whenever you are."

She is staring at the coffin.

"Amy?"

She shakes her head as if waking from a dream. "Sure. We'll go ahead and get you home now."

"Thank you."

"I enjoyed it. I'm glad I finally got to meet you," Amy says.

I'm reaching out for Amy's wrist and freeze. "Meet me? Amy, who are you. You look awfully familiar to me. An aunt I haven't met possibly?"

"Nobody." She smiles as her eyes glisten with tears.

"Tell me, please," I beg.

She sighs as twin tears slide down her cheeks. "You're beautiful like I always thought you would be."

"Amy, please—"

"I'm not supposed to tell. He made me promise."

She means my meddling grandfather. Still, knowing the identity of my other guides helped with perspective. Why would Amy be any different? "Amy, I promise you he will never know."

She draws a deep breath, pushing her shoulders back as she favors me with an unconvincing smile. "I'm the daughter you never found time to have."

My throat constricts. "I'm sorry?" I croak. "I don't understand. Did you say daughter, Amy?"

"That's right."

"I—I—" There's no oxygen in the room. My energy has left me as I feel seconds away from collapsing in a heap on the floor.

She frowns. "He's right. I shouldn't have told you. I'm sorry."

"No—I—sorry."

"No. Don't say that. There's nothing to be sorry for. Everybody sets their own priorities. Yours just didn't include me."

My arms hang motionless at my side. Amy moves closer and embraces me as she places a kiss on my cheek.

There is no swirling of colors. Just darkness. Quiet, peaceful night.

Chapter 46

Puppy wakes me up by going in and out of his doggy door. While I lie in bed, I hear him run outside again.

I try to remember Amy's visit last night. I can remember the details of events, yet her face eludes me. It's like mist. As I believe I am seeing her, the vision falls apart again.

Puppy comes running back into our apartment. He places his frozen nose on my left leg that is out of the covers.

I reckon he's excited about it being Christmas morning. Kids have the toughest time waiting until everybody gets up.

The second time he jams his pup-sicle nose on me, I decide it's time to get up and see what's going on at the big house.

I go to pick up my slippers, and he grabs one out of my hand and shakes it violently as if he is killing a rat.

"I get it. You're excited and frustrated." I forgo the slippers and pad into the bathroom. "But your mommy has to pee and brush her teeth first."

As I sit down on the commode, my slipper rolls out of his mouth. His expression turns to one of disbelief. I'm sure it rocks his world that his cute antics don't get him what he wants immediately.

Puppy is definitely a male.

As I start brushing my teeth, someone knocks on my door. Puppy twirls a one-eighty and does his best Cujo imitation.

Having completed Grandpa's "this is your sucky life excursion," I feel safe there isn't a fourth ghost. I unlock the door and open it, finding Mama standing there in her Christmas sweater.

"Hey there," I say.

"Merry Christmas, baby."

I hold my toothbrush to the side and give her a hug. "Merry Christmas to you, Mama."

"Oh. Okay." She returns the embrace in a delayed response.

"I love your sweater."

Her brow creases. "Thank you?" Mama gestures with her hand. "Is it okay if I come in?"

I snort. "Well, yeah. I was just brushing my teeth." I walk back toward the bathroom.

"The boys cooked up some sausage patties with biscuits and gravy."

"Let the fattening begin," I say, then spit out my toothpaste.

Mama walks over and sits on my bed. "Yeah, I'd say it's just the holidays. But those boys would cook like that every day if they had time."

"Let's hope it doesn't catch up with them someday." I can tell Mama wants to tell me something. She doesn't make it a habit of crashing in on me unless she thinks I really need her, or she really needs to tell me something that's bad news.

It is Christmas morning. There are rules against giving terrible news on Christmas morning. Or if there aren't, there should at least be a law.

"April, have you heard from Lee by chance?"

"Not in the last twenty-four hours. The last phone call, he told me he wanted to conserve his battery for when the storm was over."

Mama nods her head. She looks lost, deep in thought.

"Why do you ask?"

"Your daddy has a lot of government and military friends up that way, and he has recruited a few of them to help. The thing is, the storm dumped another four inches last night, and the winds picked back up."

"I know, Mama. Believe me, I've been checking the weather regularly."

"One of your daddy's friends used to be in the 10th Mountain Infantry. He lives in Millersville and goes snowmobile riding in Canada regularly."

I pull on my robe and snatch up my slippers before Puppy can grab them again. "That's nice."

"Ace, that's your daddy's friend, found a Ford Bronco registered to Bob Felix. Isn't that another pitcher on Lee's team?"

"Mama, if you're going to tell me that Bob's Bronco was rolled, I already know that. The last time Lee called me, they had just wrecked Bob's SUV, and they were headed to a barn for shelter."

Mama covers her mouth with her left hand as her eyes get watery.

"What is it, Mama?"

"Ace saw a barn in the distance, and when he checked it out, there were signs that somebody had been holed up there."

"Had been?"

"They were gone," Mama whispers.

I shake my head in confusion. "That makes no sense. They would've just waited until the weather got better. This guy probably is at a different barn. Not the one they were in."

"Ace said it cleared for a few hours yesterday. Then the second whiteout came and trapped hundreds more on the roadways. He thinks they might have made a break for it during the lull. They would have a hard time without transportation or shelter if they were caught in the second storm."

I'm really regretting freezing my crystal now. But the crystal won't help. Well, it would tell me where he is, but I still can't help him get home.

Maybe that isn't totally true. Hadn't I just been pulled around in spatial displacement by ghosts for the last three nights?

I've done it before, myself.

Of course, I was asleep at the time, and it was just me. Still, I did appear on the same plane as Liza and save her life one night. So, it can be done.

No, that's a stupid idea. First off, I don't even know if I have enough power to bring one of the men back out alive and in good condition. More importantly, what if one of them loses their grip on me and they drop off into the void. I couldn't live with having been the demise of Lee or one of his friends.

"I know it's a lot to take in, baby. That's why I hope you'll come to have breakfast with the rest of us." She stands and gives me another hug, this time less awkward. "I really would prefer if you wouldn't be by yourself right now."

Mama is right. I don't need to be by myself, but not for the reason she thinks.

If I'm alone in my apartment, I know for a fact I'd be chipping the looking crystal out of the ice before she gets back to breakfast with the boys.

The itch is intolerably intense and convinces me that the last thing I need to do is use the crystal. I definitely understand now what Nana was warning against. Once the crystal gets its hooks in you, it will ride you into the dirt.

Chapter 47

Breakfast with the family is an uncomfortable affair. We are talking about everything except Lee, baseball, the weather, or barns. At one point, Daddy talks about the Metcalfs buying a new combine. He says they had to put up a new "red wooden structure" next to the old "red wooden structure" that had fallen down to keep the combine out of the weather.

I don't know whether I should be thankful they are conscientious of my feelings or get aggravated at the lengths they are going. It's not like I'm some sort of thin-skinned girl from *The Princess and the Pea*. Lord knows I've taken my fair share of hard knocks in the last six months.

Even so, I think having the love of your life die in a snowstorm might just be more than I can handle. At least it is more than I want to attempt to deal with.

Did I just say that Lee could be dead? Is that a real possibility? No.

Clear that out of your head, April. You can't give that life.

Lee is strong, resourceful, and intelligent. He's on his way home right now.

After breakfast, we move into the family room and open gifts. It is even difficult for me to get happy when I open Mama's gift to me. The pair of red cowgirl boots I had been hinting about for the last two months.

I nearly break down and cry. I wanted the boots, so when I talk Lee into going line dancing with me, I will look exceptionally sexy.

I must be like a dark cloud over the morning festivities. After we open gifts and it is time to clean up from breakfast, the four of them insist they do not need my help in the kitchen. I would argue the point, but my sadness is sapping my energy. I curl up on the sofa and stare blankly at the TV as *The Waltons: Homecoming* plays.

I'm in a severe funk. But why shouldn't I be? It is Christmas, and my boyfriend is MIA. Three ghosts have shown me that I am a horrible person who will die alone without friends or family.

I might be rich—but I have nobody to share my life. It is a most depressing forecast for the April May Snow future.

I must believe I can alter it. Surely, I can improve my future. I must be able to. Otherwise, why would Grandpa Hirsch even bother putting the visits together?

Why come across the veil and rub my nose in my inadequacies and doomed future? Who does that?

How do you even begin to change the trajectory of your future? How do you make up for being too self-centered and selfish? It seems too large of a task to set things right now.

A voice from the past comes to me. They are the words of my other grandpa, Grandpa Snow. If he used the phrase once during our summer visits, he used it a hundred times.

"How do you eat an elephant?" Grandpa would ask.

Chase would always answer, "With a big fork." Dusty said, "With an army." I would laugh at their silly response since we all knew the correct answer.

I sit up and dial a number on my phone. If I'm to eat this elephant one bite at a time, I might as well get started now.

"Hello?"

"Merry Christmas, Liza!"

Liza laughs. "Too weird. I was just thinking about you, April. Merry Christmas."

"I want to know, do you have plans for Christmas dinner?"

"Not really. I think Tres Tacos opens back up at noon. I was considering a couple of bean burritos and calling it a Southern Christmas."

"Would you be open to being our guest for dinner?"

"Oh, I don't know, April. That's sweet of you, but I don't want to impose on your family event."

"I called you. Besides, I have a little something for you, and I'm too lazy to drive over to your house," I say.

"You do? Now I'm intrigued." She huffs. "Well, I guess if I must."

"Awesome. We are eating at two. But you can come any time before then."

That feels so good. As I hang up with Liza, I text Jacob. "Merry Christmas, have a safe shift, and looking forward to having dinner with you."

While I'm on a roll spreading Christmas cheer, I text Lee, too. "I'm having a blue Christmas without you. Please hurry home. Love, April." My face starts to twitch as I hit the send button, and the tears begin to fall.

That boy better make it home.

Chapter 48

The men in my family outdid themselves again. The aromas in the kitchen are absolutely mouthwatering. The only complaint you could have is that no plate is large enough for all the different casseroles, vegetables, ham, and loaves of bread.

The one silver lining with Lee not being able to make it home for Christmas dinner is that I'm not embarrassed to undo the top button of my jeans. I'm contemplating how much of my zipper I'll have to let down to make room for both the pecan and the lemon meringue pies when the truce between Nana and Granny finally breaks down.

Nana wrinkles her nose. "Loretta, everybody knows that your church moved Christmas to the winter solstice so that they could claim the celebration the pagans had every year."

"No." Granny clinches her teeth. "Pauline, that's just a bunch of hogwash people cooked up to slander the church."

"Ladies, is it such a bad thing to share the day? The way I see it, the church moving Christmas to the winter solstice allows Christians and pagans to celebrate together." Daddy smiles at his mother and mother-in-law. "Because there's enough love in this family for all viewpoints."

Peaches. Daddy doesn't show it very often, but when he does, you are reminded just how sneaky and slick he can be with diffusing situations. My two grandmothers share one last look of contempt but drop the argument.

My phone vibrates, and I hold it under the table while I check the caller ID. Phones are taboo at the table any time, but especially during holiday meals. I don't recognize the number. More robocalls.

"Jacob, what's been going on in your world?" Mama asks.

"Just pulling a lot of shifts with the holidays."

Mama carries a pie to the dining table. "Nothing interesting?"

"Just the run-of-the-mill stuff. Speeding tickets, disturbing the peace, and a DUI or two." His chin ticks up. "Of course, there's the Dottie Castle case. That one's sorta crazy, but April would be able to tell you more about that."

"What has that nasty woman done now?" Granny says with narrowed eyes.

"Granny," I scold.

"Granny, yourself. That woman has wrecked more marriages than a second-rate NASCAR driver has wrecked cars."

Chase howls with laughter. "What happened to 'if you can't say something nice, don't say anything at all,' Granny?"

"Vivian, can you give your son a piece of pie so he can put something in his mouth?" Granny looks at Mama pointedly.

Chase's mouth drops open as Barbara and Dusty burst into laughter.

"Loretta is right. That woman had a few years where she was hopping into so many beds it was hard to keep up with her," Nana adds.

Interesting. This is information that I never would have dreamed of obtaining. It might permanently scar me because Dottie Castle will always be a shriveled-up, condescending elderly woman to me. Still, given the crime she's accused of took place twenty-five years ago, it's helpful to know as much about her past as possible.

"What did they pinch her for?" Granny asks me.

"Well, they haven't gotten her for anything. They're charging her with the murder of her husband. I'm her defense attorney, and I'm going to get her off."

Granny and Nana share a look. They hoot with laughter. "Good luck with that," they say in unison.

"Actually, there's a lot of historical facts indicating Mr. Castle was involved in money laundering. It's not too much of a stretch to think he might have gotten sideways with his employers."

"Oh, that's rich." Nana leans back and laughs harder.

"If Gil Castle was a money launderer, I'm a center on a WNBA team," Granny scoffs.

"I'm just repeating what I heard," I tell them. "I heard it several times that his criminal clients were responsible for his demise. I believe I heard they were concerned he would rat them out to the FBI."

"Everyone knows Dottie killed him," Nana grumbles.

Granny crosses her arms. "Who told you he was a money launderer and his boss killed him?"

I think about it and can't recall. "I don't remember."

Granny's eyes sparkle. "I guarantee you heard it from Dottie. She was pitching that story from day one."

"No. I didn't." I don't think. I hope I didn't.

"Why don't you look so sure she didn't kill him?" Nana asks.

I snort in frustration. "The autopsy hasn't come back from the Doc Crowder yet."

Nana narrows her eyes. "I meant, why didn't you just read Dottie for yourself? You do have a *skill* for that."

I glance quickly at Barbara, making sure she missed Nana's code talk. Barbara is halfway into a piece of pecan pie. Good.

I gesture toward Barbara and favor Nana with a "what are you thinking?" look.

"I'm just saying people should use all their talents when they are trying to solve a case." Nana turns to Jacob. "Don't you agree, Officer Hurley?"

Jacob raises his hands. "I appreciate the meal, but if I'd known it was going to get me into the middle of a family dispute—"

"Oh, please. I'm sure you've answered enough domestic disturbances that you can at least weigh in on this," Nana continues to push.

Jacob slouches in his chair. "Yes. You should use all the talents available to you—that are legal."

Nana's lips purse as she considers Jacob's finer point. The fact is, there are no statutes written on the use of clairvoyance in determining someone's guilt.

The trouble being, even if I were to know that Dottie Castle killed her husband, I'm still her defense attorney.

That means I can't knowingly lie. Still, my job remains to make sure I blunt the district attorney case sufficiently enough to keep a jury from convicting Dottie. Since that is my lot, all things equal, I prefer *not* to know if she killed Gil.

Besides, I like winning, and I must believe that in a group of twelve jurors, at least one of them will find it reprehensible to send an eighty-year-old woman to prison. We only need one heart full of mercy and compassion for a little old widow.

I notice Jacob staring at me in my periphery. "What?"

He guffaws. "Can you really tell if Ms. Castle is lying?"

"No. It doesn't work like that," I say.

Nana points her finger at me. "You see how her left eye does that—"

"Twitch," Jacob finishes. "I know she's lying. The left side of her lips droops, too."

I cover the left side of my face with my hand. "Y'all are full of it."

"You're the one full of baloney, Snow. When I think of all the time an ability like that would save me—not to mention never charging someone without cause or letting a dangerous criminal back on the street."

"I hardly consider Dottie dangerous," I say.

"Tell that to, Gil," Jacob says. He frowns while shaking his head in disapproval.

Fine. He's shamed me into it.

I don't like the idea because it isn't right to read people without their knowledge. Still, knowing the truth about Dottie will leave me a clear conscience in the future.

The next time I meet with Dottie, I'll use my "gifts." Nobody else needs to know what I glean from her memory.

Tuesday will be a busy day. I need to convince Rhonda Applewhite to take the plea bargain Lane offered.

Some people just don't know a good deal when they see it. Rhonda doesn't understand she is looking at some serious jail time, and Lane has the videos to prove it was her.

Then, as much as I hate to, I'll go have a friendly conversation with Ms. Castle and make sure to touch her while we talk so I can read her memory.

In my heart, I know my grandmothers are right. I believe Dottie is as guilty as the day is long. Especially when you throw in the fact she was having affairs.

The affairs may have precipitated a threat of divorce from Gil. An impending divorce would be more than enough motive to commit murder for someone like Dottie, who is overly concerned about money.

"Anyone need seconds of pie?" Mama asks.

"I have room for a piece of the pecan pie, too, Mama," I say as I inch my zipper down a few more teeth. Hey, don't judge. Mama doesn't bake pies every day.

Not to get overly optimistic, but as I'm enjoying my second piece of pie, I watch Chase and Barbara out of the corner of my eye. Mama sat them together, and it seems like their chairs are closer than necessary. And from time to time, they take turns whispering something in each other's ear.

If they are trying not to look like they are still in love, they are doing a lousy job of it. I don't know I have ever seen a couple be so chemistry-perfect outside of Mama and Daddy, and possibly Granny and Grandpa Snow. It makes me want to stand up and scream, "Why can't you see what everybody else sees?"

Dusty clears his throat as he lowers his coffee cup. "Liza and April, I forgot to tell you that I got a call from Heather White this morning."

"She called *you*—on Christmas morning?" Liza asks.

Dusty crosses his arms. "Yeah, I'm afraid she beat me to the punch, and now we have a bit of a situation down there."

"She's really ticked about those chairs we burned?" I ask.

Dusty's chin ticks up in acknowledgment. "Well, she wasn't exactly thrilled about that. But when I offered to pay for the replacement, the more we talked, I think she can get around that with the historical society. No. the problem is she won't clear us to use the material we documented."

"Why? We did everything we were supposed to do," Liza objects.

"She says we didn't keep our end of the bargain by expelling the ghosts."

I keep silent and clamp down on my lips. Lest an unhelpful "I told you so" carelessly tumbles from my mouth.

"We expelled an entire hallway of spirits."

"I know, I told her that. The thing is, she claims she had one of the plaster contractors in there on Christmas Eve, and their scaffolding collapsed. One of the workers ended up with a broken ankle and a second one had a broken arm."

"What does that have to do with us?" Liza asks.

"The workers reported seeing a ghost pull the cotter pins on the base of the scaffolding, causing it to fall."

That would be the sneaky evil specter that was excellent at hiding from meters. I feel like I should have pressed the matter more urgently with Dusty. I hate to hear that people were hurt. Still, I know that everyone, including Dusty, was ready to get back for the Christmas holidays. I did what I could.

I shudder as I remember feeling that something was watching us, waiting for us to leave. I could feel the sick, perverted glee its energy sent out as we began to leave the theater. Just the thought of it now makes me feel dirty and violated.

"What theater are you talking about?" Jacob asks.

"The Imperial up in Shelbyville, Tennessee," Dusty says.

Granny groans. "There's some bad juju in that place."

"What's with the awful walk down memory lane tonight,

Loretta?" Nana Hirsch asks.

Her lips narrow until they disappear. "I don't know, Pauline. You know what they say. If you don't bury the dead right—"

"They're sure to come up," Nana finishes.

It feels like someone runs an ice cube down my spine as the hairs on my arms stand up. My grandmothers confirming there is something evil in the theater gives me the willies.

"We'll need to head back up there this weekend or the next," Dusty says.

I don't want to go back. I'm done with the theater. "Dusty, what are we supposed to do? You said you were going to get her a priest to bless the building."

"I know, April." Dusty sighs. "But she says she won't sign off on the films unless *we* clear the entity out of the hallway."

Bless it. Heather knows her leverage points and she uses them for maximum advantage.

Mama stands at the end of the table. "How about we take it into the living room. We can continue to catch up with one another over cider and rum or Irish coffee, whichever you prefer."

Alcohol sounds good right about now. I don't care what Dusty says. If I never go back to the Imperial, it'll be too soon.

Whatever I felt hiding in the corner of the ceiling was desperate to stay in the theater. I don't care to find out what happens if we anger it by making it move to the other side of the veil.

Chapter 49

Puppy is already in the den on one of the sofas, sleeping off his meal. I sit down next to him and knead the fur around his neck. He doesn't wake up.

Daddy and Howard tell us a story about a Christmas afternoon when they detached an old crank telephone from their grandmother's house, then paddled out into the middle of the lake with it. They dropped two electrical lines into the water, and Daddy cranked while Howard netted the stunned fish floating to the top. Everything was going fine until the game warden came by and figured out what they were doing. He confiscated their grandmother's phone and the fish, and took them straight home to the farm.

"Dad promised Game Warden Eaves he would take care of us. But as soon as the warden left, Howard began pleading our case to Dad, and before long, he had Dad agreeing with him that it was a good idea and perfectly safe."

"Mom was a different story," Howard says with a smile. "She grabbed us in turn by the wrist and commenced to try and slap our butts while we ran around in a big circle."

"I did no such thing," Granny glowers.

"Yes, you did," Daddy says. "I remember because you hurt your hand and couldn't sew for a whole month."

"I thought you boys would be the death of me."

Howard bust out laughing. "I think we both thought *you* were going be the death of *us* that day."

I have heard the story maybe four or five times, but it is still funny to me. It also symbolizes a legacy story to me.

Fifty years later, my daddy is still taking stuff apart and figuring out beneficial uses for them. At the same time, my uncle pleads people's cases to get them out of imminent punishment. Essentially, they are the same boys, just men now and doing their thing on a larger scale.

As if I summoned him with my whimsical thought of him and my daddy, Howard comes over and sits next to me. "We have a bit of business to attend to this morning, April," he says below the din of the other conversations.

"We do?" The last slice of pie I scarfed rolls over in my stomach. All of our open cases flash across my mind. Dottie's case is the most obvious for an emergency Christmas morning discussion.

Howard holds out an envelope to me. "You'll need this."

I swallow hard as I wonder what evidence Howard has found on our client. Evidence I am sure will make it ten times more difficult to argue her innocence.

It's a check. I pull it out as I reread the name and amount. "What is this?" I ask Howard as I turn to him.

"Your quarterly."

Shaking my head I struggle to comprehend. "Quarterly?"

Howard raises his eyebrows. "Partners quarterly distribution. That's for the fourth quarter."

Looking back to the check I read it again. "Howard—this is— twenty-two thousand." I look back to him. "I'm not a partner."

Howard smirks. "You may not have the title, but you are *my* partner." He shrugs. "Besides, it's important you know what you're giving up when you leave. An apples-to-apples comparison."

I'm not even going to argue the leaving point with him. I grab him in a hug. It has little to do with the money—although that is appreciated, and I can put it to good use—and more to do with him acknowledging how hard I have worked for him. That and I know he appreciates it. "Thank you, Howard."

"No. Thank you, April. You more than earned that." He pats me on the back, stands and walks over to my Daddy.

I'm completely blown away. Because I do the books for our little firm, I know we have gone from a tight cash flow situation to a healthy profit the last six months. Still, I never thought that any of that additional profit should be mine.

Howard thought otherwise. I'm so humbled and grateful I feel on the verge of happy tears.

Barbara stands and stretches. "I better be getting home. I've got an early shift tomorrow. Thank you for inviting me. It was wonderful."

That brings me back to earth. The sister I wish I had is leaving and I have no clue if this is a one-off or if she might become a regular at the Snow home again.

We all tell her goodbye as we give her a hug. As Chase walks her out to her car. We all run to the side window, jockeying for a position as we crack the blinds just enough to see through them as we watch the attractive couple talking.

Barbara is leaning with her back to the driver's door of her car. Chase's toes are flush with hers as they talk. He braces his hands against the vehicle on either side of Barbara, and my heart rate increases dramatically.

Chase leans in, and they kiss for an unimaginably long time without coming up for air.

A thousand butterflies take flight in my stomach.

That would be one of the best Christmas gifts ever if Chase and Barbara got back together. I know. It's none of my business, and likely it is just another one of my foolish fantasies. Still, I would be ecstatic if it worked out for them.

My phone vibrates again. I stare at the screen. Another wrong area code. I hit the disconnect button and push it back into my pocket just in time to see the longest kiss on record end.

Wow. Those two know how to kiss. They need to do a You-

Tube video on erotic kissing.

Barbara gets in her car. As she drives down the driveway, we watch Chase wave at her.

When he turns and starts back toward the house, it is like everybody wakes up from our voyeuristic dopamine rush. We scramble from the window as if playing musical chairs.

"Barbara wanted me to tell you thank you again, Mom and Dad, for letting me invite her over," Chase says.

"Is everything okay? You were out there for a while," Daddy says with a smirk.

Chase's ears turn red. "I was checking to make sure she hadn't had too much to drink."

"Does your tongue double as a breathalyzer?" Dusty asks, barely able to contain his laugh.

Chase's eyebrows come together. He looks over at the window, the blinds all askew. "Guys. That's so not cool."

We erupt into laughter.

"What can we say? Inquiring minds want to know," Howard jokes.

"Fine. Y'all just laugh it up. I'm good with that. I got a kiss tonight. That's more than what most of y'all can say."

Liza stands. "I better be heading out, too."

"Are you going to walk her out so we can watch you through the blinds as you lay a big smooch on her?" Chase asks.

Liza's porcelain skin flushes red. I feel awful for her. Chase doesn't know what discomfort he has just caused Liza with his "too close for comfort" quip.

"Some of us are gentlemen, Chase," Dusty says.

Chase is about to say something, stops, and cocks his head to the right.

"What?" Dusty asks.

Chase gestures for Dusty to be quiet as he concentrates even harder.

At first, I mistake the loud noise as being inside my head. I think it is a replay of the beating on the back door of the Imperial. Soon I can tell the noise is coming closer and becoming louder.

"He sure is low," Daddy says.

The noise continues to increase until it sounds like it is directly over our lake house. It does not move away, remaining precisely over us as the commotion continues to build in volume until I feel the vibration in the floor.

"What the heck?" Jacob says as he races for the sliding glass door. Chase and Dusty are hot on Jacob's heel. The rest of us fall in behind them.

Now it is no mystery. We have a helicopter, dangerously close, directly over our house.

As we congregate onto the back porch, we shield our eyes and look to the sky. An army green Huey hovers a hundred feet above our roof with a ladder hanging forty feet from the cabin door. A crew member stands on the bottom rung in a red flight suit, swinging precariously as the Huey moves closer.

"What in the world is that fool doing?" Howard asks.

Daddy shakes his head. "I don't know. But he's either crazy or has some major cojones if he flew in on that ladder."

"Probably a little of both," Jacob says.

The Huey flies closer toward us and begins to descend. The downdraft whips grit into the air. I feel it sting my face as I cover my eyes while turning my head. The blades create a deafening sound, making it impossible to think.

I hear and feel the blades pull up and away. I look over my shoulder as the Huey quickly gains altitude. The airman at the door pulls up the rope ladder.

"Ho, ho, ho, baby."

I turn to the familiar voice. When I see Lee, I scream as my fist pistons up and down while tears of joy fill my eyes.

"I tried to find some flying reindeer, but the helicopter was the best I could do."

He is dressed in a Santa outfit, and he *is* the Christmas gift I hoped for all along. I launch myself into his arms.

"Did you miss me much?" Lee whispers against my ear.

My voice is choked as the tears begin in earnest. "A little bit."

Lee laughs as he squeezes me tight, lifting me off my feet. "You should've known I wasn't going to miss Christmas with my girl."

"You can't ever be gone this close to Christmas again," I tell him.

"I think that's a great idea." He adjusts his stance as he looks above my head. "Well, will you look at that?"

Following his eyes, I see the mistletoe he holds above my head. He won't have to ask. I lay a hot, steamy kiss on him that curls my toes.

I suppose the Snows are just born with the erotic-kissing gene.

The End

Never miss an April May Snow release.

Join the reader's club!

www.mscottswanson.com

Coming April 1, 2022
Foolish Games

Have you read the prequels? *The Gifts Awaken* stories are the prequel series to the *Foolish* novel series of April May Snow.

Click to get your copies today!

The Gifts Awaken Prequel Series

Throw the Bouquet

Throw the Cap

Throw the Dice

Throw the Elbow

Throw the Fastball

Throw the Gauntlet

Throw the Hissy

M. Scott lives outside of Nashville, Tennessee, with his wife and two guard chihuahuas. When he's not writing, he's cooking or taking long walks to smooth out plotlines for the next April May Snow adventure.

Dear Reader,

Thank you for reading April's story. You make her adventures possible. Without you, there would be no point in creating her story.

I'd like to encourage you to post a review on Amazon. A favorable critique from you is a powerful way to support authors you enjoy. It allows our books to be found by additional readers, and frankly, motivates us to continue to produce books. This is especially true for your independents.

Once again, thank you for the support. You are the magic that breathes life into these characters.

M. Scott Swanson

The best way to stay in touch is to join the reader's club!

www.mscottswanson.com

Other ways to stay in touch are:

Like on Amazon

Like on Facebook

Like on Goodreads

You can also reach me at mscottswanson@gmail.com.

I hope your life is filled with
magic and LOVE!

Made in the USA
Monee, IL
30 December 2021

87538281R00177